Bone Lab

JM Meigs

ISBN: 978-0-9963544-1-7

This is a work of fiction. Names, characters, places and incidents either are the product of the authors' imagination or are used fictitiously, and any resemblance to actual persons, living or dead, businesses, companies, events or locales is entirely coincidental.

Acknowledgement

So many people have played a part in the development of the Rhyjl Martin Mysteries, I could write a novella just listing them.

Foremost, I want to thank my husband, Earl, who has encouraged me for the last thirty four years to turn my stories into books. My daughters and my friends, who have read so many drafts of each story and have been caring enough to be honest and critical while still encouraging me.

I want to give a special thanks to Karrie Ross who spent hours turning my ideas into an awesome book cover.

Also my fellow authors, especially Mark Henwick, creator of *The Bite Back Series*, who was always there to remind me that all my blood, sweat and tears are worth it.

Last of all, I want to thank all those during my academic years who taught me how to read the stories the bones tell.

Table of Contents

Table of Contents

Prologue

Nine Years Prior

"I found this boy."

Maggie McKenna had already made note that something was wrong. It was the way Rhyjl crossed the yard from the old barn, her eyes cast down, shoulders slumped. Her restless pacing and inability to stay seated once she entered the kitchen, cinched it.

Maggie pushed the pastry board aside. The half rolled pie crust would have to wait. She swiped the dusting of flour from her hands to the front of worn jeans and sat. "At sixteen shouldn't they be looking for you?"

Groaning, Rhyjl gnawed on her left index finger.

It was a gesture so reminiscent of her mother, Maggie's heart gave a little catch. She shut her eyes, her thumb and second finger pinching her nose between them, while her forefinger gently massaged the wrinkled bridge. "Okay." she said, returning her hands to her lap. *Lead, don't push*. She took a slow deep breath imagining the calm she'd find there. "I swear this air is stifling hot. Why don't you grab us both a cold lemonade and tell me about it."

Maggie wasn't sure what to expect. An icy niggling in the pit of her stomach was too reminiscent of the past. Rhyjl was a solitary girl preferring the company of animals and books to other people, especially teens her own age. Whether she'd always been that way, or just since coming to the ranch to live, Maggie didn't know.

Truth be told, Maggie hadn't known much about her only grandchild except for an occasional school picture tucked in brief notes from Carolyn. She knew even less after her daughter had died almost three years past. It wasn't that Maggie didn't care. Oh my God, she cared! That bastard Carolyn had married hadn't even mustered the decency to notify her until six months after Carolyn's passing. She'd written back, of course. Asked details. Never a word. She'd said her prayers nightly for the girl. Asked God if it wouldn't be too much trouble to put an end to the father.

God, Maggie knew, has His own timing. Two years later, almost to the day, a storm rode across Montana driving a deluge of freezing rain along with a soaked waif of a girl to Maggie's door.

"I saw the wolf first," Rhyjl said, returning from the refrigerator, taking her seat and sliding one of the lemonades across to her Grandmother. "I'd taken Carmen for a ride along the high pasture. I was hoping to catch a glimpse of that cougar and her kittens. I've seen her tracks for weeks... and before you say anything, I *was* being careful. Besides, Carmen's no green horse. She's quick to sense things. I knew if the cat was close by, she would alert me. That's why I was so surprised when I spotted the wolf. There wasn't even a flicker of an ear or tremor running along Carmen's neck."

Maggie shut her eyes, transforming Rhyjl's words to mental images. Just like Carolyn, the girl had an insatiable need to know.

"I pulled up on the reins and sat watching him. He was awesome! He was gray and white and must have weighed over two hundred pounds. And god, the way he moved! I've seen pictures and once I saw some wolves at the zoo. They weren't anything like this guy. I didn't move, didn't even breath. Amazingly, he hadn't sensed us! He seemed in a hurry. Not hunting, but knowing where he was going. I waited until he moved along, then cautiously followed. He skirted the trees along the ridge above the river, then paused briefly before leaving their cover. I saw his ears prick forward sensing something, but not us. It was like Carmen and I didn't exist.

"You know that big boulder that sits in the clearing? The one you said Grandpa used to call his thinking place?" Rhyjl, once more gnawing at her finger, forced her eyes to focus from the beyond back to her grandmother's.

Maggie nodded, but said nothing that might disrupt Rhyjl's narrative.

"It was there he dropped out of sight. I know I shouldn't have." Squeezing her eyes shut, she took a deep breath. Her hands had begun to shake, her face growing paler. "I knew if I tried to follow any further on horseback, I would probably spook him. I dismounted, left Carmen ground tied, and walked slowly toward the rock. That's when I saw the boy. He was sitting with his back against that boulder, the wolf laid down beside him, placing its head to rest on the kid's leg just like your old Newfie, Rooter, does with you.

"It was all so...so weird! Like a staged scene out of some natural history museum. I could see the snowcapped, jagged peaks of the Absarokas in the distance. That was wrong! It's too late in the season. The grass was spring green around the boulder. Not brown like it is now. Part of me knew that! If for one minute, just one minute, I'd been listening to what my rational brain was saying, instead of being completely caught up in the vision before me, I ..."

Maggie reached across the table enfolding Rhyjl's

trembling hands in her own. Tears fell freely as the girl's head bowed over them. "You don't need to finish."

"But I do," sobbed, Rhyjl. "I … I must have seen it for a reason."

"Sometimes there are no reasons. Sometimes it's just enough to know, your Granddad used to say."

Minutes passed. Water beaded and ran down the outside of the untouched lemonade glasses. The room grew warmer in the late afternoon sun. Finally drawing a deep breath, Rhyjl lifted her eyes once more to something only she could see.

"His raven hair hung down in two long braids. Tied halfway up one braid, a hawk's feather fluttered in a breeze that didn't exist. I knew then I was no longer in my own time. He was so handsome, Grandmum! His skin was warmed by the sun, and like his wolf, he was well muscled. I'm guessing he was about my age. He was working a cut sapling into a bow. Or at least I think that's what he was making.

"The wolf reacted first, his head leaving its resting place, the ears pricked forward. Then, as if one, the boy and the wolf leapt up. They shot down the hill toward the river. I knew, that just as I couldn't feel the breeze, whatever sound had alerted them, I couldn't hear. There was no longer need for caution. *I* was not really there … at least, in *that* time. It was like watching a really intense movie. I mean, this was his world and I was only observing. But for just that moment, I wished with my whole heart, I could have really been with him. If I could have stopped him, I would have. Or … perhaps I couldn't have."

Sobs racked her whole body. "Oh god! Oh god! I watched as the small village below erupted. The soldiers in blue charged across the river screaming in silence and firing their guns. Women scattered from their tasks. One old woman, sitting by the river's edge, was run over before she could even make the attempt to rise. I saw another young woman with a baby tucked to her breast running from the soldiers. Suddenly she was jolted by the impact of a bullet. She fell forward twisting at the last moment so she wouldn't land on the child. She curled into a ball to protect the baby even as she was dying.

"There had been no warning, no reason. I could see hatred and a sick glee in the men as they stormed the village. There were only a few warriors. It had been more like a grouping of the boy's family: Father, brothers, uncles. This was not a war party! Outnumbered they fought. The boy and wolf right in the middle of it all. I saw several soldiers fall. The wolf took down two, their throats gaping. The boy's knife flashed faster than I could believe. He was really good! I know that sounds kinda bad, but I admired him. I don't know, he must have killed or wounded four or five before a sixth sent a bullet his way. The bullet exploded just below his left shoulder, throwing him back and spinning him around. The wolf, his mussel frothing pink, launched toward the attacker. A second shot caught the wolf midair, but wasn't enough to stop the massive body. The soldier's last scream was torn from his throat in a flash of teeth. It was done.

"I half ran, half fell, down the hill yelling and screaming. When I reached him, I knelt beside the boy, helpless. I raged at the soldiers as they went through the village kicking the fallen to see if there was still life and tending to their own wounded. One pushed the body of the young mother from her baby with the toe of his boot. Then he raised his gun. I couldn't watch. I was sick! I saw two others viciously kick the wolf off the body of their comrade. A third came walking toward me. I was so angry I wanted to pick up the boy's knife and use it. Instead, I threw my body over his. He was dead! He'd been dead for a long time. Still … I needed to do something! I glared at the man waiting for what I was afraid he would do. But, for some reason he stopped and turned away to scavenge and loot.

I don't know how much time passed. Somewhere a hawk called. A raven answered. My body was stiff and cold despite the heat of the afternoon sun. Lifting myself from the rocky ground, I saw it was not a rock I was clenching, but a bone. It was an arm bone. His! Looking down, I saw where my fingers had clawed it from the earth. Saw also that next to it, I'd unearthed what remained of a mandible. The wolf's. Hurt and dying, it had still managed to drag itself back to the boy. I didn't think I had any more tears. I was so wrong! I raised my face to the sky and howled."

"Howled?" Maggie asked, her voice choked, her own tears falling freely.

"I don't know how else to describe it. It was a raw sound. It hurt my throat. There was no one, but me to mourn. No one cared that they had died and been left. I placed both bones reverently back in the indentation they had come from. I smoothed the clawing marks from where my hands had repeatedly clenched."

Rhyjl shot from the chair toward the bathroom. Maggie heard her retching and felt again the growing uneasiness in her own mid-section. More than anything else, she wished her husband was here. He would have known what to say, how to say it. He'd often said it was something you had to experience to understand. Maggie felt just as impotent as the day Carolyn had experienced her first vision. Wrapping her arms around herself, she stared out the window and wondered how many times history would repeat.

Chapter 1

Just One of Those Days

Rhyjl Martin was on top of the world. This would be her final year at Down East University. Come spring, she would be off to Sweden to put the final touches on her doctoral thesis. But for now, she smiled, there's no place prettier than Down East Maine in the fall.

To celebrate, she'd donned her backpack and spent the weekend getting a last reprieve from the insanity the start of the new academic calendar would incur. Her plans had almost bellied-up. Fortunately, she'd known a couple other people heading off and was able to snag a last minute ride. Barely! It was beginning to look like her decrepit old scout might not see her through the winter. Greg had taught her a few things to keep the old rust-infested bucket going, but not enough. If not for her status as a student and resident of Montana, she'd never have been able to keep the Maine State yearly inspections at bay. She really didn't have the money, or desire, to invest in another old clunker. Not with Europe on the horizon. She'd need to do something about it. Not today. "Sufficient for the day," as Grandmum always says. Today, she had other plans.

She'd found a nice camping spot a short hike from a pond. Back home it would have been called a small lake. Life was a lot different in Maine than in Montana. Even though she'd spent most of her childhood in Maine, she'd actually felt as if she'd encountered more culture shock from the move back than she had when visiting another country. You were expected, after all, to hear and see different customs when abroad.

It was a definite high exploring the rolling hills, rocky promontories, and boulder strewn beaches in and around Mount Desert Island. In a couple of weeks, the scenery would transform into a kaleidoscope of oranges, yellows and reds mixed with evergreens. The small lakes dotting the island would reflect not only the vibrant blue of the sky, but a mirror perfect image of the autumn foliage. The loons who skimmed their surface all summer would depart for the ocean, morph into their winter identity of gray, even muting their red eyes. She wished she could have come then, but there wouldn't be time once classes were in full session.

There were a lot of people who thought she was a bit of an introvert preferring to seek out quiet places far from the maddening crowds. Perhaps, she was. If truth be told, the majority of people didn't realize that most enclosed places, especially if they had been around for a while, were actually more crowded than they could imagine. Even out in the open, there was always the chance of coming across scenes as she called them. She'd pretty much learned to catch them early and not get drawn in. Sometimes, she let herself be lead. Sometimes they fit in so naturally it was hard to tell. Once she'd seen a tall ship off the coast of Cornwall. She'd thought it was from the past only to discover, as several more appeared on the horizon, it was part of an annual Tall Ship Race.

She'd slept well in her little tent, enjoyed the simple food she'd brought along, blackened her little kettle over the open wood fire and thought, as she sat there sipping her steaming tea, it had never tasted so good. If there had been any scenes during this trip, she hadn't noticed. In a way, with all the history of the island, it was strange. She would count it a blessing and not be overly analytical. There would be plenty of time for brainwork once she returned to the campus.

*

Monday came too soon. Muscles still aching from the weekend exertions, her current trek was toward the administration building. Today represented part of her yearly transition from the freedom of being outside, at a dig or in the hills, to the subdued teaching assistant and lab dweller.

She was a dig junkie. Exhausting as that might be and often taking its toll leaving her edgy and unsettled, she was happier there than anyplace on earth. In the field, she let herself be pulled and immersed into the scenes unfolding before her. Pulling stories out of the past was the best part of her job. It was like being caught in a fast paced novel.

The lab, while interesting, was like re-reading and re-hashing parts of the same novel until they lost that grip. This visit to the Dean this morning was going to change that. If anyone could pull strings to get some of the specimens from the museum in Visby, he could. With those in hand, her thesis might be fast tracked even more than she dared hope. She drew in a deep breath and let it out slowly, imagining how her findings would rock …

"Rhyjl you're just in time!" exclaimed Sara, a bouncy red-head, and Rhyjl's roomy. Coming alongside Rhyjl, she locked arms and step with her. "Heading over to Admin?"

Rhyjl glanced at her speculatively. "Yeah, what's up? And could you slow down some? I don't have those nice long legs that you have."

Sara slowed, if only minimally. "Nothing! Absolutely nothing!" She released Rhyjl's arm so her own could flutter above her head. "The Witch left a memo … a damned memo saying all students planning on taking Osteo this semester are supposed to come to orientation this morning before actual classes even begin!"

"So," Rhyjl shrugged, "That's nothing new. Why the fuss?"

"Because! BECAUSE! It's M A N D A T O R Y! No show, and you are out!"

"Again, nothing new, so cool your jets, Red."

"Cool my jets?" Sara grabbed Rhyjl's arm and brought them both to a standstill. It was akin to hitting a brick wall. Rhyjl could already feel the headache coming on. "Cool my jets! That orientation was supposed to be at eight AM. Do you realize what time it is? Well, do you?"

It was a rhetorical question. However, a watch to glance at for some sort of comic relief would have been nice. A large freckle on her arm would have been better. Only, Sara was the one with freckles. "I'm guessing after eight?"

"Uuuuugh! Damn right! It's eight-forty and there must be a dozen students outside the lab and no teacher. The door's locked, even the shade is pulled. Evidently," Sara's voice was dripping venom, her eyes narrowing to cutting slits, "SHE neglected to read her OWN memo."

"So what are you doing here? You are her TA this year. Get over there."

"Not a chance. I'm not going to clean up her mess. I'm headed over to the Dean's right now and spill the whole thing. Want to come watch the fireworks?"

"Sara, think! The only ones that are going to get the

shaft from this are the students. Go back to the class. You can do the orientation if she hasn't arrived by the time you get back. Then you will be the hero, the students will get the requirement satisfied and ..."

"*And* she gets off scot free?"

"No, you can speak to the Dean later. It will hold more significance giving you more power."

"Uh uh! No way." She'll claim that she expected me to handle the class from the beginning. You know she never takes responsibility for *anything* she does unless it makes her look good."

"She's not the only one," muttered Rhyjl.

"What?"

"I said, 'She's not the only one who can teach the class.' So why don't you go prove you can. Big kudos!" Lifting her right hand and prompting a high-five.

"Nope!" Sara snapped, pointedly ignoring Rhyjl's gesture. Pivoting on her heel and bee-lining for the Dean's, she declared over her shoulder. "The class can rot! It's her responsibility and she's dropping the ball. The Dean needs to know while it's happening."

Rhyjl drew in the moist morning air looking for calm. Follow Sara to the Dean's and wait in line? Or ... Turning, she reversed her path and headed toward the Archaeology building.

*

Erik Arneson's strategy had worked better than he thought. It wasn't as if he was stalking her, well, maybe he was, but not in that creepy way people thought of as stalking. He'd bumped, quite literally, into her on Friday while wandering through a maze of student cars and U-

Hauls between Engineering and the dorms. She'd almost run him down as he rounded a filled-to-bursting SUV. Flustered and apologetic, she hurriedly helped pick up the stack of books she'd knocked from his arms. Then dusting off the last one before handing it back, she smiled.

It was the smile. Yep, the smile. Something had gone "ping" and now he didn't seem to be able to get that smile out of his thoughts.

At their first encounter, he'd watched her skim across campus and disappear behind the big brick building that looked like it had once been the estate's stables. Classes wouldn't start until the middle of next week, but he sensed she knew her way around. He mentally ticked off new student, briefly considered returning student, and hoped she was faculty. If the latter, he'd get the chance to meet her at the faculty dinner on Saturday.

She'd been a no show and that's when his interest peeked even more. Casually, or what he hoped was casual, he asked a few people if they knew someone matching her description. He'd been told there were a few profs who hadn't attended.

"She might be someone from the Anthropology Archaeology Department. They always seem to be late coming back from their summer digs or some such thing," groused Harold, the dowdy little fellow from the Economics Department sprouting a rectangular protuberance from under his dinner jacket that most likely was a pocket protector. "That lady over there," he stated, with a pretentious hand flip toward a mature woman with long salt and pepper hair flowing loosely down her back. "She might know. It's well known their department would collapse without her."

The fellow was so stereotypical it was laughable.

Glancing around at others in the room, he wended his way toward his target. Curiosity heightened, he spied several others who almost announced who they were by their attire, the way they combed their hair, stood or gestured. Did he look like an electronics geek? Was it stereotype reflecting human behavior or the other way around? Was he going to someday spout white hair that stuck out in all directions, and have that lost Einsteinian look about him? Sobering thought.

Henry's "lady" turned out to be Magena Loring. Erik's first faux pas was to address her as Doctor. What else was he to think? She exuded presence. Hell, if he hadn't known better, he'd have thought she was the Dean.

Her laugh was infectious and several of those standing around her caught it. "Me! A doctor? Oh heaven forbid! We have enough of those head cases here. Someone has to stay grounded to keep them in line. That's me. So you're new? What can I help you with Doctor?" To which there was another outbreak of laughter.

His second, was his ineptitude at being able to produce a calm, coherent sentence.   For whatever reason, he was reduced to a stuttering school boy. "I, ah … I was looking for a girl, ah … I mean a woman." Erik wasn't sure he could still blush, but the grin on Magena's face would have been ample reason.

"Oh, a woman!" She winked at the group enjoying his discomfort and asked if the woman had a name?

Erik admitted that he didn't know her name, only what she looked like and thought she might work in the Anthropology Department.

"Well, we have been known to have a few of those over there. Could you be a little more specific?" Magena smiled encouragingly. From another woman, it might have come across as demeaning. He might have taken it as such. The feeling here was companionable. She was secure in who she was and there was no challenge inherent in either her body language or tone.

However, far too many people were enjoying this exchange. Shifting his shoulders back and squaring his stance so his full six foot, three frame looked a little more solid, he began. "Young, curly hair, about so high." His hand tapped even with his shoulder. He followed with a quick synopsis of their meeting, omitting his personal observations, of course, and finished lamely. "She seemed to be stressed. I just was wondering if she was Okay. Sorry to have bothered you."

Magena, her voice softening, answered as he turned to leave. "I think you may mean Rhyjl Martin."

Turning, his smile met hers. Imagination perhaps, but in that moment, he saw, no felt, a sense of deep approval. "Thanks."

A quick exit would have suited him. Martin was common enough, but how many woman had the name Rhyjl? If that name really did belong to the woman he was searching for. He still didn't have an answer to how she fit into DEU's structure. At least he had more leads than before. Ms. Loring hadn't hesitated volunteering a name. So it was a fair probability that he was on the right track with the Anthropology Department.   She wouldn't be that hard to search out. He'd start by doing a quick search on the campus web site. Then a little Google.

He was hijacked halfway to the exit by the head of Engineering and Computer Sciences. "Erik! I was wondering when you would show." George Annaker moved into his personal space, and shoulder to shoulder, he was herded as effectively as a sheep by a collie.

There were still people to meet, social amenities one should observe. It would have gone so much better if Rhyjl had just been there. He downed the remainder of the slightly too-sweet red wine in his glass, vowing that on Sunday, he would spend some time picking apart the campus website.

Everybody loves the new guy. He felt like a bitch in season with everyone circling around to get a better idea of who, what and where. Yes, he'd been offered two teaching positions. One had been at MIT and the other here. Why DEU instead of the other more prestigious school? Not so much because it was a better position, but DEU drew the kind of students he wanted to work with. The kind of atmosphere he hoped would allow him to inspire others while being inspired. It was a small university, small town. He liked the feel.

Invariably, and inevitably, someone put Boston together with Arneson. That was another driving factor in his choice of DEU. It was further away from Boston, meaning fewer family and social expectations. It also was further from his father. Not something he was willing to broadcast, but was always an underlining factor for a lot of his choices in life.

The more financially driven types like Stewart Faulkner sagely nodded as if they understood why he could *afford* to turn down the more lucrative MIT offering for DEU. "Being rich." Their slanted, close-mouth smiles and nodding heads affirmed. To some extent they were correct. DEU wasn't about money. His mother's prudent investments had left him well enough endowed, at least to cover modest expenses until he came into the family fortune his father would grudgingly leave behind some day. But that was another item best left buried. So, he continued waxing eloquently about merit and ingenuity. DEU's recruitment of bright students, rich or poor, for their academic acumen was akin to others recruiting athletes for their athletic prowess. Consequently, the classes were smaller and the students were more likely to be serious. Not that college shouldn't be fun, he added, but he hoped his students would rather get their kicks from experimentation in their field of study, not the beer bust at some local frat. To put it bluntly, he wanted students like himself.

Returning home that night, he pealed his evening wear off on the way to the shower. The socializing had left him feeling dirty and irritable. He felt pimped out; work under the guise of enjoyment. Chalk up another phobia thanks to good ol' Dad.

As the hot water steamed over his body, thoughts of Rhyjl resurfaced. He had the rest of the weekend to find her. He would find her.

By Sunday night he knew more about Rhyjl Martin than probably anyone else who'd ever crossed his life path, other than his mother. It had only whetted his appetite for more. That's when his current plan had begun to form. She lived on campus. She worked as a TA for Dr. McClellen in Anthropology and Archaeology. If on Monday, he stationed himself mid-campus, there was more than a better shot, he'd run into her.

Now, here she was. Coming straight toward him. She wasn't exactly *his* kind of girl, whatever that meant. He'd always thought he would find some tall, blond, classy … or was that his father's choice? That type certainly had been who he'd thrown in with throughout his dating years. Dating years? Whoa, that didn't sound good. Okay, tall, sexy socialites were part of his venue until he'd left for

Caltech to do his grad studies. Then there hadn't been time
for the ladies. Which, if he was honest with himself, was
fine by him. Some of his friends in California were still of
the opinion he was gay, especially that guy, what was his
name? Oh yeah, Jason, who had flirted with him so
shamelessly. Last he'd heard, Jason was at Los Alamos
with some physicist who was the love of his life.

No, Rhyjl, was completely different. It had taken
awhile, but through the campus website and a few other
searches, he'd gleaned further information including that
she was indeed Rhyjl Martin. A doctoral candidate in
Archaeology, Rhyjl had written several papers he'd found
fascinating. Seeing someone with that kind of compassion
for her subjects was something he hadn't come across in a
long time. She spoke about the lives of people from two
thousand years ago as if she had known them personally.
As if she had known their suffering and hardships as well
as their joys. He knew it was a labor of love. She was
amazing!

Now she strolled along the faux brick-stamped
asphalt seemingly lost in thought, just another student.
They must be happy thoughts, her smile seemed to grow
as she drew closer. That incredible smile. His own smile
grew to mirror hers.   She wasn't much over five foot two,
just as he'd described her to Magena, well give or take an
inch. Her hair was a soft warm hickory brown, and curly.
Not tight curls. Soft wavy ones. The kind he could wind
around his fingers. He couldn't judge its length, both times
she'd pinned it up. More than likely it would be long. He
liked that.

"Get a grip! You need to meet her before you start
imagining that luscious hair spread across your pillow."
Startled by the sound of his thoughts, he glanced around.

No one was near enough to have overheard. What did they say about people who spoke to themselves? Oh hell, maybe he was losing it.

She was about twenty yards away. Time to take action. It wouldn't do for it to look like he was just hanging there waiting for her, which of course, he was. Was this adrenal rush due to the pursuit? He'd never experienced that before. He'd honed his skills perfectly to the art of avoidance. This time, he had to make the moves. Something like walking toward her, his interest caught in the campus map he was holding. Yeah, that would work. He would conveniently collide with her. "Oh, funny bumping into you again. Say, I'm a bit lost, would you have a minute or two to show me around?"

Four strides brought him to an abrupt stop. Some carrot-top had bounded up and snatched his goal right out from his grasp. The gal was animated, her long arms flying around. One of those people who wouldn't be able to speak with their hands tied behind their backs. Rhyjl was listening attentively. He also sensed she was a bit annoyed. Again, he was struck with the smile. It wasn't quite genuine. Not like the one she'd previously flashed him, nor been wearing only moments before. No, this was strained. Kind of like the one he imagined he glued on his own face when attending one of his father's parties. There also seemed to be forbearance as well. He studied the interaction. Friends, yeah, but not close. No, not close. Miss carrot-top was … um … yeah, he knew that look. She might not be bubbly blond, or sable brunette, but she hovered in that society sphere. The Rhyjl he'd been researching would feel as out of place in one of those society gigs as he did. He was sure of it. She comfortable outdoors and in the sunshine, and not necessarily idle on the beach either. She was grounded. A deep breath of fresh mountain air like that area in Montana she came from. Something that had been missing for far too many years of his life.

The redhead had obviously failed to pull Rhyjl into whatever had her in its grip. She brushed past him, a woman on a mission. Now was his chance to move forward … but as he diverted his attention from the redhead back toward Rhyjl, his hopes evaporated. He was wrong. Whatever the other woman had said, Rhyjl had reversed direction and was zeroing in on the Archaeology building. To pursue her now would have truly crossed the line into active stalking. He wasn't quite ready to cross that line … yet.

Chapter 2

The Bone Lab

True to Sara's word, by the time Rhyjl reached the second floor of the turn of the twentieth century stable, now Archaeology building, there were approximately a dozen students milling around outside the Osteology lab. Detouring, she retreated back to the main floor and the department reception area. Empty. Well, that would soon change as the year progressed. This was the heart of the Anthropology Archaeology building. Unfortunately, the electrical charge that kept it all running, affectionately known as Mags, was nowhere to be seen. Considering her current undertaking, she would've liked Mags' blessing. Under the circumstances, she didn't feel she had the time to find her.

Skirting around the half-circle Formica counter, Rhyjl entered Mags' inner sanctum. There was no door nor gate to Mags' office. It was open to all. Yet only those who knew they had permission would have thought to trespass. This was a testament to the respect and awe most of the students and faculty held for Magena Loring. The open area reflected the efficiency and order of its occupant's personality, as well as her whimsical humor. Just inside the entry, hanging on the side of a file cabinet under the counter, was an eighteen inch by twenty inch sheet of plywood decorated in early Passamaquoddy glyphs and a half dozen pegs holding keys to various labs throughout the building. Dr. McClellen, the department head, often joked with new students that Mags, a powerful shaman, used the glyphs to curse any who took the keys without permission. Mags, when asked, only smiled neither confirming nor denying the truth of it. Rhyjl's hand went instinctively to the peg expecting to grasp the plastic skeleton normally hanging there. All faculty members had their own keys but these keys were designed for student use. Since all the keys looked the same, each one had been given a visual aid as a key ring. Zooarchaeology, had a gorilla and Anthropology had a blue, purple and pink psychedelic question mark. Rhyjl's favorite was Chip, the little chipped teacup from Disney's Beauty and the Beast attached to the pottery lab key. The one she needed now was a small plastic skeleton for the Osteology lab. Mr. Bones, Mags had dubbed him.

It appeared to be a day for things and people to be missing. First Professor Kendricks, then Magena and now Mr. Bones. There was nothing it seemed she could do, except head back up the stars to face the openly disgruntled students. Her mind crunched on how to address them. Reaching the top stair, relief washed over her. All the students had disappeared and the lab door was open.

How she had missed her, she didn't know, but there was Mags. She and several of the students were occupied in tossing about rather ribald jokes about Manny. Poor old Manny had been the butt of many student and faculty jokes for as long as Rhyjl had known him. He'd always taken it stoically. But then, what could you expect from a skeleton?

Mags waved Rhyjl over, placed Mr. Bones in her hand, and introduced her to the new disciples. As Rhyjl engaged the students, Mags pulled off a bit of magic, vanishing as efficiently as Sara had. Rhyjl took it as her blessing. Or, at least she hoped it was. With some trepidation, she looked out over all those expectant faces.

The orientation was not a challenge. She knew the material inside out. A deep breath, an adjustment to her smile, pushing her shoulders back and head held high, she felt her confidence, tinged with satisfaction, swelling. Someday this might be her class. When she was ready, when it suited her. To be honest, she rather imagined that she knew the subject matter better than Dr. Kendricks. For this reason, Kendricks had more or less banned her from this lab. How many times had she challenged Kendricks? She'd lost count. Kendricks, as Sara accurately described, would turn the challenge to her advantage as if she'd only been testing the students while inwardly nursing her growing hatred of Rhyjl. If Kendricks came in now, there was likely to be fireworks.

"Welcome to Human Osteology 400," Rhyjl began.

She was well past the speech concerning class expectations, grading, lab familiarization and procedures, and was about to move on to the first presentation of lab specimens, before the lump in her throat subsided. Kendricks hadn't materialized on her broom. All seemed well.

"Now, before I introduce you to a friend of mine, are there any questions?"

"How come you were so late," complained a smug-faced young man who looked like he belonged in the gym not the lab. She should know him, but for the moment, the why was escaping her.

"I do apologize. Dr. Kendricks has been regrettably detained. I wasn't notified until the last minute that a substitute for her was needed."

A rather mousy girl with a pale complexion and limp hair raised her hand. "I don't mean to be disrespectful, miss, but is this likely to happen again?"

"Not likely," Rhyjl answered, smiling. "Are there any other questions concerning what I've gone over so far?" There appeared to be none.

The next step was to lay out a specimen on an exam table. Rhyjl chose DR 106. She'd worked with all the remains they had in this lab. Still, Matilda remained special. "This is The Crypt," Rhyjl said, using a key attached to Mr. Bones to unlock what looked like a closet door. "It is in here we keep all the lab specimens." To the casual observer, it didn't appear to be any more elaborate than a good sized walk-in closet lined with shelves bearing identical boxes. Each box was marked with a number. It was on one of these shelves that DR 106, a.k.a. Matilda, rested in her accustomed place. Pulling down a box a little larger than a full sized apple box, she returned to the closest of three backlit tables that were each about eight feet long and four feet wide.

"I cannot stress enough, the time involved in this class. It's hard to explain, but as a student you might spend weeks, or often a whole semester learning every detail you can about one individual. You get to know them intimately. Their features will be more familiar to you than your lovers. Their illnesses and injuries will plague you, pun intended." To which there was a collective moan. "The work they each did, and if a female, whether she gave childbirth and how many times. Lastly, how they departed this world. To many, it might seem that to study these individuals, we have no reverence for them. I can assure you, that as you get to know them that will not be true.

"You might say," Rhyjl continued, pulling on a pair of purple non-latex examination gloves, which visibly reinforced lab procedure, "that Matilda was my closest companion during my time in Osteo 400. I can honestly say, I might not have made it through class without her. As you work this semester in the Osteo lab, one of these citizens of The Crypt will also become your constant companion. Even when you are not in the lab, which," she winked at her audience, "will not be often. Don't plan for any other social life once you have entered here. There is a reason this is a six credit hour class."

Lifting the top off the container, she pulled out the mandible. The U-shaped lower half of the jaw was missing half its teeth and had a long-healed fracture on the chin. As expected, Matilda's familiar touch was there; a soft, muted melancholy, like a lullaby carried from afar on a breeze. Rhyjl placed the mandible, chin down, on the table. "As I lay out Matilda, I will give you a brief overview of her life. She had been a slave on a sugar plantation in the Caribbean. She suffered from malnutrition, several bouts with childhood ailments ..."

A female hand shot up. "How do you know about the childhood ailments?"

"Good question," Rhyjl nodded approvingly. "Anyone have a guess?"

Leslie, one of the brightest students Rhyjl had previously had the privilege of working with as a TA, answered, "Obviously it must leave some kind of mark on the bones."

"Yes! Every serious illness leaves a signature. Not your common cold, unless it was accompanied by a very high fever, but smallpox, measles, tuberculosis and in a society where sexual promiscuity was common, evidence of STDs."

"Is that a social judgment, *Ms.* Martin?" It was a challenge. The tone, acidic and insolent, as if his question was of a personal nature.

While he looked vaguely familiar, Rhyjl couldn't place him. The fellow was medium: medium height, medium weight, medium all the way around. Other than a well sculpted physique he must have spent hours cultivating in a gym, he was just another of the thousands of average guys.

"No, it is just a statement of fact." Rhyjl's arms and shoulders grew taunt. Fight or flight. She wasn't a child anymore. Draw a deep breath. Exhale slowly. "I make no social judgments, and a professional archaeologist or forensic anthropologist shouldn't. Let me make this quite clear, here and now. We are not priest, judge or jury in this lab. We are observers and reporters."

Silence ruled, except the shifting of feet and the palatable hiss of rage heat coiled around her challenger.

The second fragment, a c-shaped zygomatic section also hummed familiarly as did the second and third fragments of the skull. Matilda had not died peacefully. "You will do well to remember we are journalists for the past in this class. Professionalism is expected. Anything less, will not be acceptable to Dr. Kendricks." Reaching again for another piece expecting the melody to continue, she jerked as her hand brushed against the maxilla. The slam shot from her fingers, along her arms, leaving splinters of glass edged with the mixed venom of anger and fear. Her voice gave a little squeak as she peered cautiously into the box.

"Is something wrong?" asked a tall, anorexic-looking, bleached-blond with her hair pulled back in a ponytail she hadn't noticed until that moment.

"Ah … a spider," Rhyjl answered, reaching back in the box and twisting her arm as if dispatching the offender to the nether world. "I'm not fond of them."

A collective groan of assent came from the females and mingled with suppressed laughter from the males. All except a string bean fellow peering through thick lenses and looking like he might keel over. "D-d-does that happen often?"

"No," she stated truthfully, "This sort of thing has never happened as long as I've been here."

Keep calm, keep calm, she silently chanted while her body strained to scream. Focus on Matilda. Even if this isn't her, focus on her story. You'd know it in your sleep. Just focus on the story!

"OK, Matilda." To her own ears, her voice sounded amazingly calm and authoritative considering the snakes slithering up her spine. She hoped that's how it sounded to her audience. "Matilda, wasn't her actual name. We don't know what her name was." One by one Rhyjl reverently removed the remaining bones from the box. Navigating a roller coaster ride of chilling jolts interspersed with the familiar, she laid the whole bones and fragments upon the table to form the skeleton. She could almost believe she was doing well ignoring each sting of incongruity. "Matilda was a slave girl on Haiti. Her life span was short. We know she was probably in her late-teens when she died because the epiphyseal fusion of her innominate is not fully complete." Her fingers hovered above the pelvis, someone's other than Matilda's. Fusion was complete on this specimen, making it a mature female pelvis.

"Are you *sure* that is Matilda?" Mr. bulging-biceps asked lifting an eyebrow and nudging the fellow next to him. "Looks like fusion is complete to me."

She should have known! Damn, of course someone was likely to notice. Too late, she now remembered too well who this guy was. He'd been the jerk last spring in Paleopathology bragging about how he could have been well on his way to his MD if he hadn't decided to switch to forensic anthropology. "Good call, Mr.?"

"Bannerman," he said, stepping closer, chest out, shoulders squared.

"As Mr. Bannerman has astutely pointed out, fusion is complete on this example. This is a perfect illustration of why we need to be very careful when working with specimens. I'm inclined to believe that this innominate has been inadvertently switched with DR 106's." Without even looking up, she knew she had lost them. The silence was stifling. Several were shifting their feet. The frail looking blond hovering near Bannerman looked embarrassed, but not for Rhyjl. The way her eyes shifted, it looked as if she was mortified by his behavior. Whatever, they had obviously come to the point where she couldn't go forward, and there was no going back. Bannerman had not only drawn unwanted attention to a situation she was still trying to reconcile with, but had intentionally used it to undermine her authority. It was best to cut her loses.

"I do apologize that I will have to end here. There isn't much more I can say since DR 106 has been compromised. I will need further time to rectify the problem and unfortunately, we appear to be short of that commodity. I'm happy to have had this opportunity to work with you and I hope you will all enjoy this class in the months to come."

The students filed out in twos. Their voices hushed. Some covertly glanced over their shoulders. Others, who appeared to be Bannerman's cronies, openly smirked. Rhyjl grit her teeth. In a one on one, she could wipe

Bannerman off the board. That opportunity would likely never happen. Which was a good thing. She really didn't like open confrontation. What she needed to do now, was figure out what the hell had happened.

A movement out of the corner of her eye caught her attention. Looking up, she saw the blond anorexic standing alone at the lab door. The girl didn't say anything. Just stood there looking sad. What did she want? To put voice to the apology for Bannerman she'd seen reflected in the girl's expressive eyes earlier? If that were the case, she didn't want to hear it. Not really. Closing her eyes for a moment against the beginnings of a headache, she took a deep breath and readied herself for the inevitable. When she opened them, the doorway was vacated.

Chapter 3

A Mixed Box

One of Dr. Amanda Kendricks' rules is to always leave the lab as you found it. That is to say spotless and everything returned to its proper order and place. It's a good rule, and as Rhyjl's friend, Greg, always says, "Bones is bones, at least to the untrained eye." Maintaining order is imperative. This, Rhyjl thought, picking up a patella whose voice was charged with static, wasn't a case of a few misplaced or switched bones. The offending bones that had been mixed with DR 106 had companions who also found their way into at least three other specimens that Rhyjl had pulled. Not just added to, but replacing them. Someone had deliberately corrupted the specimens. But why? Only two possible scenarios came to mind. One was an elaborate and rather sick hoax to embarrass or discredit. She didn't even have to mull that one over. Bannerman flew right to the top of the list. Where would he have found the bones? The second scenario was even more sinister and one she didn't want to entertain.

Wearing exam gloves and keeping her distance did little to deflect most of the impressions. Rage! Fear! Loss! They all mixed into an intoxicating cocktail. Being familiar with each, only made them more personal. Loss, that kind of cold that stilled the heart, turned the blood to ice, pulling the bearer deeper into the abyss where no light could penetrate, was palatable within these intruders. These bones were new. The feelings were raw. They may have been doctored to give a semblance of age, but no amount of chicanery could alter an individual's vibrations and images.

Most of the skeletons in The Crypt were like old friends at a party. She knew their life stories, the joys as well as the fears and desires, all mixing and blending into the background of her thoughts. This individual, had crashed the scene and was screaming to be heard. Besides the volatile emotions, this woman's voice was laced heavily with confusion. She was refusing to let go. Rhyjl, was refusing to join in. She hadn't signed up for this. She only worked with the long departed not the recent ones.

*

His plan foiled, Erik reluctantly trudged back to his new house to see if he couldn't get settled; not just physically, but mentally. The place was pleasant enough, a small New England cape overlooking the bay and only a stone's throw from the campus. Standing out on the weathered white deck, he could see there was a storm brewing. In spite of the warm sun overhead, the bay was pewter etched by line after line of waves, many capped with white. He'd spent enough time growing up near the Atlantic to know she was building for a blustery night or morning. At the moment, her mood suited him.

"What has come over me, stalking this woman like some raging hormonal teen?" The house only offered silence. He needed to focus on something else, anything else. The coming gale was as good as any. Pulling out his smart phone, he began a voiced list. "Batteries, candles, bottled water." He paused. Better also check the local hardware to see if they had generators. Then the grocery for some things to eat that didn't require cooking. "Bread," he resumed, "cheese, veggies." A nice wine, he thought and then groaned as he flashed on Rhyjl and wondered if she preferred red or white or possibly didn't drink at all. "Red wine," he told his phone. "White wine. Beer." Well that took care of the evening. Now he needed to focus on breakfast. "Cereal, milk, fruit..."

*

Magena was in full swing when Rhyjl returned to the office. The Xerox machine was humming and spitting out papers, most likely a syllabus, and two amber blinking lights on Mags' phone indicated she'd placed some unhappy individuals on hold while she fielded a third call. "That is extension 208. Would you like to be put through? One moment please," Mags said, fingering in the extension and forwarding the call, while smoothly moving on to the next. "Thank you for holding. How may I help you?" She reached for a pink post-it while nodding in Rhyjl's direction and holding up her index finger to effectively let Rhyjl know, even without a light, she'd been placed on hold as well. "I'm sorry, Dr. McClellen hasn't come in yet. I can take a message or put you through … Yes, I'll do that Dr. White." Mags scribbled on the post-it. "University of Arizona. Yes, I'll make sure he gets the message as soon as he comes in." Mags' finger pointed up a second time and pushed the other amber-pulsing button. "Thank you for holding … Ah, that information can be found …" She rattled off the department's web site address, then turned expectantly to Rhyjl as she hung up the phone.

"So Marc still isn't in?" The question was rhetorical since Mags had already relayed that information to Dr. White.

"Nope." Mags shook her head while reaching once more for the phone. "Down East Anthropology-Archaeology Department, Magena speaking, how may ..." Finger up, once again, placing Rhyjl on hold. "Dave, line two."

"How was class?" She turned to Rhyjl holding her hand out for the key. When it didn't materialize in her outstretch fingers, she looked closer at Rhyjl. "Oh?"

"Interesting." Rhyjl wasn't sure quite how to approach the subject. Her first impulse was to blurt it out. However, several students had walked in during the phone interlude. Mr. Bones' angles were cutting into her palm as she held back. "Mags, we need to talk. Privately," she added, indicating the presence of the others with a tilt of her head.

"This way," Magena said, taking the lead down the hall to a storage room. "Did Sara ever show up?"

"No, but we have another problem," Rhyjl confessed, as the storage room door shut behind them.

"Damn right we do! Half of the staff is MIA. So what's your fire? Did Manny walk out?" Magena's hand was reaching for a ream of pastel paper on a lower shelf.

"No, I think someone else has taken up residence," Rhyjl countered a little more sharply than she intended.

Eyes, as sharp and deep as a night sky turned to capture Rhyjl's. When Mag's got that look, it wouldn't have surprised her if Dave was right about Magena being a witch or a shaman. She'd watched Magena work magic out of chaos in the department so many times. Her look could stop students, and professors alike, cold. If there was anyone who could soothe a bad situation, it was Mags.

"Who took up residence?"

"That's just it," Rhyjl said, shrugging while shaking her head. "I don't know, but there are at least four Crypt residents whose remains have been compromised by bones that don't belong. There might be more, I - I just didn't take any more time to look. Mags, I uh, I think someone has been murdered and hidden in the lab."

"Be careful! Are you sure someone didn't make a mistake and mix the specimens together?" Magena's hand rested on the pale blue paper now forgotten.

"Yes, I know all those bones. These, well these, may look old, but they're not."

"There's a lot of bones in there, are you absolutely sure?" The older woman, her voice not much more than a whisper, moved to Rhyjl and firmly, but gently, placed her hands on Rhyjl's shoulders.

"Yes." Rhyjl whispered back. It's not that the bones have been jumbled. The bones I found don't belong there, have never been there, EVER!"

"Um, follow me and don't say another word." Magena led the way back to the reception area, pointed to a green rump-worn chair that probably dated back to the seventies. "Stay." she commanded, rounding the desk.

Like a reincarnation of someone's canine companion, Rhyjl sat. The desk divider acted like a wall to obscure what Mags was doing. It wasn't necessary to guess, however, as the rapid tapping of the keyboard and then the phone pad, struck like a tiny sharp blows to Rhyjl's confidence. She had better be right about this it tattooed. The pit of her stomach was tightening. What if.... NO! No matter how improbable, she was right. She was right. SHE WAS RIGHT! Her face dropped to her hand. Even if she were blind, there was no mistaking the feel: the seething, confusion, anger!

"I'm trusting your instincts on this one," Mags stated.

The air was tense. It enveloped her like a thousand prickling needles. To remain seated was agony. Leaving the chair, she paced the room's parameter twice before coming to rest, elbows braced on the counter. She studied Mags, envying the decisive composure enveloping the intrepid lady.   Maybe that sense came with age. Whatever. At this moment, her condition was a mixture of relief and trepidation running hot and cold through her veins. Her lips parted not knowing what to say. The decision was stripped from her when Mags' indomitable finger once more demanded silence.

"Yes, Jean, give me Dean Jacobson, and no, it can't wait."

*

Mind racing on a hamster wheel while waiting for the police to show, Rhyjl kept picturing the newcomer's bones. Yes, it had been the feel of them, that sharp energy that had alerted her. She could hardly tell the officials that, now could she. Once alerted, she had gone in search of them, felt them the traditional way, being careful not to linger, for the power was too raw. Its nettle-like sting draining. What could she tell them, show them?

The coloring was correct, a rusty brown with splotches of yellow. To an untrained eye they would look no different than the others. Someone, had even taken the time to print the ID numbers on the bones and then covered it over with clear acrylic nail polish.

"Mags, I'm going back to the lab. I will be more help there than cooling my heels here. Besides," Rhyjl said before Mags could post any objection, "It will be easier for the officers when they get here. I can separate out the boxes with the new bones from the others."

It was just an excuse to get back to the lab and look more closely. She needed to be able to point to something credible when asked. Heart racing as if she had just run a mile, she entered the lab, locked the door and pulled the shade. The snakes that earlier had been traveling up her spine were now a roiling mass in her stomach. This was ridiculous! She was doing nothing wrong. Yet somewhere deep inside, she knew she was. Still, she had to do this. Had to have a reason to explain to them why these bones were different. The alternatives? They would think she was crazy and ignore the situation or, they would simply ignore it, harboring the suspicion as Mags had, that the bones between specimens were somehow misplaced. Either scenario was pretty much the same. The results would be that the poor individual who was hidden would remain hidden. Why she was so sure about that was another question that would have to wait until later. A criminal would go free. Neither of those were acceptable.

In her undergrad years, her first archaeology professor, Gerald Grant, had been of the old school. She'd always felt privileged that the year spent under his tutelage was the last year he taught before retiring. Gerry was quite the character. It wasn't hard for any of his students to imagine him in his earlier years as the prototype for Indiana Jones.

One day, while going through some recent finds for the Smithsonian, Gerry did the unthinkable while demonstrating morphology: He removed his gloves, closed his eyes, and caressed the bone.

Matthew, one of Rhyjl's fellow classmates, looked

horrified and called the professor on it.

"Are you suggesting I'm doing something improper, Mr. Giles?" Professor Grant's eyes sparked with challenge.

"Ah …" Poor, hapless Matthew, still believing he was correct, but not wishing to take the challenge on, spoke barely above a whisper. "Your gloves, Sir?"

"Um. How very astute of you, Mr. Giles." Gerry Grant closed his eyes and continued to stroke the specimen in hand. "Tell me Mr. Giles, have you ever made love to a woman?"

Several of the guys snorted or snickered. Rhyjl and another girl managed muffled giggles. Matthew blossomed in crimson from his clavicles past his ears.

"Yes, well I surmised as much." Gerry Grant continued, in spite of another round of humor. "Bones, gentleman and ladies," he said, nodding to the only two females in the class, "are like a woman. Would any of you fellows make love to a woman with these on?" He held up the white latex gloves. "No, I didn't think so." He then threw the gloves down. "If by chance you were stupid enough, and clearly none of you are or you wouldn't be present in my class, think how much you would miss. Is she soft? Dry? Are there any fine scars only detectable because of a subtle change in the texture of her skin? What do you think, Mr. Giles? With your gloves on would you notice the subtleties?"

Smiling at the memory, Rhyjl stripped off the gloves and reexamined the bones she had left out on the table earlier. There, she sighed deeply, buried beneath the pain, anger and confusion that were battering at her mind, the bone was smooth and moist. Not moist like with water, but all bones exuded a fatty oil when they were fresh.

Depending on how long or in what fashion they had been exposed to the elements or in this case, she guessed, chemicals, the bones would still exude that oily substance for a period of time. Matilda and her Crypt companions were all well over two hundred years old. They had long since ceased to bleed. Only traces of it remained behind in the earth which had interred them, turning it darker than the surrounding soils.

"Got it!"

*

Once again taking up occupancy in the green chair, Rhyjl waited. Waiting, in this instance, was more unnerving than the clunking sound her car had made before the U joint went out and left her hoofing it everywhere. She been told the police would want to speak with her. So what was taking so long?

Something analogous to a small earthquake jarred her from her thoughts. "Hey, Rhyjl! Come up for air and talk to me. Do you know anything about why there is a police car and ambulance here?"

Um, the very individual who was to blame for her being in this situation. "Sara! Where the hell have you been!" Rhyjl groused.

"Oooooh testy are we? What? Did the witch show up and cast some dark spell over you? Did you let her have it? Do I dare hope she is the reason for all the flashing lights?"

"Ha! Funny! No, she didn't show up, but it would have been nice if you had."

"But you did well with the class. You always do." Sara, stated while focusing on her fingernails and worrying a cuticle.

"Eyes narrowing and nose wrinkled, Rhyjl threw mental daggers in Sara's direction.

Noticing Rhyjl's lack of verbal response, Sara paused in her nail scrutiny to look at her friend. "Ah." she said, raising a quizzical eyebrow. "Class didn't go so well, I take it? I'm sorry, but you took it of your own volition. I didn't ask you to." Sara flopped down on the avocado-colored faux leather sofa and propped her crossed legs on the low table in front of her. It didn't appear to bother her that in doing so, her feet fell on a few magazines scattering them on the table.

"You're right, Sara, I took it because *you* didn't care enough to."

"Wow! It must have gone really, really bad. So who is he?"

"What?" Rhyjl's head was beginning to ache. Strange how this seemed a normal occurrence when she was trying to carry on some kind of conversation with her roomy. "What makes you think there was a guy?"

Sara's cat-green eyes twinkled. "Because there aren't many women, including 'ol Kendricks, who can get to you. However, you don't deal well with men, unless …" Sara swallowed her next words. She knew that look. It was Rhyjl's one more word and you-might-find-a-dead-mouse-in-your-bed look. "Ah, so what did happen?"

"You haven't been up to the lab, I take it?"

"Nope! Just got here." Sara's eyes narrowed to slits. "Uh, you didn't do something … I mean I was just joking about Kendricks."

"I don't know if I can talk about it."

"Can't or won't?"

"Well, let's just put it this way," Rhyjl said,

twisting a rubber band she'd found in her pocket around her fingers. Someone unexpected did show up in class today. A very unwelcome guest!"

"Ha! So there was a guy? What did you do? Call the police? Hit him? I want to hear all the details." Sara uncrossed her legs, letting them drop to the floor and leaned in closer to the chair Rhyjl occupied.

"That, my dear friend, is the mystery," Rhyjl sighed, beginning to feel like this just might be the longest day of her life.

"Yo!" A masculine voice interrupted. "Does anyone know what's going on down at the bone lab? The place has sprouted yellow crime scene ribbon and has uniforms crawling all over it?"

*

The summons came through Billy, the campus' weathered security officer. Until today, Billy's primary job was to ticket vehicles not displaying current parking passes. Rhyjl didn't know much about him, but she had often passed a few words with him when working late. Her sense had always been of a man who felt his boat had long since sailed and he was just putting in time. As he approached her now, his stride was surer, his posture more erect, forcing his normally stooped shoulders back, and there was a healthy glow to his face. "Miss Martin, if you would come with me, please."

Both Sara and Rhyjl rose to follow in line. Billy turned, stopped, and wearing a deep frown, threw a warning glance at Sara. She promptly ignored it and the trio continued to the bone lab.

The deputy at the door to the lab was a different

story. He was probably of equal age to herself and Sara. His sandy brown hair, hazel eyes and tanned rugged face were attractive. His stance clearly said he was no Billy. "Ms. Martin," he pronounced formally standing aside to let Rhyjl pass, then smoothly inserting himself between her and her shadow.

"I'm with her," Sara stated, failing to maneuver past him.

"Oh good. Then you can keep me company out here until she comes back," he replied, winking.

Another time, Sara might have been flattered. Another time she would have wasted no time chatting this fellow up until he was eating out of her hand. Another time. This wasn't one of those. This attractive hunk of masculinity wasn't a game or conquest, only an obstacle to what Sara wanted.

Coming down the hall, Rhyjl was thinking that the deputy's facial morphology and coloring probably placed his heritage as British Isles, most likely Scot. He certainly had the broad shoulders and barrel chest. It was a little game she played. Later she might ask him where his people came from just to see if she was correct. She'd done the same with people's accents. There were always the chameleons who took on the guise of those they were around. She was one of them. That had never been more apparent than when she'd spent a summer in the UK. Oh that she had a dollar for everyone who'd thought she was Canadian. As she nodded politely, a second observation manifested. She'd had dealings with this same officer only last week when he'd stopped her because the scout had a blinker out. The quirk at the corner of his mouth and the wink as she passed, said he remembered their last meeting as well.

Rhyjl only hoped as she crossed the threshold into the Osteology lab that Sara wouldn't be up on charges for assault and battery. Her voice was rising in volume and irritation. "But I'm in charge of this lab until Professor Kendricks returns."

"Sorry, Miss," the deputy replied firmly. "I'm sure your turn will come."

At which point, Rhyjl imagined that Sara had tried to push past. "Get your hands off me, you oaf, before I have you up on charges of sexual harassment!"

Poor Sara. One of these days she might learn to quell her temper.

"Something funny, Miss?"

This wasn't the first time Rhyjl and seen Sheriff Buchard. Usually it was coming in or going out of Perfection Confections in town or Mel's, the small diner that catered to most of the locals. He was an ample man that had caused Rhyjl on more than one occasion, to imagine the stress to his bones that his excesses were causing. At other times, she had wondered how much longer it would be before he was forced to start wearing suspenders. The alternative being ... well, best to leave off that thought before she would have to confess to a different reason for her smile.

"Ah, no sir," she replied, forcing her face into as much placidity as she could muster. She knew she was one of those people who should never lie or play poker until she could learn to school expressions by keeping direct eye contact and the quelling of her rapid fire thoughts.

His eyes narrowed momentarily before transferring his attention to the notepad in his beefy hand. "So let me get this straight," he said, flipping open his notes. His eyes moved rapidly then stopped. "Says here that you taught the introduction to the class today. Is that correct?"

Rhyjl nodded, but otherwise kept silent.

He looked up to note her response, then back to his scribbling. "I don't see you listed as one of Dr. Kendrick's teaching assistants. Are you?"

"No, sir."

"Are you in the habit of teaching classes for which you have no authority, Miss Martin?"

"No!" she snapped, feeling the stinging heat along her neck and too late, heard the defensive edge in her voice.

His eyebrows raised. Her outburst was due to her earlier ego hit from Bannerman, but she couldn't bring that up in her defense. Seeking composure, and wishing to erase the sharpness of her voice, she rubbed her lower lip. "No, sir," she replied, in a more subdued tone. Unfortunately, there was no masking the hard edge or boldness in her eyes. "I am not. However, Dr. Kendricks was not able to be here. One of her assistants asked if I could cover as I am *more* than qualified to teach this introductory class."

"I see. And why didn't this assistant teach the class?"

"She … she needed to see the Dean."

"So you come in to teach a class, that is not your responsibility, and find bones, *you say,* don't belong. Do I have that correct?"

Rhyjl felt the sting again as the muscles along her neck and shoulders tensed. "Look, sir," Rhyjl crossed to a group of observers standing around the table she'd laid the bones out on. "I know these bones like you know Perfection Confections," she continued, in spite of a muffled groan from behind her. "This bone, for example is not the bone of an eighteen old slave girl, yet according to the numbers identifying it, that's exactly what it should be. The innominate of a young slave who died over two hundred, fifty years ago. Even a junior attending this introduction noticed the discrepancy."

"And as I understand it, called you on it. Isn't that correct, Miss Martin?"

The punch was hard. Internally she felt herself staggering, but she knew she hadn't moved even a hair's breadth. "I recognized the discrepancy, but was hoping I could bluff my way through the rest of the introduction without drawing attention to it."

"So you say. Yet as I asked, and you were so eager to point out, anyone with knowledge of bones would have noted it. Why the charade, Miss Martin?"

Why had they spoken with the students before questioning her? Or had Bannerman jumped at the chance to offer his findings just like the ambulance chaser slime he probably was? "Because I needed time to think of how to handle the situation?"

"Miss Martin, I will ask you again, are you faculty?"

"No, but ..."

"No!" He snapped. "Are you a forensic specialist?"

That was a loaded question. The enamel on her teeth was bearing her anger.

The sheriff mistaking silence for agreement, continued. "Then Miss Martin, do you know the penalty for falsely reporting a crime. No? Well you are about to find out."

The proverbial shit had hit the fan. To her way of thinking, what further damage could be done if she threw another hand full of it? "With all due respect, sir, which is more than you've given me, I've been studying archaeology for seven years. Four of those years, have been dedicated to Osteology and Zooarchaeology, the study of bones, both human and animal, sir."

He held up his hand for her to stop, the hard tracks of annoyance carving deeply around his mouth and eyes.

She was having none of it. She was right and no man had intimidated her since her father. She wasn't about to back down now. The suppressed anger she rarely allowed to surface, gushed forth in a fountain. "As I stated before, I know these bones! This one," she held up a radius and shook it at his nose. "This specimen's radius was broken in two places. It healed misshapen, because none knew how to fix it or didn't care. Does this bone look like it was ever broken? No? Well, how astute of you. And this rib," she brandished it like a blade. "This rib is much more robust than what it should be for a half starved woman." She was shaking as she stared him in the eye.

"If you are quite through, young woman," the sheriff growled. "As *I* said, we only have your word on this. You are not faculty nor an expert, only a student at this facility. I can see now that you do believe this story of yours, so it will be looked into. You may go Miss Martin and hopefully compose yourself." He snapped his notebook shut and turned dismissing her.

"Sheriff, would you know if a woman in a dark room was your wife?"

Before he could answer, the young deputy who had left Sara noticeably outside the shut lab door, and was gaping at the two bones Rhyjl still held, replied, "Anyone would know his wife in a dark room." Amid the guffaws, hoots and a few strangled groans, the young officer realized just exactly what he'd said. "I mean, well," he stammered, "it's, it's that she is just so …" To which new snickers erupted.

Buchard's face was the color of a pomegranate and just as sour. "We will discuss this later, Mr. Camron!" he snapped. "As for you!" He turned on Rhyjl.

"I'm sorry. I meant no disrespect." She hurried on, "I just meant that when you spend time with people, you'd know them even in the dark."

"If I may, Sheriff," a feminine voice of composure rose above the mirth. "I'd like to discuss these findings in more detail with Miss Martin."

"You can have her." Buchard dismissed Rhyjl like soiled laundry.

The woman speaking was one of half a dozen people who had congregated around the exam table. Rhyjl's first cursory appraisal of her had been that she was a crime scene photographer. Not an unrealistic expectation considering the high tech digital camera slung around her neck and that she'd been snapping numerous photos from different angles.

"Hi." She offered her hand to Rhyjl. "I'm Dr. Alice Merks, ME. I'm with the state coroner's office." While Rhyjl was still openly trying to grasp that this woman before her, decked out in Prada and coveted title of doctor, was probably the same age as she, Dr. Merks added, "Allow me to say, Sheriff, considering the complexity and unusual situation this case presents, Miss Martin is correct in that she most likely is the expert here."

*

"There are two hundred six bones in the human body. If those bones have been broken into fragments …

well, you get the picture." Rhyjl was saying, then apologized. "I'm sorry, I guess I'm still in lecture mode."

Alice Merks, grinned. "You're good. Tell me about the bones here in the lab. How many specimens are housed here?"

"DEU has a very small group. Sometimes we have visitors to The Crypt on loan from other sources, but for the most part, we have twenty five individuals. Around half of those are complete."

"Complete?"

"Well, yes. All of ours are characters from the past. I don't believe we have a skeleton in here that doesn't date back over two hundred years. It's not like in your business where you have …" Rhyjl paused looking for the word. Fresh? No. New? Not really. "Ah, recently deceased, and a complete set. We lose many parts to decay, rodents …"

"As we do in some cases," Alice Merks inserted. "Especially if exposed to weather or predators. Don't you ever watch TV?"

"TV? I'm sorry, but what does that have to do with …"

"Never mind, if you have to ask, I know the answer. So continue. You have twenty five individuals, half of them are not complete. How many are female?" Alice tapped something into her smart phone.

"Of the complete, probably five. Of the partial, another six." Rhyjl tapped her finger to her lips. Her brain was running the hamster wheel mentally extrapolating how many specimens would have been corrupted if indeed an entire person had been hidden among them. "What? I'm sorry I was lost in thought." Rhyjl responded to the partially caught inquiry of Dr. Merks.

"I asked how many specimens you checked before

you convinced yourself to have us contacted."

Rhyjl shifted her weight. Her eyes narrowing and lips drawing together as if she'd just sucked a lemon, she admitted, "Four females. I suppose you are going to tell me I shouldn't have?"

"Perhaps you have seen a few shows." Alice laughed, as confusion remodeled Rhyjl's face from hard core defense. "No, I would have done the same, had I been in your shoes. My boss might not see it that way, but we girls have to stick together. So they were all salted with the new bones?"

"Yes, but if we are dealing with a complete individual, then there are still quite a few missing, or they might still be in with the others I didn't have time to check."

"Such as?" Alice's finger was flying over the face of her phone.

"I've found no dentition."

"Now why doesn't that surprise me? Other than dentition are there enough fragments to attempt facial reconstruction?"

The tsunami struck, sending Rhyjl reeling and clutching blindly for the chair she knew must be close by. Hands grasped her shoulder and arm. Words buffeted her with no meaning. The face swam near. The eyes pleading, lips stretched in a silent scream. Searing pain scorched every inch of her. Then, just as quickly as it had hit, all sensations receded, leaving only the urgent need to find the bathroom. She was going to be sick.

*

Erik checked his phone list again. He knew there

was something he must be missing. Food, water, a generator, he decided flashlights and battery powered camp lanterns were a better bet than the candles. Yet, a few candles would add a warmer atmosphere that was absent from colder lights. He left the small local Ace Hardware and was crossing the street when he noticed that a few doors down from his parking spot was a bakery— Perfection Confections. Well if that isn't a challenge. He stowed his purchases in the back of his Tesla and set his sights on an apple fritter he just knew was calling his name. Still absorbed in his thoughts, he absently reached for the door handle. It was torn from his grasp by heavy set uniformed man still clutching something loaded with powdered sugar. Another uniform, looking far more fit, bobbed his head in acknowledgment as he followed in the wake of the first. Minutes later, lights and sirens blared as an EMT vehicle and a Maine State Coroner's car joined the sheriff's cruiser.

"Wow, somebody is having a rough day." Erik said, to the pretty brown-haired, cocoa-eyed girl at the glass display case.

"Something at the University. Probably a drug overdose. Little early in the year for that sort of thing, though. So what can I get for you?"

Erik chose two fritters and then on a whim, added two Texas-sized sweet rolls he thought might make a good breakfast addition.

Blue Harbor was a quaint village that wasn't going to make it on many maps unless they were the kind that showed every cow path located within the state of Maine. Most people stumbled on it either through its association with Down East University or got lost on their way to or from Mount Desert Island. But once found, it was a jewel.

During the winter months only the locals and the college people took up occupancy. In the summer there was just enough tourist trade to make up for the lack of college residents. In other words, it stayed stable neither ebbing nor flowing. Events at the university were the main topic in town most days.

The town boasted one sheriff, two deputies, three, if you counted Officer Albright who served as dispatch and public liaison during the day. Erik had met the latter a month ago by way of his first introduction to the quaint town while looking into a place to stay. Just because a town is small, doesn't mean finding a location is easy. After circling around the village for what had seemed like an eternity, he'd grudgingly inquired at the sheriff's office how he might find the local real-estate agent. He didn't feel near as embarrassed when he learned Blue Diamond Properties was located above Mel's diner. Or, that from the street, it was no more than a two by three Plexiglas-faced bulletin board hung on the wall next to a blue door leading up a flight of stairs. So much for the preconceived notion that a real-estate office would have its own building.

That the sheriff and EMT response time was so closely timed, made complete sense to Erik as he drove out of town. The fire station was all volunteer and located in a two story barn structure directly behind the lovely Georgian period home, now housing the city hall and sheriff's department. Once upon a time during the village's heyday in the nineteenth century, they had both been part of some sea captain's residence or a prosperous farm. What nagged at the back of his mind, was the State Medical Examiner's vehicle. He supposed it was possible that an ME lived nearby …

The main entrance to the university was blocked by

a patrol car where the lovely deputy Albright directed all traffic away. Too where? Who knew? Erik slowed wondering if his status as faculty might get him a pass? He decided he'd be better off going around to his house. He'd put away his groceries and other purchases and then head over to see what could be learned.

An hour later, and his physical hunger needs met by his second apple fritter, Erik made his way to the interior of the campus. To say his heart didn't pump a little faster or a jolt of adrenalin hadn't shot through his veins, would have been a gross understatement. He'd been expecting the activity to be over. At the very least, the tail end of it being wrapped up. He'd also harbored the expectation that one of the student residences or even Main would be the center of activity. He was not prepared for law enforcement to still maintain a presence, as did the EMT and ME vehicles, outside the Anthropology building.

This definitely called for a little gossip mining and Main was the best place to begin.

Chapter 4

One Man's Plan

Rhyjl had no idea how long she'd been chilling on the bench located along the campus green across from Main. The strange episode in the lab had not only drained her, but she couldn't remember ever having anything like it happen before. It was not the usual scene where she was an observer. True, more than an observer, for she often had a sense of the emotions that went along with the scene. But to actually feel as if she was inside the person? Really experiencing what they had endured? She shivered violently and not just from memories of what had transpired. The sun was much lower on the horizon and while still shedding a crystalline light, had lost what little warmth it had offered earlier. Her thoughts, as was not unusual, had run away with her until her body began to complain about becoming stiff from the chill her sweater had long ceased keeping at bay. Somewhere in the recesses of her primal survival instincts, she knew she needed to move. She was working on it, when a shadow fell blocking what little of the sun's rays remained.

"Are you alright, Miss Martin?" an unfamiliar male voice inquired.

He was tall. She guessed at least six feet since from her sitting position her eyes were level with his belt. It was good quality brown leather with a gold buckle and went well with the rest of his attire. His coat was rust colored, half knit, half suede, casual, but classy. The pants grey wool and the shoes were brown loafers. Rhyjl's eyes traveled from the well scuffed shoes to a face that was vaguely familiar. "Do I know you?"

"Well in a roundabout fashion, I suppose." The man smiled. "We ran into each other several days ago out in the parking lot. My name is Erik Arneson."

"Oh yes." Another one of her preoccupied clumsy moments. "Sorry about that. If there was any damage to one of your books …"

"No, no. Nothing like that. Look, I don't mean this to sound creepy or anything, but I have a confession to make."

Rhyjl didn't feel much like conversing. She wanted to be alone. Wanted desperately to somehow cleanse herself from the residual trappings of the day. Now this fellow shows up and wants to make some kind of confession. Could her day get any stranger? No, don't even go down that path. Grandmum would say, *'If you ask if something could get any worse, it usually does. Don't invite trouble.'*

He took a step back sensing he was encroaching too far into her space. Or was he expecting she might find exception to what he was going to say and desire a quick exit? "I don't quite know how to say this, but I've been trying to find you ever since then."

"Why?" She was studying his face. A strong face, an elongated oval; the forehead, high, the cheek bones as well. His brow ridge was strong, but did not protrude Neanderthal-like and blended aesthetically with his long straight nose where his wire rimmed glasses perched. A trim, rusty-iron-colored beard and mustache swallowed most of his mouth and effectively hid his chin. Decidedly of Scandinavian descent, even if he hadn't given his name.

"Because I want to get to know you." It was the

plain and simple truth.

"Okay, I'll bite." Her voice dripped with the exasperation she was feeling. She saw him wince, felt a tinge of remorse, and softened. "Look, I'm sorry, but right now isn't the best time for me. I've had a tough morning."

"Yes, I heard." He reached in his pocket. Felt the small smooth stone waiting to give him security just as it had since his mother's death.

"What?" She shot to her feet.

"I was over at the SUB to get something to eat, when I overheard a couple students talking about you." Well, it was a half-truth. He had ordered a coffee chaser for his earlier two fritters.

Great! Just great! Now she was the subject of gossip. "Might I ask what they were saying and who they were? For that matter, do you often listen to other people's conversations or were they speaking directly to you?" She really didn't want to know. Not really. So she gathered her pride to leave.

"Look, I …" he placed a gentle, staying hand upon her shoulder. Behind his wire rimmed glasses, eyes the color of the winter sea expressed concern along with a disarming smile which was half hidden. "I'm not trying to be intrusive here. I just want to get to know you. I'm awkward at this. It appears my tongue has forgotten how to articulate. It would seem to me that you might just need someone to talk to. Nothing more. Perhaps we could talk while we eat, or I could at the least get you a coffee?"

"Didn't you just tell me you'd come from the cafeteria?"

"Yes, I did," he said, offering his arm. "I didn't say I'd eaten. I heard this trio talking and spotted you outside the window. Look, treat's on me. No strings, just some conversation."

"Do you make this offer to all the young women on campus?" she asked, wondering at the same time why she was slipping her arm through his.

"No, only the damsels that appear distressed."

"White Knight syndrome?" They had begun walking and it occurred to her, and was strangely pleasing, that while he had long legs, he adjusted his stride to match hers. She could have sworn his eyes twinkled with mirth or mischief before he adeptly turned the focus back to her.

"Possibly, I haven't really stopped to analyze it. So I gather there was an unexpected surprise today in the Archeology orientation you were hosting?"

Bannerman! She stopped abruptly. "Was that the gossip? No one is supposed to know until the police are finished." Then realizing what she'd just done, she groaned and bit her lower lip.

"Police? Here on campus? Now how did I miss that? It's not as if this is a large campus. Word does gets around. Plus you must admit it is pretty hard to miss flashing lights and sirens. You'll have to tell me more. Or not." He quickly amended, feeling her stiffen. "Unless you want to, that is. But to answer your question, I was standing at the counter in the SUB waiting my turn to grab something to go. These three, rather raucous and immensely immature young men sitting close by, were enjoying a big laugh at your expense. I'd heard your name, and shamefully, but not apologetically, listened in. The one was bragging about how you didn't know one bone from another. Something I know isn't true."

They reached the double glass doors leading to the cafeteria which was located in the north wing of the main building and had once been one of two formal dining rooms when the building had been a private residence. Erik casually skirted the first dining room known as the Student Union Building and proceeded to a second dining room further down the hall. The SUB was a casual gathering place with a couple of pool tables, lounging couches and studying tables. It served prepackaged everything and looked out on the campus center. The second cafeteria, or the Victorian as it was known, had retained much of its grandeur of the past. The one exception was a serving counter at the far end. Even that was made of beautifully carved, dark, rich wood that perfectly blended with the paneling and parquet floor. She felt a little contented sigh, looking out the tall windows framing a majestic view of verdant lawn dropping off into the wind tossed cove. Yes, she did love the class and beauty of bygone eras. Even going back to the Nordic halls of the Vikings, it had been important to bring depth of ownership into the structures. To her, much of the contemporary architecture was cold, impersonal, assembly line. Then perhaps cold and impersonal did reflect contemporary owners.

"Penny for your thoughts or would that be a half dollar these days?"

"Um, just wool gathering as my Grandmum would say. And wondering why you seem to know so much about me?"

"Because," he grinned, a slight blush warming his cheeks, "as I started to say, I've taken an interest in you since our collision in the parking lot."

"That sounds a little unerringly like stalking to me." Rhyjl went to take a chair at a nearby table and felt slightly embarrassed and taken aback when he pulled it out for her.

"Don't look so shocked," he offered seating her,

then chose the opposing chair. "Some of us were taught manners. I came from a proper Boston home. My Grandmother, the matriarch, made sure I even knew which of the forks to use at dinner."

Ice began to melt. The beginning of a thaw her body was craving. She laughed. "Well that's more than I can say. At our table we only had one fork." His demeanor was infectious. Grudgingly, she had to admit, it just might be what she needed.

"So what will it be? Coffee? Full meal?"

"I don't drink coffee," she shrugged.

"Tea, or my favorite, hot chocolate?"

She agreed a hot chocolate would be nice. He left her sitting while he went to the counter to place the order. She watched as he walked away, his strides eating up distance. Again she was struck by how he had tempered that. Once more the gentleman. Had he also been discrete by avoiding the other room guessing that Jerk Bannerman and his companions might still be there? Most likely.

So he'd thought about her. Why? She hadn't given him a passing thought. Then she usually didn't give guys much thought. Truth was, she didn't have time for any complications except her work. And just like the Jerk, men were often just that, complications. She knew that sounded like she hated men. Well, maybe in part she did. There were exceptions. Her friend Greg. Yeah, he was okay. Part of her wished he wasn't in York England, but ... well, he was more like a brother. She also knew what she wanted. Someone who shared her interest in Archaeology. Probably a co-worker. A face came to mind. She quickly dismissed it and chose instead to focus past the windows out to the ocean.

"What are you planning on knitting?" He asked,

returning with two hot chocolates and a large poor boy sandwich on a tray.

"Huh?"

"You were wool gathering again. You must be going to do something with it?"

"Oh, ha, funny! No, just wondering why you seem to know about me, but I know nothing about you. Are you a student? Are you with the Anthropology or Archaeology department?"

"Hardly. I'm an engineer. Your science is too abstract for me. I prefer knowns and constants. Much easier for my simple brain to wrap around." He looked at the sandwich and then up at her with a nonverbal question.

She shook her head.

"You're sure? There's more than enough for two here."

It did look good and she hadn't thought she was hungry until that moment. "Well maybe a quarter of it if you don't mind?"

Erik cut the long over-stuffed roll in half and magically produced a second plate from under his own.

"You planned for that, didn't you?" she accused, as he slid the plate in front of her.

"Moi?"

"Either that or you're a piss poor excuse for an engineer. That's a lot more than a quarter."

"You asked if I was a knight. I'm not, but I was an Eagle Scout."

"Ah," she said, before biting into her half.

As she ate, Erik shared how he had come to DEU. He'd first learned about it from an old professor friend of his who was now retired and living in Portland. "I could have chosen something out California way, but I'd miss the New England winters and the changes of season," he shared. "I also wanted a smaller campus."

He *was* at home in New England, just as the setting they were in now was perfect for him. With the exception of his jacket, the rest of his appearance; full mustache, beard and even the way his thick, wavy brown hair combed back from his high forehead, made her wonder for a moment if he wasn't one of her aberrations. Then, one didn't eat sandwiches and interact with aberrations. He was real enough.

Even though they were both aware he knew more about the day's events than he had mentioned, small campuses being what they are, he neither poked nor prodded. Small talk of the weather, class schedules and good places to eat, flowed smoothly. The exception being the best pizza joint that ended with them laughing.

Another two cups of hot chocolate, and the topic switched to their own academic goals. He broached the subject first. "I assume you've chosen your doctrinal thesis project? So what's your focus on?"

"Which one do you mean?" Rhyjl answered, as she stirred the hot chocolate to a swirling eddy. "The one my advisers all are pushing for, or the one that I secretly want to do?"

"Two? My, you are ambitious. Why don't you tell me the secret one? That sounds most intriguing."

"Well, I don't know about intriguing, but a little paradigm shaking and also dangerous. It could cost my PhD and black ball me from working in archaeology, other than as a digger."

"Ouch! That controversial?" Erik was folding his hands on the table and settling in for the long explanation he hoped for. He was enjoying her company. Enjoying her wit. She was easy to be with and just as earthy as he had presumed.

"My work started out as a study to understand the stress placed on Nordic women during the Viking period."

Erik leaned back in his chair with a chuckle. "My great grandmother could have told you that."

"Right!" she grinned back. "Maybe your great grandmother several generations back. But seriously do you really want to hear this?"

"I'm sorry, I just couldn't resist. My great grandmother came over from Norway when she was no more than sixteen. When she arrived like so many others in East Boston just prior to the First World War, she was, as she put it, 'terrified, yet resolute.' My great granddad, born to Norwegian immigrants, was working in the ship yards. He took one look at that bedraggled gal and scooped her right up. He'd said he wanted a woman that would be willing to work like a man right alongside him. Together, they worked and saved until they had their own flourishing ship business, courtesy of the First World War, and the rest is history. She was a lady who knew stress and handled it well. She lived to a hundred and four and was sharp as a tack right up to the end."

He was proud of his family, obviously. A sentiment which had eluded her with the exception of her grandmother. She knew nothing of her dad's family and very little of her mother's. Grandmum hadn't been much for talking about the past. She'd bring up Grandpa from time to time. He'd been a Scot and proud of it. She'd also mentioned, when Rhyjl was struggling, how he would have been able to answer many of her questions. He was dead, of course, and …

"I'm sorry, that was rude of me," Erik broke into

her thoughts. "So how is that controversial?"

"What? Oh, you mean my thesis? It's not, and that's what my advisors would like to see me publish. It's what grew out of my research that ruffles academic feathers." Rhyjl closed her eyes and punctuated a long pause with a deep breath. "Look, I'm not sure I want to go in to details about that right now."

Erik shrugged. "Okay." He left it at that, even though it was the second time today his curiosity had been placed on a diet.

"So, tell me more about you." She was happy to switch the focus. "More about your family, your work, I don't know."

"Isn't much more to tell. As you might have guessed, I was very close to my great grandmother. I spent a lot of time with her."

"You were lucky to have her it sounds like?"

He shifted in his chair, his right hand dropping below the table. "Yes, she was special."

"And the rest of your family? Brothers? Sisters? Parents?"

"Only child. My parents weren't close. I've often wondered what brought them together. My father always said it was because she was the most exquisite woman he'd ever met." *She was certainly better than any of the air-head-bimbos he was always pursuing.* The tension in his jaw was doubling in PSI. "Mom never talked about him. I often wondered if it was because he offered her freedom to pursue her career. It wasn't that easy for a woman like her to balance family and career during the early eighties."

It didn't take a physic to see his parents weren't an easy topic for him. At some point a stone had materialized in his right palm. As he spoke, the agitated movement of his fingers polished it. It probably was akin to the same embarrassing gut niggling when the topic of her parents came up. "That's an interesting stone. Mind if I see it?"

Erik looked at the stone in his fingers as if he was surprised to see it there. "It's an agate," he said, handing it over to her. "A small token my mother gave to me many years ago."

Rhyjl let the warmth of the stone settle in her hand a moment. The energy surrounding it was extremely uncomfortable. She handed it back and changed the subject. "Tell me about the grandmother who taught you about forks?" She nudged the one sitting next to his untouched sandwich.

It had been the right move on her part. With the shift in topic, so went his mood and the stone evaporated into his pocket.

"Oh, she was a tyrant. Obsessed with our family standing in Boston society. Probably a hangover from the days when being *nouveau riche*, they were still fighting to prove themselves in polite society. The crash of twenty-nine helped with that. So many of their quote betters lost everything. My great grandparents were prudent investors." He winked. "Their newly acquired wealth, remained quite solid."

"You say she was a tyrant, but I get the impression you were close to her."

"Oh, I was. She used to say I was the spitting image of her father. He'd been sort of a partner to my paternal great grandfather. Also Norwegian, he'd a good eye for financial figures that earned him the head accounting position in the company. Later his daughter married the only son of the boss and well …"

"You were lucky you were able to know her."

"Yes, very fortunate to not only know, but love her. But then I'm lucky in many ways." He wanted to move on. He'd never spoken so freely about his family.

"How so?"

"Well," he said, gesturing with his hand to their surroundings. "I'm working in a profession I love. As a kid, I was addicted to puzzling out answers to difficult problems, inventing and proving to others that what they thought couldn't be done, could." Especially his father, but he omitted that.

"That last sounds a little conceited, doesn't it?" she teased.

"Not at all! I am, by most accounts, the very essence of humility."

"Really?" she coughed, tilting her head slightly, her eyebrows raised.

"Yes," he replied. "In earnest, one has to want recognition for what they do and push for it. They want to believe in their own superiority. I, on the other hand, want to make things work. To understand what makes them tick. I am a seeker, a detective, if you will. My reward is stepping up to the challenge and discovering a viable solution. That's what drives me and keeps my interest. For example …"

His passion for his work was contagious even though more than half of what he postulated was way beyond any understanding she had. As he spoke, she also was struggling with her earlier perception of him. Physically, he still fit into their Victorian surroundings. Listening to him talk about his goals, put him so far into the future, she wondered why they were still earthbound. Wrapping her mind around the apparent inconsistency, she realized almost anyone who might have sat in this very room with Nikola Tesla would have felt the same.

Eventually, his stomach reminded him that his sandwich remained untouched, along with his third hot chocolate. "I apologize for running on so. I get carried away at times."

"No, no, don't apologize." she sighed, and let her hands scrub over her face and push a few strands of hair away. "It's been a long day, and while I've thoroughly enjoyed our conversation, I think I'd better head back to my place."

He glanced outside the window and winced. Beyond the glass, evening had spread a dark cloak. If it hadn't been for the glow of the eighteen-hundreds-replica streetlights evenly spaced along the paths, the campus would have been swallowed.

He was out of his chair and offering to assist her in a blink. "May I escort you?"

"Very gentlemanly of you," Rhyjl said, rising as he pulled her chair back. "But I only live across campus in the cottages.

As they left Main and turned north toward the student housing, he seemed reluctant to leave her side. The weather was changing. A storm would most likely hit later tonight. The air felt thicker and carried the tang of salt in it. Hugging her sweater closer around her, she watched as several early crimson leaves swirled and danced across their path in the pool of light from one of the lamps. "Really I'm fine, you don't need to go any further."

He paused, looked toward the gathering of old cottages, then rubbed his hands together. "I'd like to take you for a decent meal. Tomorrow night maybe?" Seeing her hesitancy he added, "I promise not to rattle on."

"Thank you." Rhyjl shook her head. "And not

because of your rattling. I found our conversation fascinating. To be honest, it was just the diversion I needed from my own thoughts."

"Rhyjl?" his voice was thicker almost sultry. For a moment, she was sure he would move to kiss her. Her breath caught. His hands encircled hers. She found herself drawn toward him.

"Another time, then." Hands parting, he turned and strode away.

*

The cape was cold and comfortless when he entered. He'd never noticed before. Pulling out his phone as he headed to the fridge, he started a new list. "Two chairs. End table. No," he amended. "Three end tables. Rugs." He pulled out a beer, looked at it as if he'd never seen one before. How would beer go atop hot chocolate? He put it back and grabbed the carton of milk. A quick search of his cupboard produced a mug. "Glasses," he said to his phone.

Tomorrow would be his first day of classes. There were fifteen students signed up for the ten AM class. His afternoon algorithms class had swelled to thirty. He'd have to look into finding a teaching assistant if he wanted to give the students his best. The chair at his desk groaned and gave a little as he sat. He flipped the red button of his electrical strip and watched his work center come to life. The computer whined and hummed as it woke from slumber. Three large, rectangular, glowing Cyclops-eyes filled the room with winter light, then displayed his dreams. On the displays before him was his child, conceived in thought and born through hours of labor. It was what, until quite recently, consumed his waking hours and, often like any child, woke him in the deep of night demanding its due. It had begun as only a seed of a question once long ago in his mother's lab. After her untimely death, it had swelled to fill the void she'd left behind, giving him purpose. It had given him the strength to defy his father. His creation was all he thought he'd needed until a few days ago.

A chance meeting in a parking lot had changed that. Now Rhyjl haunted his nights. Her presence intruded into his thoughts and even at this moment, she was the reason he saw the sparseness of this room; why there was no warmth, no soft amber glow. He looked over at the wall and saw the fireplace dark. "Order wood." He added to his list. A vision appeared. In it, he knew what he wanted. It would become real, of that he had no doubt.

Chapter 5

Dream Scape

Sara was screaming! She was so far away. Drifting further from Rhyjl on every receding wave of pain. The darkness, cold, so very cold. No longer was the knife flashing, stabbing, bringing heat, consuming heat. Sara's voice surged! Urgent! Demanding!

Rhyjl tore herself from the suffocating shroud. Despite her efforts, it clung, cloying ribbons tangling with the present. She threw out her arms no longer in defense, but in a plea of freedom. Her right arm connected. A howl and curse.

"Damn you Rhyjl! Wake the F-ing up before you kill us both!"

With a jolt, she was back on the couch in their cottage. There was warm pine and red curtains holding back the darkness. She was no longer in the white room. The room with faux gold brocade drapes. The room where pain and the flashing knife assaulted her. Sara was still cursing her from a distance. But only as far away as the kitchenette where Rhyjl could hear running water.

"If I don't get a black eye from this, it will be a bloody miracle!" Sara groaned, returning to stare down at Rhyjl with her one good eye. The other was hidden behind a wet kitchen cloth. "God, I thought, you were being murdered in here!"

"I was!" Rhyjl muttered.

"What!"

"In my dream, I was being murdered."

"Freaking hell! Who was killing you?"

"I don't know. I didn't see them. Well, not really. They were kind of a hazy outline. All I know is there was so much anger coming from them. I can't imagine that kind of anger, so wild, so out of control."

"Ugh! So do you remember anything else?" Sara plopped herself down next to Rhyjl, her hand coming to rest on her friend's shoulder.

"Really, Sara," Rhyjl flinched at Sara's touch. She wasn't ready. She needed space. "I'd just as soon forget it. I'm feeling a little sick."

"I don't know. They say, Rhyjl, that it is good to talk it out."

"Good for whom, Sara?" She stood and did her best to ignore the sensation of the room tilting beneath her feet.

"Just saying, it might help if you talked about it."

Rhyjl didn't need to see Sara's pretty face to imagine the drawn pout of her lips. "Okay, but there isn't much to tell. I was in this room …"

"This room!" Sara unfolded her lean model figure to rise from the couch and follow Rhyjl's retreating back.

"No, it was like a hotel room." Rhyjl said, reaching the bathroom. "Someone was stabbing me with a knife over and over again. They were screaming at me … or was that you? See, it's all a jumble and fading."

She shut the door. For just a moment the face looking out from the mirror was the one she'd seen earlier in the lab. Then it wavered and faded to her own pale haunted features.

*

It was growing late. Or early, depending. Sara had long since found her bed. Only Rhyjl sat in the dark letting the thoughts that would not be silenced tumble over each other. Not since her first experience with the boy and his wolf had she been held so emotionally captive. She still saw them. Made a point to go back and visit. Neither were there anymore. Dr. Fendler and his team had excavated the site the same summer she had shared her findings. She watched them exhume the bodies. She listened to them summarize what they found. Some of what they said was so exact, she had wondered, if like her, they could see the events unfolding. She knew it was just as Fendler said. "You study, you research and the bones, the artifacts tell the story." It was the summer that changed her life. At first she had been sad to see them separate the wolf from the boy. But that was silly, she knew. They had long since been united in a way no one could ever separate them. To her they still roamed the hills, played in the river. Their presence grew fainter as time passed. Their story had been told. It had changed the history books. Not that anyone cared other than a hand full of scholars. She cared. That was enough.

There had been so many since then. Matilda and her fellows from The Crypt. Sven and Helga from her first dig in Sweden. She had learned to read the evidence. To tell their stories from the artifacts and their bare bones. What others, including fellow students, her colleagues and advisors didn't know, was she saw and felt so much more. Only Grandmum knew and even she couldn't completely comprehend. Curse or gift? Possibly a little of both. What she was feeling now, felt more like a curse. Who was this woman? Why had someone done this to her? Why me?

The dreams of the past, as Rhyjl had come to think

of them, had always been third person. She touched the bones or went to the site. She witnessed their stories play across the big screen of her mind. At first, and almost always, she observed the silent scenes. Rarely had she been more in tune and heard as well as seen. What was happening now was new territory. It was as if she was reliving this woman's death in the first person. Her stomach felt like cold steel. She took another sip of her camomile tea to warm it away. It was little comfort.

*

Heavily laden clouds scudded across the sky. The trees bowed and swayed to the whims of the wind. It was a good day to stay in with a good book, a good hot drink and a warm fire. Of those three, Rhyjl felt she only had the hot drink.

Marc wouldn't be needing her this afternoon, *if* he was back from who knows where. True, his classes wouldn't start until Wednesday afternoon, but it seemed so unlike him to put things off until the last moment. She made a mental note to swing by the office and ask Mags if she'd run off the syllabus.

Her first course of action was the Dean's. "This morning, I will not get sidetracked!" she asserted aloud to the universe. She had procrastinated long enough as it was. One day here, a day there, didn't seem like much in the long term, but added up quickly. She needed to get this moving before she lost her nerve. Once she had the specimens and their documentation in hand, she could get what she needed to add to the Blue Hill site. Crystal, her associate and friend at the University of York, had already agreed to run the DNA. Without that, her skeletal evidence alone would never stand up. Her strongest evidence, of course, would fly like a one ton stone. How to explain, she had seen the voyage of the girl and her deep longing for her native soil rather than this new land? Ah, she might as well sign her own commitment papers. So that evidence would remain her secret, but without it, she'd never have pursued this course. Whether that was a curse or a blessing would remain to be seen. Okay! Back to the present and needing to keep first things first, which meant securing the Dean's commitment to obtaining the bones from Visby. Once that was accomplished, she just might go over to the campus book store to see if she could find a good book. Two out of three wasn't bad.

Main was a flurry of activity. Merging with the flow until she could break for the stairs leading to the south wing and administration, she threaded her way through the crowds. The book store was already a sea of humanity wearing away the towers of text books in restless search to fulfill their syllabuses. For a moment, she doubted the sanity of her earlier thought of entering there on her way out. Then reminded herself that the kind of book she was most interested in, would be cloistered in the back, not in the center of the storm.

The wait outside of the Dean's office was short. He agreed to meet with her almost immediately. That alone should have been a clue. But her mind was focused on her mission and she had intentionally put the events of the previous day in a closed vault with every intention of leaving them there.

"Rhyjl, thank you for coming in this morning." He was standing behind his desk looking out over the ocean when she walked in. Now he turned with an open-handed gesture for her to take the chair opposite his. The massive mahogany desk separating them had always reminded Rhyjl of an ornate alter. For worship or sacrifice, she was never sure. She imagined it most likely had to do with a person's business here.

"I, of course, have had the official report from the police. I would much appreciate your first hand take on this." Supporting his weight on his fingertips, he leaned heavily across the desk toward her. "I'd like an explanation. How do you think those bones got into the lab?"

For a good three quarters of an hour they did a dance. She had no answers for him. At least none that were anything, but pure speculation. She didn't know why Kendricks wasn't available. No, she hadn't been scheduled to take the class. Hadn't he already been through that with Sara? Yes, the lab was kept locked. Yes, there was a key available to those who needed it. Did she have any idea who might have done this?

When the intercom in his office buzzed informing him of his next appointment, Rhyjl felt the serpent coiling around her relax. She wasn't free, but for the moment, it wasn't choking the life from her. Dean Anderson's reluctance to let her go was palatable.

"Damn, damn, damn!" She chanted going down the stairs. She hadn't asked for this, but she sure as hell was stuck with it.

The book store off to left was still teaming with bodies. Bodies, she shuddered. That was the last thing she wanted on her mind. The bones had been a body and recently. A body that wanted to tell her. "Stop!"

Several people did. They looked around to see if there was something amiss and then at her, their brows furrowed or raised. "Are you okay?" asked one girl who looked a bit retro. Her hair was pulled back with a headband. The close fit of her sweater combined with the A line of her skirt accentuated her Barbie figure.

"Just great!" Rhyjl answered, fleeing the close confines for the salt-laden assault of the wind.

*

Erik spotted Rhyjl outside Main on his way to class. She had confided the night before she intended to speak to the Dean. Even from this distance, it didn't look as if things had gone well. She was standing alone, her head tilted toward the sky, not stooped like most against the blow. His steps faltered. His gaze torn between her and the entrance of the Engineering building. The vice squeezing his chest urged him to go to her. The sharp exhale of resolve, moved him forward to his class. He'd seek her in the afternoon. That had been his plan anyway.

*

Rhyjl needed a diversion. Someone, or thing, to interact with other than the maniacal hamster in her mind.

Thoughts scattering like the leaves caught in the fickle wind, she headed for the Archaeology office. Mags sat on her throne paying audience to all those who entered either by door or phone. "Morning Mags, are any of the MIAs back yet?"

Magena replied with the expected index finger pointing heavenward. Then let it fall back to the keyboard to assist the other hand which hadn't lost a stroke.

Rhyjl idly leafed through random papers from several stacks scattered across the counter. Some were class schedules with room numbers, others were announcements from different campus clubs and organizations. They served as minor distractions like mosquitoes, not really holding her attention past a few swats. Her usual patience with Mags' routine was becoming like wet tissue paper.

The thought of going upstairs to see if the crime tape remained outside the lab door flitted at the periphery of her thoughts. What purpose that would serve, was negligible. She knew nothing about this cop stuff, other than what she had seen yesterday. That hadn't impressed her much, except for Dr. Merks. But she really wasn't a cop, was she. While many of her fellow students had raved about shows like CSI, she'd never cared to watch them. She didn't own a TV and that's how she liked it. The only brush she'd had with mysteries, were a few sorties over the years into classical Agatha Christie novels her mother had owned.

Past the horseshoe counter was the hall she'd traveled down the day before. Had it been less than twenty-four hours ago? It seemed like an eternity. This time she passed the storage room and headed for the third door on the left. In passing, she noted the other four doors lining the hall were dark. She didn't need the gold lettering on their opaque windows to tell her who was absent. There was light at the end of the hall. It spilled from under the closed door and permeated the frost. Closing her eyes, her heart raced a little faster. He was there.

Dr. Marcus McClellen was one of the most brilliant men she knew. It didn't hurt that he was also one of the most attractive. Every year his introduction to Archaeology class was filled to capacity with freshmen, mostly female. This was her third year as his TA. He was also her thesis advisor. Today, she wanted something more from him. She wanted his counsel and his compassion. He always cared. Not just about her academic status, but what was happening in her personal life. Hadn't he been supportive when her grandmum had her heart attack? He'd even lent her the funds to fly back to Montana.

Before knocking, she listened for a moment to know if he was speaking with someone either in person or on the phone. There were no audible voices. Actually, there didn't appear to be any sound coming from the other side of the door. Maybe he isn't in, after all, she thought, pivoting to go.

"Who's there?" Barked the familiar voice.

Rhyjl cracked the door and poked her head in. "Just me. I was wondering if you had a few minutes?"

"Well hello, Rhyjl!" Marc said, turning from his window overlooking the rocky shore. "You've created quite the stir around here, I hear. Come in, come in. Make yourself at home and tell me all about it." He took his own chair as he gestured to the one across from him.

The similarities of the two meetings were almost so Deja vu that it was unsettling. Taking a deep breath, she remained standing. "I'd rather not, sir. I've already had a session with the Dean this morning. I came hoping for some distraction."

"Um," he said, leaning forward and forming a steeple with his fingers. "Did you have anything specific in mind?"

He'd aged since last spring. Was that a touch of grey at his temples where there had been none before? The way his jaw muscles worked, said he was chewing on stress even though his voice remained steady and calm.

"I was hoping you might have something for me to

do."

"Well, classes haven't started as you are aware, so there are no papers to grade, Mags has taken care of the syllabus, and I have nothing planned for the class tomorrow that would require any kind of set up. But let's be honest. You really want someone to talk to about yesterday that won't pester you with questions. Isn't that so?"

"Yes, no! I'm really sick of it, but at the same time, I don't seem to be able to get it out of my mind."

"That's perfectly reasonable," he said, picking up a pen and tapping against the edge of his desk. Tossing the pen back down he asked, "So why don't you just start and tell me what it is you want to sort out. You have that look about you, you know. The one you get when you're deeply engrossed in some kind of puzzle."

"Ah." She nodded, he knew her so well. "I guess that's true. It feels like people somehow want to blame me for those bones. All I did was find them."

"I can see your point, but I guess the question is why was it *you* who found them? Why where *you* there? See, you were somewhere you weren't supposed to be. Sara should have been leading that class in Kendricks' absence. That's what has people confused. You may not have put them there, but you were on the scene, and you are the one who brought them to every ones attention."

Rhyjl gnawed on her finger and stared unseeing down at the desk before her.

"Look, I know you and Sara are friends and roommates. I'm the last person that's going to ask you to say something you might feel disloyal. Let me also tell you it is already known where Sara was at the time. I don't need to be clairvoyant to know why she was there. There's no love shared between her and Kendricks, any more than there is between you and Kendricks. Amanda is a difficult person to get along with. I should know. We've known each other, and often worked together, since grad school right here at DEU. Truth be told, I think I understand why you were there and so does Mags. Others, however, who don't know you as well, will wonder."

"So are you saying, that if Sara or Dr. Kendricks had been there, they wouldn't have seen the discrepancies?"

Marcus shrugged. "Sara? Possibly. She's not as astute as you, Rhyjl. Kendricks? Well, let just say she's taught that class for the last fifteen years. When you've taught something that long, you often go on autopilot, so to speak. She may have if, and that's a big if, she had chosen to pick up the bones and spoken of them individually rather than collectively. From what I understand, you chose your old friend, Matilda. How could you have not noticed? And you chose her because you are most comfortable with her. Do you see the difference?"

"I suppose, but where is Kendricks?"

"That, I'm not at liberty to tell you and before you wrinkle that forehead of yours, let me advise that it is really none of your business. Ah! Ah!" He held up his hand to stay her protest. "I will go so far as to say, that at a major conference we both attended, something came up. She had to make an important side trip. I expect her to be back in the next few days. Which under the circumstances, is just as well, since I've been told the lab will not be released for use again for, at the minimum, another week.

"Let me add, thanks to your excellent, if not unsettling orientation, the eleven students in this year's osteology class have gotten their money's worth. Chalk that up as a win for the department."

"Eleven? But there were twelve? Did someone drop out?"

"I was told eleven. If there were twelve there for orientation, I don't know anything about it. You'll have to ask Mags. I'm sure she has the information."

*

"Yes, there were twelve in the class, Magena replied to Rhyjl's query, loading paper into the copy machine.

"So someone did drop out? Who?"

Mags' eyes appeared fixed either searching her internal data base or debating on how much to say. Marcus was correct that none of this was her business. "Melinda LeFevre." Mags nodded and went back to scanning something on her monitor. "She was absent when I opened the classroom. She hasn't put in an appearance this year. That's what I told the police."

"I'm not familiar with her. What does she look like?"

Mags paused again. "Cute in that faerie sort of way. Tall, blond, mid-twenties. Had a tough time settling on a major if I remember correctly. Too many interests. That sort of thing."

"Really skinny, anorexic almost?"

"Yes, most of that is due to that boyfriend of hers. Um … what is his name?" She looked as if she were searching some unseen attendance sheet. "Bannerman. Yes, Dirk Bannerman. Rarely do I dislike a student, but I wouldn't mind if he went somewhere far away."

"Got that." Rhyjl grunted. "She was at the class. I

saw her hanging just behind him. I even saw the look on her face, all apologetic when he put on his Mr. Hot Shot routine."

Mags looked up sharply. "You saw her?"

"Yes, and I'm sorry she's dropping. I would like to get to know her better. Is she going to be in any of Marc's classes?"

"Rhyjl," Mags hesitated. "Are you sure you saw her?"

"Yeah, she even hung back when everyone else had filed out as if she wanted to say something. She didn't and when I looked away for a second back toward the bones, she'd vanished."

"Rhyjl this is important. The police have been trying to find her. They want to speak to everyone who had access to the lab. No one here on campus has seen her. They tried contacting her parents, but they are away on a holiday somewhere. Are you sure you saw her?"

"Oh, wow, is it that late? I've got to go. Later." Rhyjl flew out of the room chased by the shadows growing in her thoughts and the churning of her stomach. Could it? Was it Melinda scattered among The Crypt residents? What did she know about the bones? Doing a rewind on the events following her discovery, what had she learned? Not much, other than they were from a recent victim, female and over twenty. It had been wrenching to handle them. The energy, for lack of anything else to call it, had been too fresh. Way too disturbing. That was part of her problem since last night. It was clinging to her like a bad smell she couldn't wash off.

Imagination in overdrive, Rhyjl fled back toward Main. Bannerman! Yeah, it wasn't astuteness on his part. He had very good reason to know the Ilium wasn't

Matilda's. He knew because he had switched the bones out. What did they say, that the guilty always returned to the scene of the crime? What had he done to her? What terrible, twisted things had he done? And yet, there she had stood behind him, silently apologizing for his jackass behavior. Tears stung at the back of her eyes. *God, if that's love, please spare me.* It wasn't the first time she'd made that plea.

Chapter 6

A Little Help

What had checked her headlong race to disaster, she couldn't say. After all, the only thing she might have accomplished by running to the Dean with her theory, was to make herself a fool. Instead of entering Main, she veered to the right, skirted the building and headed to the cliff path. Sun bleached grasses bowed low over the hard packed trail in obeisance to the building storm. Few trees grew here, mostly because they had been cut away so as not to obscure the view from the people who spent their days in Main. The path dipped and wound along the worn cliff edge. Here and there small offshoots led down the rocky outcrop to the pebble and bolder strewn beach some twenty feet below. Another day, she might have chosen one. At present, the tide was high and even without the sea's furious onslaught thundering at the cliff's base, there would have been little space to walk without getting wet. Even at this height the buffeting gale caught up the errant spray of the waves creating a heavy misting that was threatening to soak through her sweater. There was the taste of salt upon her lips and small droplets gathered on her eyelashes like tears. Here, in this wild place, she let her raging hurt meet and match the ocean below.

It was so easy to stuff the pain when she could immerse herself in study or focus on the primal beauty that surrounded her. Human interactions seemed outside her sphere. Strange that, considering her chosen field was married to Anthropology, the study of humans. Or perhaps not. Possibly, deep within, she wanted to understand. Just not close up and personal. She'd learned to distance herself from the past, both hers and that of her subjects ever since the incident by the river. She could observe, and while not completely immune to the emotions they evoked, she could, most of the time, walk away and leave it in the past where it belonged. Not always. But most of the time. That was good enough.

Hurrying along the trail, she soon reached a bend that turned in to a bank of mixed native jack pine, pitch pine, ash, and maple. This small strip of woodland separated the cottages from the ocean. After a few hundred feet, the trail turned seaward again to breakout on a point that divided the two coves. In this place, she truly felt she was away from the world. The thick fiery hued underbrush tangled beneath the pines and maple formed a substantial curtain from the hustle and business of the campus. The crashing pulse of the sea drowned out the thoughts she wanted to escape.

She leaned into the vibrant voice booming against the rocks below clearing her mind of everything, but its presence. Soon her breath matched its ebb and flow, followed by her heart. Many like Sara and her friend Greg, found it disturbing. They saw the primal anger like clutching fingers or pounding fists wanting to pull them in and under. She felt the surge of strength like a love wooing her to be calm. The lover she longed for, but so far had eluded her. Or was that kind of man a fantasy like dragons and fairies only to be found in movies and those bodice busting romances?

To hear her grandmum speak, Grandpa had been such a man. Not perfect perhaps, for he'd been prone to bouts of moodiness. According to Grandmum, he'd been able to see and speak to the departed. She wasn't sure she believed that. It was possible that Grandmum had misunderstood. More than possible that her Grandfather hadn't been able to communicate just what it was he experienced. She could relate. Not in defining it for others, only herself. If true, and he was capable of carrying on whole conversations with the dead, it would leave any man's or woman's soul heavy. Just as she needed this isolated place on the Maine coast, he'd sought the rock overlooking the river back at the ranch. Was there something cleansing in the water?

She wished, oh how she wished, she knew more about this gift or curse. She'd spent hours upon hours researching and searching for the answers only to become more frustrated by all the literature and propaganda written on the subject of the paranormal. It soon became clear most of the so-called experts had no idea what they were talking about. Except for what she was personally experiencing and gut feel, how did someone go about ferreting out what was and wasn't true?

Opening her eyes, she looked out toward the turtle-backed islands dotting the horizon stretching out toward the far shore across the hand-shaped bay. The two larger islands followed by the three smaller ones had always reminded her of a family of turtles treading the waters. Today was no different, other than their journey wasn't quite as tranquil as on a sunny day. Her breath caught just for a moment as she spotted the lone fisherman or lobster man off the point closer to town. What was he doing out on a day like today? True, she didn't know much about that time honored trade, but couldn't his pots have waited? He was so alone weathering it all in his bright yellow slicker and hat. He'd become a staple of her walks as much as the islands. It would have been abnormal had she not seen him. She let the tension drain as he easily handled the stormy waters much as the islands did. Still …

She couldn't imagine why watching him riding the waves made a wave of loneliness sweep over her. Did anyone care that he was out there? Why did it matter to her? He obviously knew the waters well. Were they so different? Did anyone care that she was out here? Did it matter to anyone? Raising her hand, she hailed him not really expecting him to reciprocate. When he left off rowing to reciprocate, her lower lip began to tremble and she would have wept had the heavy clouds above not done so for her.

*

Erik was surprised to feel the tension draining from his head to his toes. His first classes as a full professor were finished for the day. Before, someone else had always set the tone. First impressions count. If he came on too strong, he could discourage some of the students. If he came on too soft, they might not take him seriously. There was a balance and hopefully he had found it. Now as the last student filed out of the room, thoughts of Rhyjl bubbled to the surface.

If he remembered correctly, she had two classes she was a TA for on Wednesday. She had a lab on Thursday and Friday. But nothing today. Well at least not scheduled. He'd head back to his place, change into some jeans and a sweater, and see if she wanted to check out one of the pizza places they'd talked about.

The clouds hung heavy with their burden as he

pulled up to the cottage. It was amazing they hadn't burst before now. The small cabin, probably no more than six hundred square feet if that, seemed lifeless and there were no lights welcoming him from the windows. Getting out of his car, he could hear the slap, slap, slap of a black shutter on the neighboring cottage as it banged against the wall in the wind. Rhyjl's cottage in contrast, was quiet and solid against the gale. He knocked twice and waited. He hoped she would be happy to see him. Knocking two more times, his hopes began to fray. When still no movement inside could be seen or heard, he turned from the cottage door cursing himself for being a pompous fool to think she would just be sitting there waiting for him. Perhaps she was at the Archaeology building? Would it be too intrusive to seek her out there? In his mind they were already a couple. Perhaps a serious couple. He doubted she'd come that far yet. Would she find it creepy or a pleasant surprise? Did he want to risk it?

Her old beater scout was parked to the side of the entry. At least it was a pretty fair guess of her ownership. The Montana license plates on it looked to be the only sturdy parts remaining. How anyone could go out on the road in that accident waiting to happen was beyond him. "Okay, Mr. Spoiled. Just because you've always had the funds to drive nothing older than a few years, doesn't mean others do." So she must still be on campus, unless she'd caught a ride from someone else.

The first drops caught him as he left the sheltering little overhang above the entry. Those few drops would momentarily be joined by others. While he'd stood there waiting, he'd taken the small Turritella agate out of his pocket and fingered its familiar surface. Tossing the polished grey and tan sandstone up and snatching it midair, he turned to go to his own car and was stuck again by the contrast of hers next to his midnight-blue Tesla.

Rhyjl saw him, but too late. The rain was driving and relentless soaking through her wool sweater that normally shed light showers. It only added to the chilled isolation encompassing her. And while isolation was something she craved, the cold wasn't. There was nothing to be done, however. He'd spotted her as well.

"You're drenched to the skin," he said, appearing by her side and attempting to hover over her as if his bulk could somehow shelter her.

Since he wasn't making much of a difference, and if anything was making her feel less at ease, she pushed past and scurried toward the warmth and security of her own space. Fingers wet and shaking from the cold had her fumbling with her keys.

"Here, let me help," he offered, extracting them from her possession.

"Hey, Boy Scout, I can handle this!" She meant it to come out as half jest. Her frustration negated the jest part and had her sounding the shrew. "I'm sorry," she amended as the door swung open and he stepped aside to let her in. "I didn't mean it that way. I'm just having a tough day."

"I can sense that. Is it the bones? The weather? Or perhaps both?"

He'd made himself right at home by heading to the kitchen and grabbing the tea pot. "Both!" she snapped deciding to let him do his caring thing while she headed for her bedroom to strip before she started steaming. Sheltered behind the bedroom door she could hear the rattle of dishes and the thump, thump as he opened and shut the cupboards.

"I'll just fix us both some tea while we decide the best way to go about our research from the other day. Do you want something herbal or with a jolt of caffeine like Green tea or Earl Grey? Those appear to be your only choices."

"Look, this is all very kind …" She stopped halfway through the process of pulling her wet tee over her head. "What research! I'm finished with this bones mystery. It's in the hands of the police now. I'm an archaeologist, not a detective."

"If that's what you want to believe. Personally I think thou doth protest too much. However, as intriguing as it may be, that wasn't what I was referring to. I suppose we could give it a try. I'm pretty good at putting two and two together."

On the other side of her door, the clatter clack thud of the mugs being taken from the dish drainer and put on the table was clearly audible. "Make yourself right at home, why don't you?" she muttered, tossing her damp shirt toward her clothes hamper. She'd deal with it later after she'd dealt with Mr. Congeniality. "So if that wasn't what you had in mind what other research are you referring to?" When there was no reply except the whistle of the tea kettle, she slipped into a baggy long sleeved tee she usually reserved for fieldwork with the logo, *Life's a Blast! Dig It!* circling an archaeology trowel.

Opening the door, she found him standing at the table, absently looking out the kitchen window where the rain was sheeting down and scooping rounded spoonfuls of brown powder into a mug. "I see you found Sara's hot chocolate?"

"Oh, is this your roommate's coco? I hope she won't mind. I'll get her another. She's almost out anyway.

It's just I'm not much of a tea drinker. Here's yours." he said pushing the pink cow mug toward her. "I picked something with camomile when you didn't answer. I didn't think you needed a caffeine hit."

Her heart gave a little glitch. It had been a long time since anyone had mothered her. At the same time it annoyed her to no end. She didn't need a mother. She hadn't had one for a long time and she'd done just fine. She was more resourceful than most knew.

"About that research." he picked up the red cup with a rose red heart against a porcelain white background. "I thought we would first hit that pizza joint for lunch you were talking about. Vinnie's wasn't it? Then we'll checkout my favorite, Pizza Pizza next time."

"Look, Erik, I appreciate the thoughtfulness, but I'm not interested in lunch today. I'm really not interested in your pizza research. I have other plans." Like trying to deal with a murder that won't get out of my head. But she wasn't going to admit to the last.

As if he'd read her thoughts, he shrugged. "Rhyjl you need to eat. You need a diversion. I can see this hasn't been easy for you. I can't even imagine …"

"Then don't! Don't try! Don't think! Just *please* let me be."

He wanted so much to hold her. To take away the pain he saw eating at her. When he moved to take her in his arms, she shied away almost stumbling over the sturdy wooden kitchen chair. Sighing, he forced a smile he didn't feel. "Alright then, maybe later."

He stood outside the door watching the rain pour in steams from the roof of the cottage and hoping they could wash away the mess he was feeling inside. He'd try again later, give her space. He remembered there were times his mother needed space. It would only make matters worse when his father hadn't understood that. He would not repeat the sins of the father.

As his Tesla whispered away with only the hiss swoosh of the water channeling from its tires and the slap, slap of the widow wipers to mark its passing, he frowned at the dark sedan that pulled into the place he'd just vacated. Slowing almost to a stop, he watched the man get out and go to the door. Green claws swiped at his heart leaving a stinging trickle of blood as caustic as acid behind. Another sin of his father's he would not give in to.

*

Sipping the tea, the tea he had so considerately made, she let a heavy sigh escape. Damn she had to get a grip. Here was this nice guy who really had been like a knight in shining armor making her tea and inviting her out for pizza and she'd been horribly rude. She could blame it on the recent bone fiasco, but deep within she knew it was just old, sensitive scares. She liked Erik Arneson. She might even go so far as to say he made her feel comfortable. It was like he knew her, knew something about her that she wasn't even sure she wanted anyone to know. Well, that was it, wasn't it? Intimacy in a way that was just too much to handle. So what? She'd run? Run fast and far? Was she that much of a coward?

Disgust leaving a foul taste in her mouth and a growling belly, she went to the fridge and opened the door to stare at its contents. Other than the cold light, there wasn't much to see. Sara had obviously eaten the last of the cold turkey and ham slices. There was a jar of jam with some rather old sticky contents that probably should be thrown out, a couple of beers, Sara's stash of course, a squeeze bottle of ketchup, a small jar of mayonnaise and some shriveled dills. And, she'd turned down Vinney's Pizza for this! Ugh! Okay, option number one, forget about eating. The grrrrowllll of her stomach nixed that thought. Option number two, find someone who could take her into town to raid a store. The rain beating a rapid tat-a-tat-a-tat on roof made that option rather discouraging as well. Again her stomach grumbled with a little squeal at the end. "Oh, yeah, full circle. You just blew that, didn't you?" She shut the fridge door in hopes of finding better foraging in the cupboard.

The knock rattled the door just as she was reaching for the cabinet handle. Saved! He'd come back. Maybe forgot something. Maybe he'd decided to try again. Did it matter? She'd just apologize profusely, and be eating pizza in no time.

"I'm so sorry!" she blurted, opening the door then stumbling back from the so-not-Erik masculine figure blocking the entry.

"Ms. Rhyjl Martin?"

"Yes?"

I'm Detective Tanner, Maine State Police." His badge flashed silver from a black case. "May I come in?"

Silly question. As if she could have stopped him. He'd already advanced two steps inside forcing her to abandon the entry before he'd even shown his badge. What was another step or two?

Droplets of rain were pooled on his black jacket. The shirt under it was stark white, the tie basic black. He looked like a cop or at least her idea of one. He wasn't as tall as Erik, probably just under six foot. But he was muscular, had broad square shoulders, a broad chest, slim waist and squared facial features. Clark Kentish. Pull off the glasses—except he wasn't wearing any—and yeah, Superman. Those cold grey eyes might even have x-ray vision.

"Is this a bad time? You appeared to be expecting someone?"

"I … no, not really. He just left. I was hoping he was coming back. I need a ride to town." Oh god, she was rambling.

"Interesting. I was hoping you wouldn't mind a ride to town with me. We have some questions for you concerning the bones you found in the lab."

"We?"

"Yes, the ME and I."

"Will it take long?" she inquired, moving to snatch her bright L.L. Bean purple rain jacket hung from a peg near the door. I haven't had lunch and I'm starving."

He was casing the room. She was fumbling with an inverted sleeve thanks to Sara. Amazing the jacket hadn't ended up on the floor or over a chair. His eyes narrowed for a moment. "Looks like you already had lunch."

Turning, she took in the scene that was her cottage. It was a jumbled mess of clothes, books and papers scattered across the sofa, chair and side table. A dish with a scattering of crumbs crowned the whole affair. Stormy, luxuriating on one of Sara's favorite sweaters, appeared to be well contented. Well, that was some consolation. She hoped the feline had enjoyed the cold cuts and Sara's sweater would be matted with fur. On the table, the two cups she and Erik had just finished, stood abandoned. "My roommate. She doesn't believe in clearing away her mess or leaving anything left behind for me." Except her mess, she silently added.

"I see."

Which, of course he probably didn't, but then what did it matter? The audible complaint from her stomach was hard to refute.

When they got to his car, she hesitated. Where did you ride when being taken somewhere by the police? The back or front? Tanner came around to the passenger side and opened the front door of the sedan. Was he just being polite or had he understood her confusion? If she had to make a guess, it was probably the later. When he got in his own side, his eyebrows rose in a question as he pointedly looked at her seat belt. She felt a rush of heat from her neck to her ears. This was why she should have been left to herself, she thought, fastening the belt like an obedient child.

Perhaps her wisest course of action would have been to decline his offer. Was it an offer? Could one say, "Gee, I'm sorry, but could we do this later," to a cop? The slap, slap, slap of the windshield wipers swiping at the rain as the car stated up appeared to reply, no, no, no! Driving off campus, her mind again wandered down a path of police etiquette. Was there a book for such things with a title such as *How to Interact With Law Enforcement*? Probably not. If there was, chances are your everyday person out on the street wouldn't pick it up. Lying back and doing a mental recap of the morning, she wasn't too pleased with her day so far. The talk with the Dean had been disappointing to say the least. She wasn't sure what she had been expecting from Marc, but she hadn't gotten it. Discovering that she might just know who the body in the bone lab might be was very unnerving. Add to that, her bad behavior which had cost her a nice lunch, a lunch, she might add, that would have spared her current situation

… yep, she definitely could put this day down as a minus ten on a scale of one to ten.

They had just turned on to the main highway leading to town, when he broke into her thoughts. "You were the one to find the bone discrepancy in the lab, correct?"

Is that what they called it? A discrepancy! Someone was dead, their bones scattered among archaeological specimens and it was a discrepancy? "If you mean did I find the bones of the murder victim hidden in the lab, then yes."

He flashed her a sideways glance before focusing back on the rain-slicked road. "Interesting that you should say they belonged to a murder victim?"

"Well, surprise! How else would they have ended up there?"

"A prank. I've heard you can buy a skeleton pretty easy on line. How do you know it isn't something like that?"

Yeah, how did she know? Oh I've been having visions of the owner of those bones being brutally stabbed. "While I didn't spend a lot of time with them, I did observe a few things. These bones are not old. They were walking around fully fleshed not so long ago. Second, there were a number of marks on the ribs and sternum indicating trauma from a knife-like edge, among other things."

"Are you familiar with crime scene investigations, Miss Martin?"

"No. Why do you ask?"

He glanced her way again a slight smile forming at the corners of those firm lips. "You remind me of someone else." he said, without further explanation. "So what is your best guess on how the bones got into the lab?"

"I imagine someone put them there. They didn't walk in on their own." Her stomach now felt like it was gnawing on her backbone and finding it audibly unsatisfactory.

"Does this amuse you, Miss Martin?"

"To the contrary, Detective Tanner. It's just that there isn't much I can tell you."

"But you can tell me why you were in the lab, teaching a class you were not scheduled to teach, true?"

Here is was again. Why was she in the wrong place at the wrong time? She wished she really knew the answer to that herself. She sat for a few moments pondering how to answer the question while worrying a lose thread of the hem of her worn Tee. Had it been a desire to help her roomie, Sara, or to help this year's Osteology students? Or was there something even deeper and less altruistic like a chance to figuratively stick it to Dr. Amanda Kendricks? She was about to go with her second choice when the detective's phone chimed.

He reached down to his pocket and pulled out his blue tooth earpiece and fastened it to his ear. "Tanner. Yes, I've picked her up. I imagine our ETA in ten minutes. Oh! So what kind of delay? Half an hour to an hour? Make it an hour. Yes, later." Pushing a button to disconnect, the earpiece returned to his coat pocket.

"So how about we stop at the Gray Whale and grab a bite to eat," he asked, slowing as they neared the village limits.

Blue Harbor wasn't much different than any other small coastal town in Down East Maine. It had been, and still was, primarily a fishing village. Grey clapboard houses with lobster pots and their colorful buoys, looking for all the world like oversized children's tops, were clustered around the cove. Rising on the gentle slopes overlooking the cove were centuries of diverse architecture including Victorian and staid Salt Box homes that stood in silent testimony to the village's endurance over the ages.

During its heyday, it had served as a fairly major port for bringing goods into the area due to its deep water cove and natural breakwaters, making it a safe port even in a storm like the one raging around them now. As a major player in the rum trade of the seventeen hundreds, numerous stories of local color had been spun like the ones of Crossbones Jack. Ol' Crossbones had been a minor pirate. Though not as well-known as his contemporary, Black Beard, he still had a reputation as a bit of a scoundrel with a tidy sum of treasure. There were some who said Crossbones had made Blue Harbor his final port of call. Rumor had it, that the treasure still existed in some hidden cave near the town and almost every summer, saw a few adventurers who would set about exploring in hopes of its recovery.

There was also the most influential resident of that era, a Captain Jacques Archambeau, who after the loss of two of his sons at sea, had retired to farming and business. Captain Archambeau had been extremely wealthy, owning most of the lands, businesses and several ships. No one was quite sure how he had acquired his wealth. Some thought he was a Privateer for the French. Others thought he might have been a slaver. Of course, there were more than a few locals who believed that Cross Bones Jack and Captain Archambeau were one in the same.

To Rhyjl, there was always that one nagging question: Why someone acclimated to far warmer climates would want to give up the Caribbean for colder New

England? Then again, if one was facing a hangman's noose, northern Maine just might be as good a place as any. It was all a fun mystery and Rhyjl thrilled at a good mystery as long as it stayed in the past, unlike her present circumstances.

The Grey Whale always invoked these ruminations on the village's past, as it was meant to. Housed in a traditional Salt Box with the front two stories sloping down a long stretch of roof to one story and dating back to the late sixteen hundreds, the building had retained much of its earlier flavor of being an ale house. The current proprietors had done their best to maintain the building's heritage. It gave diners the feeling of stepping back into a 'true New England pub'. Besides the promise of easing her distraught stomach, it was a much appreciated distraction.

The pub was favored by tourists and college students as well as the locals. Of the four nearby restaurants: Mel's, Vinney's Pizzeria and The Cap'n's House, The Grey Whale was Rhyjl's favorite when she could afford it. It was famous for its clam chowder that was the best to be found within two hundred square miles, or so everyone said. Evidently Detective Tanner was one of them.

The hostess knew him by name and seated them without any wait at a plank table near the open hearth and a cheery crackling fire. True, it wasn't packed to capacity but Rhyjl had the distinct impression that even if it had been, there would have been a table for her companion.

"The usual," asked the waitress who hovered over their table, "or would you like a menu?"

"I'll have the usual. Miss Martin might like a menu, however." The waitress noted the formal use of Rhyjl's name and gave a polite smile.

"No, that's fine. I'll have a bowl of the clam chowder and a small salad."

"Anything to drink?"

"Water's fine, thank you." Rhyjl had mentally calculated how much money she had in her purse and figured a hot drink would have to wait.

"Same." replied the detective, then turned his attention back to Rhyjl. "So how long have you attended at DEU and how long have you been studying bones?"

"Before we get back to 21 questions, can I ask one?"

"Shoot." He extended open palm up as if offering her a gift.

"Is this a lunch date or a last meal before you arrest me?"

"Neither. We are just killing an hour and to be quite frank, I've never heard someone's stomach complain so much. I will be expecting you to pick up your share of the tab."

"Understood." She answered as the waitress returned with two glasses of iced water, a wedge of lemon floating on top.

"I've attended DEU for the last four years ever since I was recruited with a full scholarship after my sophomore year at University of Montana." Rhyjl offered.

"Nice. Did you study bones there as well? Is that how you got the scholarship?" He said, unwrapping his silverware from the blue napkin and extracting the spoon.

"Yes, I did." Rhyjl watched as he seemed totally absorbed using his spoon to first push down his wedge of lemon below the ice cubes and then freeing it so it could float back up to the top.

"So would you say you are the ambitious type?"

Rhyjl closed her eyes for a moment taking a deep breath, then slowly exhaling. "Not really. I like what I do and I'm good at it. If I appear ambitious it's an illusion created by my insatiable desire to learn. And you, Detective, are you the ambitious type?"

He looked up from his lemon, a hint of a smile ticking the corners of his mouth. "I used to think so, Miss Martin. Now I just like to do what I know and do it well."

When the waitress returned, she set almost identical meals before them. The only difference was that while Rhyjl had a small dinner salad, Detective Tanner had a full blown Caesar salad, smothered in a generous amount of grilled chicken.

As they ate, their verbal match dwindled. Which was worse, the endless questions or the pregnant bloody quiet? When it reached a point of expectancy she couldn't handle, she set her fork down with a loud tinny twang. "Not much of a dinner conversationalist are you?"

"I enjoy my food," he answered, with only a slight pause between the plate and his waiting mouth. "But if *you* want to talk, be my guest," he replied, the fork descending for the next bite.

When the waitress brought the ticket," Rhyjl snatched it, quickly added up the price of the chowder, salad, taxes and her share of the tip and set the bills and coin on top. While not outrageously expensive, Sara was on her own this week if she wanted anything more than peanut butter sandwiches.

"Ready?" He stood, grabbed the ticket allowing Rhyjl's share to slide freely to the table.

"Ah, excuse, me?" she said, following his retreating back while still casting confusion over her shoulder at the money he'd left behind. "Do you have a tab here or something?"

"No, I'll pay at the cashier."

"But what about my share?"

"It will be a nice tip for a hard working lady. You have a problem with that?"

Yes! No! Shit! What could she say? Her stomach was full. She'd paid for her meal. If *he* wanted to leave behind her entire portion of the bill as a tip, what was that to her? Nothing, but a little niggling worm whispering that the waitress would be eating better than she for the rest of the week. She also harbored no lingering doubts as to why he was given preferential treatment. None what-so-ever.

The heavens opened up as they set foot outside the restaurant as if waiting for them. Hard hitting mega drops quickly turned into a hammering barrage drenching them both by the time they slid into Tanner's sedan.

Sitting in a brooding silence, they waited for the rain to slow. It would have been reckless to put the car in motion when there was no chance of the wipers being able to clear the windshield. It was reckless to talk so freely with this man. She'd never been faced with intense scrutiny. Always in the past if someone wanted to ask about her, she was happy to speak without reserve unless it had to do with her parents or her gift. Her life with her mother and father were old bones better left buried. Her gift, well, it just wasn't something to admit to unless she wanted a one way trip to a psychiatric hospital.

"So would you mind if I ask who we are meeting?"

"Sorry, I thought I had mentioned it. We are meeting with the coroner. She has some questions for you." Tanner was staring at the windshield willing it to be dry or at the very least, clear enough to see through.

"I must have missed that. Look, I'm not versed in crime, I don't think I've even had a parking ticket …"

"You haven't."

"Uh, okay, so as I was saying, from what I do know, this doesn't seem …"

"Normal?"

"You know," she said, twisting in her seat to look him square on, "I don't think I like people finishing my sentences for me. In fact, I think it is somewhat rude."

He shrugged, glanced briefly in her direction before returning to his communion with the windshield.

"So I'm not a suspect." She paused, fully expecting him to interrupt again. "I've already told you what I know. What more do you need and why the interview with the coroner?"

Tension rang with the dissonance of a poorly tuned guitar string.

"Finished?"

She didn't answer.

"This isn't a normal case. YOU aren't a normal witness. To be honest, this is a procedural nightmare. Think about it." He said, as she opened her mouth, then pressed it shut. "A bunch of bones scattered amid a bunch of bones. No normal person would have even spotted them, but you are not normal and I don't mean that in a negative sense. From my investigation up to this point, you are by all accounts a gifted lady in your field. Then there is your field of study. A room that can be locked, but for the most part, might just as well be open to the public since the key is kept in clear view. A baker's dozen of possible suspects, any of whom could have had means and opportunity, but without the victim's identity, we don't know about motive. You are a key. I don't know what you will open, but Lady, I have this gut hunch you have the answer."

At some moment during this little speech, the rain had ceased to drum on the car. Rhyjl had this vision of herself looking a bit like a fish, her mouth opening and shutting numerous times. Tanner reached for the ignition and the sedan, wipers swishing, pulled from the parking lot. Obviously, she wasn't the only one who was manifesting a headache.

*

It was just after three when they pulled up to a stately two and a half story symmetrical white building with a semi-circular portico supported by four large white columns. Black shutters posted like sentinels, guarded both sides of the sixteen windows facing the street. A sign, with a definite colonial air, announcing that it housed the town offices, sheriff's department and fire station was posted near the intersection of the curbside and walkway. Captain Archambeau had wasted no expense building his Georgian home.

Inside, however, with the exception of the vaulted ceilings, and the beautiful carved moldings, the charming period ambience had been replaced with casual, and a bit shabby office efficiency. A glass door marked Sheriff's office was the first door on the right. Detective Tanner opened the door and stood back waiting for Rhyjl to enter.

At a circular desk in the middle of a room that at one time had probably been the dining room or drawing room, sat a pretty blond woman not much older than Rhyjl. Her hair was tied back, natural, not dyed, and the color of flax. The uniform of khaki cotton did nothing to hide her feminine curves. She was country girl: gorgeous with strong bone structure and delightfully natural teeth not molded by metal into one of those artificial smiles so common these days.

A polished brass plaque on the desk identified her as Officer J. Albright. A series of three glowing computer screens, two types of keyboards, multiple line phone, headset, and focused concentration, indicated competency. Sheriff Buchard and his deputy might be the brawn of the department, but J. Albright was the heart that kept it all working.

The walls around the brightly sun painted room were covered in posters toting warnings like a benign "*Click it or ticket it*" poster with its fasten seatbelt. And the more disturbing ones: "*Is that text worth a life? Don't Text and Drive*" showing a crumpled car that obviously no one could have escaped alive, and a "*Dare not to take drugs*" with a series of pictures showing the devastation of continued meth use over time.

Did meth really ravage people that drastically in a few short years? What a high price for escapism.

Directly across from Officer Albright, hanging above four olive green and pewter colored chairs, were posted two large maps. One of the county, the other of the township. Rhyjl wondered if the chairs were part of the set sitting in the Anthro. Department. There must have been a redecorating frenzy during the '70's or a great yard sale in the '90's. Fortunately, Officer Albright's seating was a bit more up to date with an ergonomically designed black leather office chair.

"Can I help you?" she addressed Rhyjl professionally. Then noticing Detective Tanner, she immediately transformed into a radiance that even surpassed the sun and left Rhyjl forgotten. "Detective." So nice to see you. You are here for your meeting with Dr. Merks?"

"Yes, Jamie, which room?" He brushed her off.

Jerk hadn't even noticed how his curtness had dimmed poor Jamie's light. What kind of detective was he that he couldn't see she was head over heels for him? Or … perhaps, he did and didn't want to encourage her. Still, he could have been a little more civil.

"She just called. She's running about ten minutes late," she replied, reverting to her professional demeanor, her smile dimming.

Tanner checked his watch, frowned and grumbled. "You gotta love Maine time. Which room is open?"

Officer Jamie Albright's eyebrows arched and Rhyjl could hear the barely restrained laughter behind her answer. "Around here, Tanner, everything's open."

*

"Okay, let me get this straight," Tanner said, for the second time. "You taught this introduction class that you are not associated with?"

"Yes." Rhyjl answered, exhaling audibly.

The room Tanner had chosen was an eggshell white that was in serious need of a touch up. Four chairs with faux tan leather seats and chrome frames were arranged around a chrome table with a soft brown Formica top. Detective Tanner had positioned himself in one nearest the door. He'd made it clear, that the chair on the other side of the table across from him, was where she was supposed to sit. Positioning yourself between the suspect and the door made complete sense. She imagined that it was all part of a mind game to remind the detainee that there was no way out, other than past their interrogator. One thing was missing, however: the large mirror which even the most inattentive knew was a one-way window. Instead, there was a three by four white board where someone had drawn a happy face with a blue marker.

"On the date in question," Tanner flipped through the note book, and nodded. "I checked and classes were not expected to begin until the next day. Is that correct?" On the ride into town and at the restaurant his questions had been casual conversation. These were forced, clipped. Just what she'd expected from an interrogation.

"That's correct. But Professor Kendricks always has this intro class a day or so before classes actually begin."

"And why is that?"

"I could hazard a guess, but I think you should ask her." Rhyjl smiled at the thought.

Tanner's face hardened. "Miss Martin, do you find this situation entertaining?"

"Hardly, and quite contrary, I'm bored. Detective, we've been over this. I can't tell you anything about why Professor Kendricks does what she does. I've never been privy to her reasons for anything, unless it concerns lab procedures."

"Which you broke?"

"Huh?" Well at least it was a new tack.

"Isn't it a lab procedure to wear gloves when handling specimens?"

"Yes." She could feel the crimson tide of guilt creeping up from her neck to her earlobes. Fortunately before she could feel anymore annoyed at herself, the door opened.

"Oh, starting the fun before I got here, I see?" Doctor Merks' entrance was like a breath of fresh air. Her voice was soft, her tone light and teasing. She looked like she was straight out of a fashion magazine. Not model thin, but dressed immaculately. Rhyjl wasn't alone in her admiration. So Tanner wasn't a cold fish, gay or numb from the waist down. He wasted no time standing, pulling out a chair and inquiring if there was anything she might like before they resumed. She accepted the chair and declined his offer by holding up a white with green motif Starbucks cup.

"Miss Martin." She nodded, placing both the cup and a notebook on the table between them. "May I call you, Rhyjl?"

Tanner rolled his eyes. It was either a great "good cop, bad cop" routine or he really was a little peeved.

"Rhyjl is fine." The heat in her neck was subsiding. So if it was the "good cop" bit, it was apparently working.

"Great! You may call me Alice if you wish or Doctor Merks. But I'd prefer the former." Opening her notebook to a scribble that didn't look like any kind of shorthand Rhyjl had ever seen, Alice Merks, continued. "So where were you two when I came in just now?"

"We were discussing the discrepancy in the timing of the class that Rhyjl shouldn't have been teaching and the fact that she broke a lab regulation." Tanner's face had returned to hard cop mode rather than lovesick puppy.

"Um, well I'm not really interested in that," Alice replied. "I suppose if you must, then I will sit this part out. I'd rather discuss the bones and the state thereof."

Rhyjl was liking Alice more by the moment. She could talk bones up one side and down the other. They were her language.

"Well," Tanner steepled his fingers near the tip of his nose for a moment, then braced them once again upon the table before proceeding. "I would like to know why fingerprints and DNA were found on the bones, that I'm sure after further tests, will confirm that you, Miss Martin, handled them."

She was guilty. He had her there. But only of breaking a lab rule not the law. She knew it was a good rule. Bones could harbor diseases for long periods of time. But sometimes rules needed to be broken. She'd promised herself that she would make it a rare thing, but not rule it out of happening again. As for this particular incident, she'd had to know for herself. Tanner could be damned.

"I'd be surprised if you didn't find my prints and possibly my DNA. As I've already mentioned to others, I knew right away the bones were not part of the collection. I could see it just as clearly as I can your face. But," she held up her hands and shrugged, "I needed to know more. I needed to understand things my eyes just couldn't see. My sense of touch can find things that are not discernable from sight alone."

"So without gloves, you just compromised a crime scene just to satisfy your own curiosity?"

That hit hard! And yes, she could fully understand his anger. It would be akin to someone taking an artifact or bone out of situ. So much information would be lost or denigrated.   How often had she or one of her colleagues bemoaned and bitched about the stupidity of amateurs? She may know bones, but in police investigations she was about as ignorant as they come. Still ... "Yes, I understand your point."

"Do you? Do you really?"

Rhyjl had noticed during their time together, that

when agitated, Tanner would start worrying the cuticle of his thumb with his index finger. Was it a throwback to nail biting?

Pausing for a moment to collect thoughts that were as elusive as snowflakes and just as fleeting if she did capture it, she tried to understand how to explain something even she couldn't quite grasp. "Yes, I understand and what I did, was wrong. I did let curiosity get the best of me but not in a morbid sense. I work with bones. I study them and ask questions to get answers. It was habit, I suppose. I wanted to know the three: who, what and where. Or better yet, why." There are just some things you cannot tell with gloves on."

"So you admit it?" He leaned across the table as if he might connect with her. "You contaminated the bones."

"What do you want from me, Detective? Yes! I did touch the bones without gloves. Do you always carry gloves?"

He sat back, a satisfied cat grin. "As a matter of fact, I do, Ms. Martin." He said, pulling two latex blue gloves enclosed in a bag out of his jacket pocket. "Evidence, clean evidence, is very important in my line of work. You also were in a lab where gloves are at every station. I know, I looked."

The atmosphere was getting so thick and charged, it was becoming harder to breath. Did she have this effect on all men or just cops? If the former, it might explain why she didn't have a love life. Unexpectedly, a snapshot of Erik flashed across her vision. Just as quickly she dismissed it.

He was still holding the gloves for her inspection, his brows raised in question.

She pushed the gloves away. "Look, I don't know

if I can explain this or not. Can you humor me for a moment?"

He looked as if he was about to protest when Alice Merks tapped her fingers gently on his arm. "I would like to hear what she has to say?"

Tanner turned to putty.

Watching the exchange, Rhyjl was impressed. Was it just Tanner or could Alice pull this off with any member of the opposite gender?

"Put one of those gloves on your left hand, Detective. You've got a hangnail or such on your right thumb you've been picking on all afternoon."

"Point?"

"I want you to feel that hangnail. With only your gloved hand, I want you to tell me about that hangnail. Is it dry, moist, hot, cold? You cannot use any other of your senses, including the feelings in your right thumb. Only what you can feel with the gloved one."

"I think I see what you are playing at, Ms. Martin, however, you were not limited to just your sense of touch. You were able to use sight to satisfy your curiosity as you put it."

"Okay, so you can use your eyes as well as your gloved hand. What do you glean from your examination?"

"I've got a hangnail and it is dry, the skin is reddened and there is a place or two where it might actually bleed or has bled recently. Did I pass?"

"With flying colors, but suppose I was to do this." Rhyjl reached into her small bag and pulled out a small white squeeze tube of Eucerin she always carried. Taking Tanner's thumb, she squeezed a drop of the white cream on the affected area and began to massage it in. She could feel his desire to pull away and knew it was costing him not to. He appeared to be a man who didn't like familiarity, especially with someone he hardly knew. The urge to resist was strained further with a knock at the door and the appearance of Officer Albright.

"Ah, new interrogation technique, Detective?"

"No!" He snapped. "Ms. Martin is making a point. What do you need, Jamie?"

"There is a phone call for you. They said your phone is going straight to voicemail. It sounds important."

Tanner pulled his hand away, reached for his cell in his pocket and looked at the glassy screen. "Damn battery! Excuse me ladies."

"I can only imagine what she might have been thinking just now," Alice Merks chuckled.

Rhyjl nodded, but remained silent.

"So what is your point? I'm assuming you aren't trying to seduce him. If so, I could always leave and come back later. I'm not really into a threesome sort of thing."

Rhyjl almost choked in response. "Hardly! I'm trying to show him that gloves limit what we can ascertain from our surroundings. I don't know how else to make clear my reasons for my blunder in corrupting the scene."

"I figured something like that, but what was it you were looking for?"

"The bones were good. If I hadn't been so familiar with them, I wouldn't have seen anything."

"That's already been established, Rhyjl. So again," she said, tilting her head slightly as if subconsciously trying to see something from a different angle, "What were you looking for?"

"The age. I was looking for the age specifically and anything else in the way of a residue that might tell me more about the bones."

"I'm sorry, but I'm not quite following. I know we can tell the age by looking at the bones just as you can tell the sex. We know she was around twenty to twenty five. You would have spotted that right off. So …?"

"Oh! Okay, I see your confusion. No, I wasn't looking for the age of the victim. I was looking for how long the victim had been dead. How old were these *bones*! They were treated and cleaned. I don't know much about forensics as in the kind of work you do. I've never worked with anything that wasn't at least a couple hundred years old. But the fresher the bones are, the more they have to give."

"And what did they have to give, Ms. Martin?" Tanner said, returning to their company.

"Can we go back to my demonstration?" Rhyjl answered, pointing to his still gloved hand.

With all three looking on, Rhyjl once more instructed Tanner to examine the torn cuticle he had earlier. "Can you feel a difference?"

"Sure, it isn't as stiff and dry. I can both see and feel that."

"Ah, but can you tell me if it feels wet, moist, sticky?"

Tanner rubbed his thumb again. "Well, I can make a guess, that it probably feels moister because it is not as stiff or dry."

"Exactly! You can make a guess, but if you really want to understand something is 'a guess' good enough? Probably not! You want to know! So it is moist? You can see that, but you are only guessing as to what kind of moist. Is it a watery moist? An oily moist? Is it slightly tacky? That's what I was trying to discover about the bones."

"Because bones that are not old will have a greasy

residue on them that doesn't necessarily show up to the eye." Alice Merks nodded approvingly. "Of course! That makes perfect sense. But that still wouldn't have given you a time of death."

"No, but it would tell me if the bones were more recent i.e. a possible murder or some antique specimens that someone had just planted to create a practical joke. For my own curiosity, and to confirm my suspicions, I needed to know if it was someone's sick, sick way of disposing of a murdered person. I needed confirmation that what I suspected was true, so I could sleep at night. Unfortunately," Rhyjl sighed, "It hasn't helped me to sleep at all. Just the opposite.

"Have you recovered all her bones?" Rhyjl asked.

"Not yet," Dr. Merks answered. "It's a long and involved process and there are a lot of bones to look through. As you pointed out, they are not easily detectable."

"And until you recover them all, you can't really understand what happened to her, is that right?"

"Well," Alice shifted uncomfortably. "We know a woman was murdered. You gave us the beginning of that. To be honest, I've had a few other bodies to contend with that have a slightly higher priority. People tend not to schedule their deaths."

"Yes, I can see where that might put a crimp in the time frame. How far have you gotten? Have you been able to narrow her age yet? She was mature, but I didn't have much time."

"What did you have time for? I'll be honest, I haven't even gotten to all the boxes yet. I need to establish cause of death and get something that will help with identification."

"The pieces I did see gave me a hint of a struggle. Possibly cause of death, but I didn't come across anything I think you could use for identification. If I was looking at her from a dig site, I'd really want to have the whole assemblage laid out before making any concrete statements."

"Yes, I need that as well. It's just the mess! It's going to take me ages to sort the bones from your lab specimens. Hopefully, no one else decides to drop dead in the next week." Alice sighed.

Rhyjl looked toward the door wanting an exit. "I could help you with that! I don't think it would take me more than a couple hours."

"Oh whoa! Now just hold on, you've done enough damage. I don't want you anywhere near those bones. Do you understand me?" Tanner ordered, looking at Rhyjl first, and then Alice.

"Well, I don't know who made you my boss," Alice responded, "that you think you can toss out orders, but I'll consider your request." She looked to Rhyjl. "Tell me your thoughts."

Rhyjl considered. "There are 206 bones in the human body. Even if you discarded the small bone and teeth, which I'm guessing our killer did, he or she wouldn't have mixed female bones with male bones. At least that is my thought."

"So they took twenty-five boxes of bones out of your lab and brought them to mine. I haven't really even had the time to notice how many were female. What are we talking about if you are correct?"

"Twelve. Twelve if I'm correct." Rhyjl nodded. "I could easily pull what you need." Rhyjl shifted as if to get up and get started on the task. Truth told, she wanted to get back to the bones. Solve the mystery, it would all be over. The restless dreams, the creepy feeling that someone was trying to possess her, would cease. The answer was in those boxes.

"Okay ladies, the fun stops here. I cannot tell you what to do Alice, but I can go over your head. As far as Ms. Martin, she is still a suspect. She cannot go anywhere near that evidence."

The proverbial pin could have dropped and sounded like a bomb going off. Both women sat round eyed and open mouthed. Alice was the first to regain composure.

"I thought it was obvious that Rhyjl was not a suspect only a highly trained witness. So what's changed?"

"I agree," Rhyjl stated. "You made it pretty clear only a few hours ago I was in the clear."

"Things change. Some new evidence has come to light."

"What new evidence?" Alice demanded, now rising to her feet. She wasn't a tall woman, but at the moment all five foot five of her was erect and in intimidation mode.

Rhyjl remained seated. She was deflated. The momentum she felt only moments before had gone out the door without her. She needed those bones like she needed to breathe. Without them, there wouldn't be closure.

As if reading her mind, Detective Tanner asked simply, "Tell me Ms. Martin, why is it you think you can do a better job with those bones than our ME here?"

Without thinking, she looked straight into those cold blue eyes and said. "Because I can FEEL them."

Chapter 7

Girl Talk

The big black clock on the interrogation room wall tick, tick, ticked away the seconds, but they might as well have been hours. Bitter cold had settled in to the very core of Rhyjl's marrow, but it had nothing to do with the ambient heat of the room. There were voices, both male and female, but they seemed far, far away. What did they have to do with her? Why not get up and walk out the door? Why? Her mind hung suspended on the word. The drop from it seemed too deep.

"Rhyjl? Rhyjl?" The soft voice was accompanied by a warm hand gently squeezing her shoulder.

In the distance, beyond her fogged mind, a door opened and clicked shut.

"Rhyjl, talk to me." The voice was persistent. The squeeze turned into a slight jostle.

Rhyjl pulled herself from the cloying fog toward the voice. Her eyes opened. Before her, Alice Merks' face appeared both friend and doctor: concern mixed with clinical detachment. Rhyjl knew the look oh so intimately well. She'd seen it in the doctors and nurses who had helped her mother in the beginning. It was that look that said, I know you are hurt, sick or scared. I care about how you are coping. I'm here for you for this moment, but it's only professional. Rhyjl knew it was the way they had to be. They have to walk that fine line between caring and letting it take over. You cannot work with hurting people all day long and absorb it all without crashing. So you draw the line. You keep it professional. Your compassion becomes a coat you put on and take off. You maintain your sanity. Your survival depends on it. Rhyjl also sensed Alice Merks was truly trying to comfort her. Unfortunately for them both, it failed.

Rhyjl shrugged off Alice's hand with a force stronger than she thought herself capable of at the moment. "I don't want your sympathy!" She felt the heat rising in her body even if her bones remained frozen. "And I don't need your understanding! I'm innocent. I'm the victim here just as much as the woman murdered." Heat, cold. Pain, anger. What was one without the other? How did you really know one without the other?

Alice stood back, her arms crossing across her breasts. "Interesting that you see yourself as a victim, here. Would you mind elaborating on that some?"

"Simple. I was going about my life. I stopped ..." Why had she stopped? Why hadn't she just stayed her course to the Dean's office? Why was it her business what happened? What was that saying, 'not my circus, not my monkey'?

"Yes?" Alice said, leaning her hip lightly against the conference table.

"I stopped to do my friend, Sara, a favor. No, not Sara, but the kids coming into that class. I knew I could do the orientation and to be honest, I like helping others. I like sharing my passion with others."

"So you took the class. You made that choice and something unexpected happened. How does that make you the victim?"

"How does it not!" Rhyjl leapt to her feet. "I should be at the University now working on MY research, not sitting here being bombarded by questions. I am not guilty of anything and yet people are acting as if I am. I'm the one that can't sleep at night because SHE is haunting me! How does that not make me the victim and in more than one way. She is dead. Nothing that happens or doesn't happen will change that. Oh sure, if you find her murderer, she will be at rest and not feel the need to haunt me, but other ..."

"She's haunting you?"

"I ... um ... the case not being solved is haunting me." Damn, why hadn't she kept her big mouth shut!

"No, you said, *she* was haunting you. You also said, she would feel at rest."

"Yeah, well that was just a way of talking. Surely, Dr. Merks, you don't believe in ghosts?"

"I believe there are a lot of things seen and unseen we don't understand. I also want to know why you are angry with me."

"I'm not!" She just wanted to get the hell out of this room.

"You are. Until the accusation Tanner made, you and I were on first name bases. Now you've distanced yourself and reverted to the formal Doctor Merks. That says you are upset with me. Resentful actually. And, well, I actually resent it, considering I've backed you from the beginning. So let's start new. I'm your ally in this. I'm pretty close to thinking of you as a colleague. A colleague whose help I could use. And YOU, my dear friend, are being haunted."

Laughter, shrouded in tatters of trepidation escaped from Rhyjl's constricting throat. "Look, Doc," she choked off the laugh.   "I'm not upset with you. I'm just upset. As for ghosts, I can honestly say there are no spectral figures, dressed in sheets, manifesting before my eyes."

"Then," Alice pushed herself away from the table. "Why don't I give you a ride back to your place and you can enlighten me so I won't make further observational blunders." When it looked like Rhyjl might balk, Alice added. "Or I can see if Tanner is still around and let him take you back."

"Sure, I'll accept your ride, but just do me one favor."

"What's that?" Alice moved around the table and was collecting her notebook, purse and a pen she'd left sitting there.

"Treat me like that colleague you were mentioning. I've had enough of the suspect role for the day."

"Done!" Alice smiled, meeting Rhyjl at the door and reaching for the knob. "You first, partner."

*

Alice's official medical examiner's vehicle was parked in the back lot behind the old mansion. Nothing fancy, and not what Rhyjl would imagine she drove in her off time. The rain had stopped. A brief respite since dark, heavily-burdened clouds hung poised as far as the eye could see. Alice snatched the key off the console between the seats and plugged them in the ignition. When she noticed the quizzical look on her passenger's face she said. "What?"

"Is it wise to leave the keys out in the open like that?"

Alice smirked. "You are joking, right?" Her brows V-ed making her eyes narrow, her head shaking. "Who in their right mind would steal an ME car? And let's face it, this isn't exactly a crime prone town."

Rhyjl nodded, sat back and fumbled with the twisted seat belt.

"Sorry about that." Alice started the ignition. "I get a little careless from time to time. Corpses don't always care if their belts get tangled."

Rhyjl's hands flew away from the belt and she looked as if she was about to bolt. Alice laughed and placed a steadying hand out. "Just coroner's humor. In my line of business we have to keep it light. Otherwise the darkness would take over."

They pulled out of the lot and headed back down the main street which looked almost deserted. Evidently most people had chosen to stay home and weather the storm. They were nearing the small Shop & Save and Rhyjl wished she had the nerve to ask if Alice would stop. Just a few things to fill her fridge would be nice. The lunch with Tanner had turned sour in her stomach and was already wearing off.

"So do you drink?"

"What?"

Alice pulled into the parking lot of the store. "Do you drink? Imbibe? Alcohol?"

"Ah, no. Not really."

"Well I do, and I'd like some wine. Mind if we stop?"

If Rhyjl was a religious person, she might have considered it a prayer answered. Instead, she just smiled. "No problem."

It didn't take long to make their purchases. Alice had picked up three bottles of wine. Red, pink and white. Rhyjl had grabbed a box of tea, a loaf of bread, two cans of tuna, a tomato, lettuce and a pound of butter.

"Lunch tomorrow?" Alice asked as they loaded the two sacks in the back of the car.

"Yeah," Rhyjl replied. And dinner and lunch and dinner.

Back in their seats, Rhyjl didn't miss Alice's grin as Rhyjl buckled her seat belt.

"You eat healthier than I did when I was in college." Alice started up the car. "I lived on pizza. Do you know that pizza, statistically, is the most commonly eaten food by college students?"

"I could have guessed." Rhyjl answered. "I hadn't really given it much thought, but it makes sense."

They'd come to the last intersection prior to hitting the highway leading to DEU. "Yes, I suppose it is pretty obvious. Dead town at this hour of the day except for Vinney's. Bet a dollar for every car there, it belongs to a college student."

Rhyjl, wishing she could have taken Alice up on the bet, scanned the packed lot around Vinney's and was pretty sure she'd seen more than half of those cars on campus. But not all were students. The sleek Tesla was Erik's.

In the same tone and not skipping a beat, the next question infused itself into their conversation with ease. "So, Rhyjl, why do you think those bones ended up scattered in the bone lab?"

"Someone wanted to hide a body?"

"But why there? Obviously it wasn't a good choice. You discovered it right off."

"Well maybe yes, maybe no." Rhyjl felt a chill running through her bones again as she flashed back to the lab and the feeling of the bones. That horrid jolt filled with unimaginable pain and confusion.

"Rhyjl?"

"Sorry, I was back at the lab for a moment."

"So tell me, why do you think it was a good place for the bones to be hidden?" Alice pushed.

"Well I guess it wasn't since I did find them. But that's just it. Normally, I wouldn't have been in that lab. And if I had been, it would have been to work on some specimens that I want shipped over from Sweden. I wouldn't have touched those bones."

"Are you telling me that someone else might not have seen that something was amiss? What about Professor ... ah"

"Kendricks? She might have if she'd been looking. She's taught that class for over ten years. It's not likely she is going to be going back over those bones until she notices a discrepancy between what she expects to find in a student's paper and the students assessment of the remains. That might not even happen until the end of the semester. Then again, she might just slough it off as the student's mistake. I mean what other logical explanation could there be? It's not as if new specimens have been added. At least that's what she would think. And, as much as I hate to say this, I think Kendricks relishes the thought that all her students are inferior and make lots of mistakes. She never makes them, of course."

"Do I detect some hostility here between you and Kendricks?"

"You might say that." Rhyjl looked out the rain splattered window of the car as the surroundings bled by. "I respect the woman, don't get me wrong. I also learned a great deal from her."

"But?"

"But she can't take criticism, and can never be

wrong. It's not that I criticized her, but there were more than a few times we knocked heads together over bones. The first time it was over cats, and honestly, I suppose the two of us looked to any observer, like two cats fighting with all the hissing and spitting that went on." Rhyjl still felt a sliver of perverse joy, considering that in the end, she had been proven to have the right of it.

"Cats? I thought Kendricks and you were into human remains?" The rain had begun its relentless onslaught again forcing Alice to slow so as not to miss the turn onto University Drive.

"She was my instructor for Zooarchaeology as well. Faunal remains are an important aspect to understanding what humans were doing. You know the old adage: You are what you eat."

"So someone was eating cats?" laughed Alice.

"No, at least the bones we were arguing over showed no signs of being munched on, but the bones were in the midden—that's a garbage pile—so they did something with the creature. My guess, it was hanging around and someone thought a lynx fur would be nice."

"Ah, that's the difference between your field and mine. No guessing, no hunches." Alice pulled over to the side of the road.

"I wouldn't say that. Something wrong?" Rhyjl scanned the rain soaked surrounding.

"Yes, I just realized I have no idea where you live?"

"It's over there." Rhyjl pointed to the huddle of about a dozen little cabins. At the moment they had the look of abandonment and where uninviting except for a few who spilled pale light from half covered windows. "The one on the far left." The one that is dark and lonely and has an empty fridge.

"So, I've been thinking ever since we passed Vinney's that we should order something out and continue our talk while we have girl's night." Alice pulled the car to a stop leaving the lights illuminating the entry.

"Let me guess. Pizza?" Rhyjl said, sliding out of her seatbelt and opening the door. A gust of wind and rain swept in spattering her coat and jeans. "I thank you, but I don't think I can. I've got some work to catch up on."

"You don't. I know your schedule. You are just politely trying to be rid of me." Alice said, getting out of her side and opening the back door to extract Rhyjl's three plastic grocery sacks and her own two reusable totes.

"God what is this? Everyone all of a sudden seems to know everything about me! When did my life become a fricken open book for everyone's perusing?"

"Price of fame, luv." Alice handed her the three bags and headed for the door. So how does Bar-B-Q ribs sound?"

*

The tuna sandwich would save until tomorrow. Rhyjl unloaded her groceries into the vacant cavern of the fridge and placed the tea pot on the burner to heat. Alice was on the phone ordering enough food to feed an army. What? Was she one of those thoroughly disgusting women, whose metabolisms worked overtime, allowing them to eat and eat without gaining an ounce? Rhyjl's jaw just about hit the floor when Alice moved on from the order of a quart of potato salad and another quart of baked beans to the ribs. Two? Yes, two buckets or ribs! "So you and what army are coming to dinner?" Rhyjl asked, coming back into the cluttered living room with a wine glass and cork screw for Alice.

Alice tossed her phone into the pocket of her slacks and began folding a pile of laundry occupying the sofa. "Just us, but I like to think ahead. Whatever is left will save time fixing a meal tomorrow. Yours or your roomies?"

"Hers."

"Her room?"

Rhyjl turned slightly to her right and pointed to the room behind her and to the right of the kitchen. "But you don't …"

"Hey, no problem and I know I don't, but I'm not going to sit here on these. Are you?"

"No, but I shouldn't have to pick up after her either!" Yet, that's exactly what she felt like she'd been doing ever since she'd met Sara.

"Rhyjl, it's your choice." Alice said, still folding and sounding as soothing as a mother with a distressed child. "You don't have to let people run over you. Take your throne back. Rule your life from it. Stop letting others make those choices for you. Do you want Sara's things all over your shared area or do you want to be able to come in and sit down on a chair or sofa without competition? With the exception of the cat." Alice reached down and stroked the cat who was favoring her with its presence.

Alice was certainly adept at folding and had the pile turned into two neat stacks in minutes. Picking up one, she threaded her way toward the room Rhyjl had indicated. Rhyjl picked up the second and trailed in her wake. When Alice entered, she looked at the unmade bed and unceremoniously dumped the load on the floor. She then turned with a smile, took Rhyjl's load and dumped them as well. "Done! Now where were we?"

Rhyjl stood, her mouth gaping at the jumbled piles and then at Alice's retreating back. If she was going to just dump the clothes, why the hell did she fold them?

"So while we are waiting for the food," Alice resumed the conversation as if nothing else had transpired, "what did you do differently, that our killer hadn't anticipated?"

Rhyjl remained standing, and still in a daze of confusion, as Alice deftly opened the bottle of red wine, poured a glass full, and took occupancy of the space only moments before holding Sara's clothes. The cat jumped up purring and rubbed against Alice as if in full approval, then circling three times, curled into a blissful ball next to her new hero.

"Excuse me just a minute," Rhyjl said, looking about her. "What did we just do, here? I mean what was the purpose of folding those clothes then just dumping them?"

"We just claimed space. We were considerate enough to politely fold the clothes, remove them and deposit them in a fashion that clearly your roommate knows. Total clutter. I had originally thought of placing them on the bed," she said, crossing her legs and taking a sip from her glass, "but as soon as I saw the state her bedroom was in, well."

"You don't know Sara." Rhyjl moaned. "This could start an all-out war."

"Only if you let it." Alice indicated a cute kitten throw draped chair across from her with a regal wave of her hand. "Your throne, Lady."

Rhyjl looked toward the door before seating herself. Please let this be one of the nights Sara chooses to stay away. Alice was correct. She couldn't just let Sara keep running over her. It had been a long time problem whether it be food or cleaning or general upkeep. She'd always made excuses for Sara. What she really was doing, was avoiding conflict. Sara was from a wealthy family. She'd always had everything done for her. The only down side, according to Sara, was that her older brother was the shining star. Sara was never able to please her folks. In a way, that was the driving force behind Sara. Proving herself and that meant excelling. When things didn't go her way, however, well … there was hell to pay. Rhyjl didn't feel up to dealing with another hell. She also didn't feel like cleaning up after Sara and especially feeding her. But was this the time to challenge the status quo?

"Hello? Anybody there?"

Rhyjl brought her mind back to the present. "Just mulling over what you said."

"That's good, but how about we mull over this unusual case? I may not be able to get your help in the lab, but anything you can share with me could make a huge difference. So back to my question. What did you do differently, that our killer wouldn't have anticipated?"

"Simple. I wouldn't have been there."

"Besides that?"

"I don't know." Rhyjl's hand waved about grabbing invisible thoughts.

"Go back over what happened." Alice's fingers played with the stem of the wine glass as she leaned in narrowing the space between them.

"Well, I was giving the lecture on lab procedures while I was laying out the bones and that's when I noticed something wasn't right. Actually, I wasn't the only one. One of the students also noticed that something wasn't what I was saying it was."

"Interesting that someone else noticed. So it was pretty obvious. Why? Let's back track a second. You say you noticed that something wasn't quite right. Then the student openly disagrees with you. That just doesn't fit. You're good. So why would you say something about a bone that a student, I'm assuming isn't as proficient as you, would so easily notice?"

"Because it was Mattie. I know her so well, that I just started telling her story as I was laying the bones out. I immediately saw the discrepancy, but didn't want to stop the lecture. I stupidly thought if I could just keep going, keep the flow moving, I could get through the whole lecture and have time afterward to go back and figure it out." Sitting back rolling her head against the back of the chair Rhyjl groaned. "It was dumb, dumb, dumb! I should have just shut down. As it turned out that student made a big deal of it and had a lot of fun at my expense."

"This student wouldn't happen to be a guy by the name of David Bannerman, would he?"

Alice held her hand up. "We can get back to that. Who is Mattie?"

"It's the name I used for DR 106. She was my project when I was in that class. I chose to display her because I know her so well." More than she could say. "So, I thought I would lay her out talking about her life. I think it helps incoming students to think more personally of the specimens. It's not just about knowing what bones look like under different circumstances. It's about piecing together someone's life."

"Another difference between your job and mine. I don't necessarily want to know their life. Just the way it ended."

"But what about this case, Alice? Don't you want

to piece this person's life together to learn who she was?"

"Only as far as making an identification and statement on manner of death." Alice leaned back and took a long, slow sip of her blood red wine. "I can't really say I would want to learn more. I try not to make it personal. Sometimes just seeing their death is hard enough. I don't think I could emotionally survive if I had to start putting people's lives together. But you do. You really need to know, don't you?"

A flash of lightening lit up the room mid-day bright followed closely by a thunder clap that rattled the windows. Alice broke the moments of silence following. "Wow, didn't even have time to count that one."

Rhyjl remained looking out the window, now nothing more than a streaked black screen with a few pale pin points of light. She did make it personal. They were people. They had a life. Sometimes it was filled with love. Sometimes hurt and anger just as her's was. Their death was only an infinitesimal fraction of that time. She could see Alice's point. What if every skeleton she looked at affected her in the same way as this woman's? She had learned to put it all in perspective after the Boy. His death had hit her hard. It had driven her in her dreams and waking hours until she'd pursued her field in archaeology. She could tell their stories and sometimes in the history books, right a wrong. The perpetrators of those wrongs were long gone, however. There was no justice, only the telling. This woman, this blond who haunted her with screams of pain and confusion, was different. Her nemesis had not been brought to justice. There was still time. Alice made a difference in the here and now. Perhaps, that was all that could or should be done. Still …

"I do need to know the whole story, Alice. Without

it, how can you understand the why? It may seem cut and dry, even a heart attack, but why? Was the individual under stress? Was it poor eating habits?"

"Most likely both in most of those cases." Alice reached for the bottle and topped off her glass. "But knowing that won't change the fact that they are dead or that there are people grieving for them. My job is to bring closure. The person died of such and such. I leave it up to the researchers to understand what brought the person to that place. Now in this case," she took a long drought of the Cabernet, "I need to know who she was and how she died. Tanner will fill in the rest. And don't roll your eyes," she snapped, admonishing her finger in front of Rhyjl's nose. "Tanner's good. Too good to be working the backwoods of Maine. He was a top investigator out of Seattle until, well, until his life took a strange twist. Suffice to say, he will catch this killer and have the motive tied up in a nice neat bundle if we can get him something more solid to go on than innuendo and supplications."

"Nice speech, Doc." The teakettle had summoned her several minutes ago with its rolling popping and ample steam, but now she really needed the tea. She'd seen the attraction Tanner had for his ME, but it appeared now as if the cool, collected Alice just might entertain the same feelings. "So are you here playing the good cop to his bad ass one?"

"He really pissed you off, didn't he?" Alice shifted with the grace of a feline to watch Rhyjl pour water from the red enameled teapot into a large mug with a loon on it. "But no, I'm not playing the good cop. As hard as you might find it to believe, I really do like you. I've liked you from the first time I saw you in that lab of yours. You intrigued me then. You still do. You might just be an exception to my rule of don't get involved with other people's lives."

Returning with the mug steaming between her two hands, Rhyjl sat in the battered wingback chair across from the sofa and shrugged. "What if I don't want you to know my life? I thought I was just here to help you find a cause of death."

Another lightning bolt split the night. The thunder, however was delayed, the distant roll barely audible over the roar of sheeting rain on the metal roof. Rhyjl, regretting her words even as she spoke them, sighed. "I'm sorry, that was rather bitchy of me. I could say it's been a long day and that storms like this put me on edge. It would all be true, but still, you haven't been anything, but nice. There's no excuse."

"We will both feel better as soon as the food arrives. Food always soothes the beast in me. So back to business or maybe for us, pleasure. I enjoy a good mystery. You?"

Rhyjl laughed and felt the tension easing. Partly due to the soothing warmth of the tea and Alice's ability to switch gears mid-sentence. "I guess you could say I do. Archaeology is solving mysteries of a sort."

"So," Alice shifted again, this time displacing the cat by an inch which it let be known was unacceptable with a low growl, "tell me more about Mattie."

"Not until you tell me about Bannerman."

"Fair enough. Not much to tell that you haven't already confirmed and probably guessed by now. Everyone in the class was questioned. He just made it a point to emphasize that you tried to hide the discrepancy between your narration and the actual evidence you were handling. He also stated you appeared nervous, and when he pointed out your mistake, you were quick to end the class. My take and Tanners too, I think, was of someone inflating their own importance."

Rhyjl nodded. Yep! That described Bannerman to a T.

"Now about Mattie. You were familiar with her because she had been your project. Would someone else have put her out on the table? Would they have noticed the difference?"

The wind was whipping in frenzy. Small branches scratched against the roof and walls of the cottage aping fingernails on a chalk board. What Rhyjl had said about storms putting her on edge was true. As a kid she'd often hid under the covers of her bed. One time, she'd even striped the blanket off her bed and huddled with it in a closet. Why people would want to live in areas frequented by hurricanes and tornados was beyond her.

"Not likely that someone else would have used Mattie."

"Then one of the other specimens?"

Rhyjl thought about that for a moment. If someone else had chosen a specimen, they would have chosen one they were familiar with. If it had been a male, then probably, if her earlier guess was correct, there wouldn't be any of the victim's bones to find. If another female, then yes, but …

"Your wheels are turning." Alice put her empty glass and the scarred wooden end table and leaned toward Rhyjl.

"I was just thinking that if I'd chosen a male, the murder would have remained unknown. So, if Sara had taught the class, she probably wouldn't have seen anything because her choice would have been the male she worked with." But there was more. Would Sara have even chosen to get an example out? Probably not. Sara and Kendricks would have done something quite differently. "Alice, I don't think anyone else who would have taught that class, would have noticed anything out of the unusual, simply because they wouldn't have gotten any of the individuals from The Crypt out. It's not their teaching style."

"Ah," Alice smiled and sat back reaching for the wine bottle again. "And you, my friend, wouldn't have and shouldn't have been there. Our killer didn't count on you. They counted on the fact that the bones might not be discovered for a long time to come. Do you remember there ever being an orientation where one of the, what did you call it?—The Crypt?—residents were brought out?"

"No, as I said, usually Kendricks does the orientation. She'd just discuss the skeletons in general. Come to think of it, I probably goofed. By talking about Mattie, I was unwittingly giving whomever was assigned her, an advantage." Kendricks would never have done that. She'd have to remember that in the future. It was one thing to get your students psyched about what they could get from bones and quite another to hand an advantage to one student over the others. Still there were only twelve students, correction eleven, and more than enough specimens to leave Mattie out.

"Now we are getting somewhere. Would you say it is safe to assume that whomever put those bones there was very familiar with the lab and not just the lab, but the habits of those working in it?"

"Yes, I've thought about that before. They would have to have an understanding of the lab workings. But then I get caught up on the who. I mean there are not that many of us. Kendricks, a couple of the other professors,

Sara, Kyle Jensen, he's over in Environmental Science now, Bruce Willis …"

"The movie star?"

Rhyjl laughed. "No, far from it. Not even a relation, as he would be quick to tell you. The poor guy gets razed about it a lot."

"Yes, I bet. What about Bannerman?"

"That's tough. He knows bones. I'm not going to deny that. He was pre-med. He'd know how to place the bones and he's taken enough Anthro. and Arch. classes to know about the lab, but not the orientation as far as I know."

"But you'd like him to be guilty, right?"

"Of all the people off the top of my head, yeah, I'd like it to be him." And for more than the fact she disliked him. She couldn't quite shake the appearance of the blond girl who was missing and who had come to Bannerman's defense. No one had seen her prior to, or since that lab. No one, but Rhyjl. A blond girl, or rather woman, who had known Rhyjl's excuses were false. A woman, that according to Magena had been cowed even to the point Magena described as abusive, by Bannerman. It was all supposition, but …

The knocking at the door was too regular to be storm driven, three hard knocks followed by a pause and then three more. Alice looked at her watch, raised her brows and unfolded her legs to rise. "I'll get it," she said, smoothing the wrinkles and cat hair from her slacks. "It's probably our food. They must not be busy tonight for it to get here this quickly."

It only took her three strides to reach the door and open it to the blustery night, but it wasn't the delivery they had been expecting.

Chapter 8

Man nor Beast

Vinney's pizza was a mad house. The rest of the town had pretty much shut down knowing that customers were likely to be few with the nor'easter blowing. But Vinney's was pumping out tasty pizza, calzone, and lasagna as fast as their brick ovens could handle. Garlic, onions, oregano and a spicy blend of tomato and something else Erik couldn't identify, captured his senses the minute he stepped through the door. *Note to self: Do not enter this place when extremely hungry.* And he was hungry. After leaving Rhyjl's, he'd gone home and threw his whole attention behind his work. Breakfast had been slightly insignificant, consisting of a cinnamon roll and coffee and had been a good ten hours ago. Looking at the choices, he saw a few that were new … well, at least to him. He'd never seen a clam and scallops pizza before, but it sounded good. The Seafood Special included crab along with the other two. It's Maine. Why not? He ordered up a large and then ordered a Mediterranean with tomatoes, feta, and spinach, and a Hawaiian with pineapple, chicken and ham. To go. Pizza was always good hot or cold, any time of the day. Even as he was thinking it, he was also hoping he'd have some company to enjoy it with. She'd turned him down for lunch, but he wasn't about to give in that easily.

Starting the Tesla, he was about to throw it in gear when smell and temptation became too much. He cracked the top box, inhaling deeply. The rising steam fogged the passenger side windows and carried a mouthwatering aroma. It was the Seafood Special. "Here we go." He said, taking a wedge oozing with mozzarella that left a spider web of broken cheesy strings behind. He knew from the first bite, he'd found a little piece of heaven. His hunger staid for the moment, he put the car in drive and whispered his way out of town.

The heavy clouds and driving rains had created an early dusk making visibility strained. Rounding a corner, he slowed when the brake lights of the vehicle up ahead flashed several times. They pulled to the side of the road and the driver's door opened. The dark clothed individual got out and crossed behind his car. He was hunched against the wind and the hood of his jacket was pulled closely around his head. Between Erik's dimmed lights and the rear lights of the vehicle, the only thing recognizable was the bulk of the man and his worn jeans.

Should he stop and ask if they needed help?

The passenger side opened. Someone half stood and half fell out. Changing drivers, Erik thought until the man ran to the driver's side, and the car spun off the graveled side leaving something behind. Erik skid to a stop and flicked on the brights. Whatever had been left was moving! The shambling bulk was struggling out of the ditch back toward the road on all fours. Erik felt a sick chill run down his spine as he sprung from the car to help.

The poor creature was wet, muddy and scared. Who wouldn't be? He clung to Erik as if his life depended on it. Erik sat on the side of the road and pulled him close. Maybe, his life did depend on it. Who knew what would have happened had Erik not stopped.

"It's okay. I've got you now," Erik hefted the

struggling body up in his arms. He was rewarded by a low whimper and a wet tongue across his chin.

*

Pizza growing cold, and the back of his car a disaster, there were two choices. Run home and clean up the mess or? He liked the alternative. Who could resist a drenched man holding a drenched puppy and three cold pizzas on a stormy night? Good chance that it wouldn't be Rhyjl. If there was one thing he got from her, it was her need to rescue. Friends, other students, and even a girl who was dead. She had a passion for life. Not just hers, but others'.

It was only a short drive to her cottage. He only paused a second when he saw the ME's vehicle parked outside her door. Official business most likely. It was after five, they would be leaving sooner than later and, he reasoned, maybe his appearance would spur the sooner scenario. He took a step back when the woman opened the door. She was stunning! Two weeks ago, she might have stirred his interest. That was before Rhyjl. That sudden epiphany was a little disturbing. Rhyjl was more a defining point in his life than he'd realized. Yes, two weeks ago he would have smiled and engaged the woman with hopes he might find something they had in common. Now she was in the wrong place and the wrong time. It didn't matter that her smile was beguiling or that her eyes sparkled with mirth. It wasn't important that her whole being from her fashionably smart blond hair glowing in the halo of the room behind her, to the well-tailored fit of her classy professional attire spoke to something he didn't even know was there. Right now she was standing in the way of him seeing Rhyjl. She was an obstacle to his plan.

"May I help you?" She said, raising her eyebrows her smile taking in both him and the wriggling bundle in his arms.

"Rhyjl?" he half called, half inquired.

"Erik?" Came the answer from behind the woman blocking his view.

"Yes, can I come in?" He did a two-step dance with the woman before they silently agreed who would go right and left.

Rhyjl rose from the chair. Her solemn face broke out into a smile then laughter as she saw him with the dog. "My god, where did you get that!"

"I just found him on the road. Some SOB threw him out. I thought," he glanced back at the woman closing the storm out, "you might help me with him. Didn't you say you used to work for a veterinarian?"

"Did you see who threw him out?" Ms. Beautiful said, coming over to lay a hand on the puppy's head. Her touch was rewarded with energetic wriggling making it impossible for Erik to contain him. *Note to self: Hit the gym more often.* Sixty some pounds of live animal was exhausting. He let the pup down and grimaced as it launched itself toward the fashion plate.

She deftly sidestepped, firmly said, "Down!" Then she rewarded the expected action with a fur ruffling pat on the head. For some reason Erik felt she would have greeted him in the same fashion.

Rhyjl was on her knees next to the pup before Erik was aware she'd even crossed the room. "Oh poor baby! He's frozen! Let's get you dried off!" She took control and the puppy followed her so closely he was almost tripping the two of them.

"Dr. Alice Merks." she held out her hand then let it drop as he held out his covered in fur and wet.

"Ah, yeah, right." Erik dropped his hand to his pants to clean it, only to find his pants were worse than his hand. "Dr. Erik Arneson."

"The kitchen is there." Alice pointed across the room. "I think you can find some soap."

Erik kicked off his loafers. The doc approved with a slight nod. It took two goes with the anti-bacterial soap before the grime was gone.

"Archaeology?" Dr. Merks asked.

In the bathroom behind the closed door echoed the joyous barking and laughter of hidden occupants.

"No, Engineering." Erik glanced at the bathroom door and smiled, then returned to address the woman. "I take it, that you are the State Medical Examiner?"

"One of them." She laughed, holding out her hand for the second time.

Erik grasped it firmly and was surprised at the strength of the grip that met his. *Note to self: Hit the gym at least three times a week.*

"Hey, I always pay my dues. I've got pizza out in the car. I thought I might just leave it here while I go get … He looked down at his clothes and then the bathroom door.

"Sure. I'll let Rhyjl know you will be right back. She should have … does he have a name?"

"No, as I said," Erik headed for the door, "some jerk threw him out. It wasn't like he was going to hang around and give me details." He slipped his shoes on.

"Right! Did you get a license plate?"

"Spoken like a cop." Erik said. "Nope, too dark, too rainy, too quick."

"I suppose you don't know the make?" Walking to the door and resting her hand on the knob, she waited.

"Again, hard to tell. Just some kind of four door sedan. Or maybe only two door. I guess as a witness, I'd fail the test."

Alice stood at the door. Was she getting his make model and license plate down to memory? Why the switch to feeling resentful toward her. Well, that was a no brainer. SHE didn't look like she was planning on leaving. In fact, he looked back toward the cottage door. She all, but looked like she was planning on moving in. So much for a quiet evening with Rhyjl.

Erik returned with the three green, red and white pizza boxes stamped with Vinney's logo on the top and sides. "Back in a few." He bent his head into the driving rain and headed for the Tesla.

*

"He's adorable!" Rhyjl said, exiting the bath with the entire front of her sweatshirt soaked.

"Who? The man or the beast?" Alice asked, closing the door.

Rhyjl could actually feel the warmth of a blush starting at her neckline as she looked around the room expecting to see the man.

"He's gone. Needed to clean up. He left these." Alice pushed the pizzas in Rhyjl's direction. "Said he would be right back."

"Oh! Rhyjl stopped to take in the three large boxes. "Why did he leave them here?"

"Don't ask me," Alice carried the boxes to the kitchen and turned the dial on the oven to low. "Should I leave? Did you have plans for this evening?"

"No, not really."

"No?" Alice slipped two pizzas onto the oven racks. "You don't sound too certain."

"No!" Rhyjl said more firmly, as she headed to change her wet clothing. The puppy trailing after her, paused as if he thought it a command for him. "I mean he did ask me to lunch at Vinney's today, but then we kind of had a quarrel."

"Oh, do tell," Alice said. "I love a good lover's quarrel tale?"

"Stop! It wasn't like that at all." This time the puppy sat confused at her feet tilting his head one way, then the other. "We are friends. Well, maybe just friends."

"Just? What does that mean?"

"I only met him less than a week ago." Rhyjl disappeared into her room.

The puppy sat looking at her, doing his head tilt thing. She wasn't sure what to think about Erik, the dog or the pizza. She tossed the wet sweat top on the floor next to the one she'd discarded only a few hours ago. Her jeans joined them a moment later. Looking at the small pile with dismay, she groaned. This wasn't her style. What was wrong with her? How could she let this all get the best of her? "Pull yourself together!"

The puppy flopped on the floor with his head resting on his two massive front paws, his back legs stretched full out behind him. She rubbed her toe against the soft, still damp fur of his front paw. "Why would someone throw you out? You are as sweet as they come." He raised his head, then licked her foot before laying it back down. His eyes remaining half open, watched as she pulled another pair of jeans and a shirt from the dresser.

She tossed the jeans on the bed while she slipped the tee over her head.

How had it gotten so crazy? She was a quiet person. An introvert actually. This gathering of friends—if that's what they were—was not her doing. Of the three newcomers, the only one she didn't feel wanted, or was demanding something of her, was at her feet snoring.

*

Upon returning, Erik was not overly thrilled to see Dr. Merks' car still parked out in front of Rhyjl's place. He wasn't going to let it deter his plans.

He'd liked the way Rhyjl had taken control of the puppy. It was just as he had predicted. He counted the pup as a blessing thrown out from Heaven. Just today, after his first class, he was thinking about getting a dog again. His house needed to be a home. He wanted it to be a home. He wanted companionship. He'd wrapped himself in solitude too long.

Something came to life for him when he'd run into Rhyjl that first day. He hadn't realized until that moment how he had locked a part of him away after his mother's death. Oh, he'd known he'd changed. He'd blamed it on his father. He'd blamed himself. If things had been different, she wouldn't have died. If his father had let him go with her that summer. If he'd defied his father and gone to the airport instead of standing there watching her drive away. He thought something in him had died that day. He knew it had when the report of the kidnaping and brutal killing of his mother and her team came back. He'd buried himself in his passion. He'd allowed research to fill the endless hollow hours, days, years. He'd chosen to defy his father at every turn.

He had everything. Poor little rich boy. It meant nothing! The ache had woken and he knew how he wanted it filled. He wanted a home filled with love.

Alice Merks opened the door when he knocked. A mouth-watering hit of Italian assaulted his senses the moment he entered. There was something else as well. Tangy. It spoke of hot summers, the beach. Was that really Bar-B-Q?

"Well that was quick. I envy a man's ability to go from disaster to proper in a short time." She smiled.

"Yes, we are lucky in that respect." Striding toward the kitchen, he glanced around the crowded room. The bathroom door stood open. "Where's the puppy?" The sack he was carrying gave a soft clank as he set it down on the table.

"He and Rhyjl haven't come out of her room, yet." Alice replied, taking over the position of host. She pulled two bottles of wine from Erik's bag, smiling when she saw the name of the wineries. "Is there anyone else we should invite to this party? We've enough food and drink to satisfy a crowd."

"Leftovers?" Erik pulled a wine glass from the cabinet.

"My thoughts as well."

Rhyjl emerged from the room looking freshly groomed. Her hair was combed and flowing over her shoulders. Her face looked freshly scrubbed. But her eyes were rimmed with a red hue and dark circles were forming under them. Had she been crying?

"Smells good. Pizza and ribs!" Her voice was bright. Too bright. She saw the unspoken concern in the two people facing her.

"Wine?" Erik was reaching for a second glass.

"She doesn't drink." offered Alice.

It was too much! These people didn't know her. "I do drink, actually. When it suits me." Rhyjl added, seeing Alice's arched brows and thin smile.

Erik's hand was paused mid-way between the cupboard and table.

"And I think I would like a glass."

"Red or white?" Erik took down a glass

"Do we have a white Zinfandel?"

"Interesting that you are here tonight Dr. Merks." Erik poured the pink wine half way up the glass then held it out for Rhyjl to take. "Do you usually give your cases this kind of personal touch?"

"No, not usually. I was actually hoping Rhyjl could help me. Being an expert."

"Yes," Rhyjl added. "We were discussing our theories."

Alice putting the food on the table paused for a moment. Rhyjl caught the warning look and sensed the stiffening.

Erik hadn't missed it either. "Interesting. I have a few theories along that line. I had thought of throwing them out to Rhyjl tonight to get her take."

"Oh?" The plates clattered a little louder than expected as Alice set them down. "I didn't know Engineers were experts in death."

"Maybe not death, but we have been known for our deductive reasoning." Erik winked.

Pandemonium crashed, howled, hissed and barked from Rhyjl's room. She reached the door before Erik and Alice had even set their glasses down.

Stormy was stationed on the top of her dresser in

full alert mode: back arched, nails extended and every hair on her normally sleek body standing at attention. The feline needn't have worried. The pup's attention had long since been adverted and was now deftly fixed on the spilled contents of Rhyjl's small heart shaped jewelry box. To her relief, he was only checking it out with his sensitive nose and not those needle point puppy teeth.

"Everything okay?" Erik and Alice chorused.

"Yes, but I think I've had quite enough of these cat and dog scenes." She didn't elaborate when puzzled silence ensued. Erik came to claim the puppy while Alice returned to the food. It was more than she wanted or needed. Alice was right about one thing. She needed to claim her throne.

Returning to the living area and leaving the door to her room blocked so the puppy couldn't enter, she asked for their attention. "Look, I'm really too tired to listen to the two of you hiss at each other. I'm not even sure why and …" She held up her hand to block a protest forming on Alice's lips. "I don't think I want to know. Can we just eat and enjoy the evening? If not, I'm going to ask you to leave and take your wine and food with you."

"I can leave. I was uninvited." Erik reached for the coat he'd hung over the kitchen chair.

"Well, actually, so was I." Alice admitted. "I do apologize. I really did want us to become better acquainted and I do need your help, despite Tanner. Perhaps, tomorrow?"

"Or the two of you could sit down, enjoy the food and we could move forward?"

It wasn't long. The antics of the puppy playing with a rolled up piece of paper like a kitten, the incredibly rewarding banquet, and a few more glasses of wine and the earlier hostilities seemed to fade completely.

"So what I haven't been able to figure out is this Bannerman guy. How did he catch on so quickly to the mistake? You can't tell me he was the only one in there with prior knowledge of skeletons." Erik leaning back in the chair, cupped his hands around his right knee as he crossed his legs.

Again, Alice shifted uncomfortably. Rhyjl understanding her reserve spoke quickly. "Erik and I spent some time together directly after I found the bones. He'd also heard Bannerman shooting off his mouth in the Student Union Building.

"Ah," Alice relaxed. "So, Sherlock, what do you think was the reason?"

"I really can't say. I've had more than a few thoughts along that avenue, however. Let's say our Mr. Bannerman is really good at reading people's faces and body language. Rhyjl isn't exactly deadpan. Could you have tipped him off, causing him to look closer or guess there was a mistake. What do you think, Rhyjl?"

She knew what she believed. That Bannerman was the perpetrator. How she could explain that, she wasn't sure. It was best to let the others lead. "Well, it's possible. My grandmother always said I shouldn't play poker. I was shocked. He might have clued in." Or he might have known because he put the bones there. She took another sip of the wine and was grateful for the chill it held at bay.

"For what reason? Just to show off? He appeared to me to be that kind." Alice tossed out.

"To embarrass Rhyjl? My other thought," he ticked one finger off with an opposing one. "Was that I got the impression he doesn't like you, Rhyjl. Could he have planted the bones knowing what would happen?"

Rhyjl flinched. Erik was close, but not for the right reasons.

Alice gnawed her lower lip. "No, I don't think that's it. For a couple reasons." She halfway mimicked Erik by ticking off fingers with her thumb. "No matter how much you dislike someone, this is a little elaborate for a hoax. Also, no one knew Rhyjl was going to be teaching until the last moment. Right?"

"Actually, I didn't even know. The class was late starting because I didn't run into Sara until it should have already begun."

"Right! Third, he could have clued in, and he could have wanted to show off. Or fourth he was part of the deception and does know who is buried, well, laid amid the other bones."

Erik's frown deepened, his brows forming ravens wings above his nose. "No, I'm not buying it. Something just doesn't feel right. I think Bannerman is just a herring among the cod. He's a blowhard. I don't think he could plan something this cold."

"Or maybe, that's what he wants people to think." Did any of them really know the guy other than what she did from Mags? Her grandmother had always said that a man who beats on a woman either verbally, physically, or both, was usually a cowardly boasting type trying to prove something. Bannerman fit that bill. "What if he did something by accident and needed to cover it up? Then when it was discovered, he could play all detached from it while looking like he's clever. Magena said he'd been abusive to his girlfriend." And now she has disappeared.

"Really?" Alice tapped her wine class. "Now that brings up some possibilities. Do we know the girlfriend? Could we maybe prime her for some ideas on how violent he might be?"

"She's missing." Rhyjl spoke barely above a whisper.

Erik choked on his wine. Alice almost dropped her glass.

"Her name is Melinda LeFevre"

"LeFevre? LeFevre? How do I know that name? Alice had resumed tapping her glass.

"Perhaps because she was on the roster of students supposed to be in that class and she didn't show?" Except to me. I saw her, but I'm not going to tell you that. Rhyjl got up from the couch and walked to the table to pour her second glass of wine. She hesitated. She was a lightweight when it came to alcohol, but she wasn't sure she wanted to continue the conversation without it. She filled the glass.

"That's it!" Erik joined Rhyjl at the table and didn't hesitate in the least before filling his glass again. "Bannerman kills the girlfriend, panics and doesn't know what to do with the body so he hides it in the lab. Who would know?"

"All speculation. You two really hate the guy don't you?"

"Is it obvious?" Erik laughed.

"I have a profound dislike for people who abuse others." Rhyjl admitted. "No, I can see some flaws. It's a knee jerk reaction. I don't like the guy. He is abusive. His girl, Melinda, disappears. No one knows where she is. What's missing is why the bone lab? I can't really think of a good reason. And my prejudice might be showing again, but I don't think he is that creatively inclined."

"I would tend to agree with you. It's interesting that you chose the word creatively. Whomever our murderer is, placing bones scattered among bones in a lab was inventive. I didn't read Bannerman as especially creative either."

"Ah, Erik, your puppy is circling. You may want to take him out". Rhyjl pointed to the pup who was indeed going round and round before the door.

"Huh! His mind still stuck on the idea of creativity, it took him a moment to realize Rhyjl was pointing toward the door for a reason "Oh! Wait boy!" He jumped up. "Don't continue until I get back."

"He's really gone on you." Alice stated, as she perused the pizza and Bar-B-Q remnants, deciding that her taste buds would win the battle over possible weight gain.

"Erik? We've only just met!"

"Well, I don't think that is an issue for him. Haven't you noticed the way he looks at you? The way he, for lack of a better word, analyzes your every move, thought? Guys only do that when they are gone, gone, gone! I'd say he would like to eat you up the way I'm going to tackle this Ocean Special." She took a bite, rolling her eyes heavenward. "Mmmmm whomever thought of this combination has become my new hero!"

She had noticed, well sort of. Probably because she didn't really want to notice. He was intense at times. Too intense as if, like Alice said, he could devour her given any encouragement. In one way, she had been flattered. In another, disturbed.

Hearing his voice drawing near, she dashed to the bathroom and met him just inside the door with one of the towels she'd used to clean the puppy before. Even that simple act elicited a look of admiration that was much deeper than necessary.

"Did I miss anything?"

"Oh we were just talking about you." Alice smiled.

Rhyjl threw her a warning glance. "About what you are going to do with the dog. You do realize he is going to be really big?"

"Yep!" Erik leaned down and ruffled the puppy's head. "I think he is a Saint Bernard or at least a cross. Do Saints have short hair?"

"Yes" Alice replied, after swallowing another bite of her pizza. "I used to have one."

Both Erik and Rhyjl looked at her, round eyed and disbelieving. "YOU!"

"What? I'm not allowed to have pets?"

"It's not that," passing Alice on the way to the bathroom with the sodden towel held before her. "I just … well, you don't look like the kind of person who would be into …"

"Dirt, shedding, slobber? Oh, he will slobber, Erik. Wait until he shakes his head and a big slimy wad flies up sticking to the ceiling."

"Can hardly wait." Erik watched as the puppy followed behind Rhyjl, tail wagging and barely missing one of the wine glasses on the end table.

"Back to Bannerman." Alice curled up on one corner of the sofa. "I think we have more or less dismissed him. Would you all agree?"

"Not until Melinda is found." Rhyjl settled into the opposite corner, her new furry shadow struggling to get up between the two women's feet.

"Okay, fair enough. I'll mention it to Tanner and he can look into it if he hasn't already."

"I don't know the lab or the faculty, being new around here, but they all have access to the lab. Could it have been one of them?" Erik looked to Rhyjl.

The thought had crossed her mind. There were

several things that hadn't quite added up. Kendrick's absence to begin with. Marc's reluctance to talk about it. "Maybe."

"Anyone in the Department would have opportunity." Alice agreed. "But motive?"

"Well," Erik came back from washing his hands in the kitchen and took up his post in the old chair opposite them. "A thought has been niggling at the back of my mind ever since Rhyjl talked about most people in the incoming class wouldn't have noticed the discrepancy except for Professor Kendricks. Add to that, her admission that Kendricks wouldn't have given it much thought until she started grading. But what if she didn't mark the students down for mistakes because she knew they were correct. She would know the observations were good considering she knows the imposters. She knows them because she put them there."

"Why, as some kind of test?" Rhyjl held up her hands and shook her head. "I mean Kendricks has accused students in the past of taking information from papers written by former students. But to salt the specimens just to catch people? She's a bitch, but I can't believe she would stoop that low."

"You said whomever put those bones there knew what they were doing, Rhyjl." Alice reached for her wine glass, frowning to see it empty.

Erik made a grab for the glass and walked over to the table for a refill. "Following that train of thought, could it be that we don't have a murder victim at all? Wouldn't Kendricks have access to bones from other sources? She could have indeed doctored them and then salted them as Rhyjl said."

"NO!" Rhyjl flew off the sofa and began pacing.

The puppy whimpered then slid off to keep pace with her. "That woman was murdered. She was murdered recently! She died violently! If it was Kendricks, then she is a murderer."

"OKAY! So the woman could be a killer or she isn't. Why are you so upset, Rhyjl? Are you that close to her?"

"Me?" spat Rhyjl, glaring at Alice. "Not on your life. It's just … Oh, I don't know what it is!" She threw up her hands. She did know, but she couldn't tell them. She'd seen the dead woman, felt her emotions. Lived her death more violently than any she'd ever experienced before, because it was fresh. The energy from it was still raw.

Erik sidestepped Rhyjl, handed the wine to Alice and resumed his seat. "So let me see if I've got this correct. You don't think she would salt the bones. You don't think she could have just found another skeleton. You are saying that she might be capable of committing murder. Would it also be safe to say that if she did want to hide a murdered victim, her bone lab might have been a good place?"

"Yes, to all the above!" Rhyjl's back was turned to them. She couldn't face them. Why had she let her frustration almost betray her? Gazing out into the black stormy night through the living room window, she wrapped her arms around herself to ward off the cold threatening to seep in again.

Alice's voice softened. "Is there any motive you can think of that she might have?"

Turning back and almost tripping over the puppy, she said. "I don't know, Alice. I don't know the woman all that well. I know she's made a lot of enemies here at the school. I know she has ruffled some of her colleagues, if gossip is to be trusted. But why SHE would want to kill someone? No, I can't think of anything off hand." She plunked onto the sofa cushion and only demonstrated minor resistance when the dog pulled itself up on the cushion as well.

Lights flashed through the windows and the sound of a car pulling up outside silenced the conversation. The door burst open and a laughing Sara being mauled by a guy Rhyjl had never seen before blew into the room.

"Oh, what do we have here?" Sara glanced around the room. "A party and you didn't even think to invite your own Roomie?"

Sara's escort pulled himself up tall and straight, but he was unsteady. He'd had more than his share of alcohol.

"Ooooh look, Troy, there's pizza and ribs! I love ribs!"

Rhyjl was about to protest that the food wasn't hers.

Troy spoke first. "Not now, babe. We can get something later. I thought you just wanted to grab a few things. Everyone is waiting."

"Spoil sport," Sara's lips pouted. "Okay, fine. I'll get some things and we'll go."

"Rhyjl! What the …!" Sara's voice exploded from her room.

"I folded your clothes," Rhyjl got up, indicating with bobbing hand for everyone else to remain seated. "Is there a problem?"

"They're all over the floor!" Sara was at the door, feet braced apart, hands on hips and with her red hair, looking like an avenging Celtic war maiden.

"Oh, that damn cat!" Rhyjl shrugged in apology. "I guess I didn't get the door shut soon enough. You know how Stormy loves your room. Sorry."

"Hummmp!" Sara spun, dipped down to pull some jeans and a blouse from the tumbled pile.

"If it's any consolation, she knocked down my jewelry box tonight."

"Rhyjl, that's a ridiculous thing to say!" Sara pushed past her and grabbing poor inebriated Troy's arm, headed for the door. "Why would I care about your jewelry box? Night all!"

The door slammed. Lights flashed. The roar or a motor competed with the hammering rain. Then only the sound of rain on the roof remained.

Erik was the first to break the silence. "Ah, what was that?"

"That was my roommate declaring war." Rhyjl looked pointedly at Alice. No other words were needed.

"You handled it well." Alice batted her eyelashes. "Have you ever thought of murder?"

Rhyjl started giggling. "More than once, but people like Tanner and jail time are a great deterrent."

Kendricks was bantered about for a while longer. She had the means, certainly the knowledge. Under her supervision the bones might have gone unnoticed indefinitely. She hadn't expected Rhyjl to be opening her class. And where was the woman? Why hadn't she returned from wherever she'd been? Was she eluding the law? Okay, so the last was out of the time sync. Kendricks wouldn't need to avoid the law if the bones hadn't been discovered. So that didn't explain her absence in the beginning.

There was enough to make her a viable suspect, the three agreed, but one thing eluded them. Motive.

"Or," Erik got up to stretch. He thought about pouring himself more wine, but quickly dismissed it when he saw all three bottles were empty. "Is she the victim?"

Both women shook their heads. "Too old. Our victim is between twenty and forty." Rhyjl sighed.

"Well, from all I've heard tonight, it seemed plausible, even probable. There's certainly no love lost for her. I'll ask around tomorrow after my classes. People love telling the new guy all about past indiscretions or current ones of other faculty members."

"This isn't a game, Erik." Alice stood and placed a hand on his arm. "You should really leave this to the experts. Someone has killed once, they could do so again."

"Ah, but the game is afoot, as Sherlock would say. Inquiring minds and all that. And how is it any different than what the three of us sat around and did tonight?"

"Look, I'm a medical examiner. It's my job. Let me throw some of the things we discussed tonight out to Tanner. Let him do his job. My suggestion," she looked from one to the other, "is that you two go on about your business as best you can. If you hear anything, let Tanner or me know. But don't go looking. Please!"

When their foray into detecting had run its course, coupled with Alice's sobering admonition, it was agreed they should call it a night. Alice and Erik packed up the goodies declining Rhyjl's help. Rhyjl sat absently stroking the sleeping form at her feet, her brain feeling like she'd just pulled an all-nighter. Something had happened tonight. She couldn't put her finger on it, but something was definitely different. Perhaps it was the wine. She wasn't used to drinking. She'd had, what? Two? Three? Four glasses? One of those had only been half full, but still, she'd always considered herself the kind that could get high from the fumes off the cork.

Alice's hand rested on her shoulder. "Are you

alright? You look kind of lost."

"Just tired." Rhyjl smiled up at her. "Thanks for all the good food and good company. I'm sorry we didn't get the things worked out the way you intended to."

"Well, your friend made some of that impossible. You know Tanner warned me about discussing or having you help me with specifics. He'd have had my hide for allowing someone else into the circle. In spite of that, we did accomplish quite a bit. And well within the realm of nothing more official than a good gossip group on a stormy night. Grudgingly, I have to admit, Erik was even insightful. I've got a lot to ponder and more than a few thoughts to plant in Tanner's ear."

"It's late, you could spend the night. I'd take the couch. My sheets were just changed yesterday." Rhyjl blurted out without knowing why.

"Thanks, but I've got a cat who gets a little miffed when I don't come home. She's liable to take it out on my Ficus or Areca Palm. I'm not sure how much more shredding they can survive. Are you sure you're okay?"

"Yeah, I guess it's like telling ghost stories. You just don't want to be alone afterward." That was closer to the truth than she wanted to admit. Between the storm and their conversation, she wouldn't be at all surprised to get a visit from her unwelcome specter.

"Well," Alice winked, "there are other options I'm sure wouldn't turn down your offer."

"You may be right, but I'm not going there. Besides, he's not my type." Tall, dark, handsome, intelligent, thoughtful and employed. In this world, what wasn't there to like?

"Whatever, you say." Alice patted her shoulder and went to collect her things.

Rhyjl, returning to her own thoughts, looked at the warm mass of fur at her feet and smiled. "You'd stay with me wouldn't you?"

The pup responded by snuggling in closer.

"That's what I thought." She stroked his soft head.

Some thought played around the periphery of her consciousness. Something had been said. Something important, but she couldn't quite recall it, nor the person who had said it. It had to do with being clever. Why would someone hide bones in a lab? Why go to all that work? It had to have been extremely time consuming; cleaning and then staining the bones. Then numbering them so they wouldn't be blatantly noticeable. There had to be a motive in that act alone.

*

Erik returned from helping Alice to her car, to grab his garb and dog. On the warm blanket draped sofa, Rhyjl appeared lost in contemplation while looking at the pup curled up at her feet. "What are you thinking about?"

"Umm …" she looked up, her eyes still far off. "I was just thinking about how things don't always appear what they seem."

That brought a little twinge of guilt deep in his belly remembering thoughts run rampant after seeing her get into the detective's car earlier that afternoon. "Anything specific? We've talked about a lot of theories tonight."

"Yes, no, I don't know. Something just doesn't seem to fit and I'm wondering if we aren't looking in the wrong box?"

"Wrong box?" He asked, perching himself on the

edge of the chair across from her.

"Huh? Oh, yeah, just what my grandmum says when you keep looking within certain parameters for an answer that is probably lying outside of them."

"I think I like your grandmother. So what do you think is outside the box we haven't been over?"

"I don't know." Her long sigh was weighted with frustration and fatigue. "I just have this strong sense that something isn't right. We are missing something. I can feel it, here." She pointed to her chest. "It's like a big lump sitting there. You know like when you have to burp and can't get it up."

"You mean women burp?" Erik tried for a bit of levity to ease the tension. It fell flat.

"Of course they do!" Screwing her face up as if seeing some particularly obnoxious bug.

"I only meant …"

"Yeah, yeah, I know. Sorry! Brain in analytical mode." She went to get up and stirred the sleeping puppy awake. "Look, I'm exhausted. I'd like to call it a day if you don't mind?"

The lights went off as if on cue.

"Was wondering when that was going to happen." Erik said, producing one of the small flash lights he had purchased the day before. "Do you have back up power or something I could help you get started?"

"Nope." She made her way in the pale blue glow of the LED flashlight to the kitchen. "I've got plenty of candles, the fridge doesn't have anything that will spoil and, I don't need lights to sleep."

"I could leave you this flash light." *Or you could come home and stay with me.* "I've got a generator at home."

"Nice, but as I said, I just want to catch some sleep. If it's still out tomorrow, I'll be over at the Department anyway. All the buildings have backup. You can't live in this part of the county and not have backup." She lit several candles and shepherded him and puppy toward the door.

He fought back disappointment, and a tad bit of jealousy, when she lavished a big hug and kiss on the puppy. He'd just have to be content with the smile she shared for him.

"Let me know what you name him. Remember, he's going to be a big boy." She didn't wait for his reply. She shut the door leaving both sad-faced males standing in the rain.

*

Within minutes of arriving at home, Erik had the generator working and was sitting at his desk with a full glass of Soléna Pinot Noir. "You are complicating my life here, boy." He said rubbing the puppy's head, his eyes scanning the computer screen. There doesn't appear to be a decent pet store within thirty miles. I suppose I could run to Bucksport tomorrow. Perhaps my best bet, however, is Amazon.

An hour later, a second glass of wine, and a three hundred dollar hit to his debit card, Erik went outside again to stand on the porch encouraging the puppy to do his business. The only problem was, the puppy didn't want to leave the protective sheltering of the porch. Erik quickly grabbed his coat and took a little stroll. Fortunately, the little beast didn't appear to like dawdling in the storm any more than his human companion. It wasn't long before they were both back in toweling off.

Sleep would not come. A myriad of neurotransmitters stimulated by the sleuthing session were crashing between his neurons. Add to that, a dog who didn't give jack what Erik wanted, but had his own puppy agenda.

"Jack?" Erik said, and watched as the pup lifted his big head from his paws. "You like that name, Jack?" Slap. slap. slap. The tail smacked the floor. "Then Jack it is."

The remainder of the night, it was Jack who was not content to sleep on the floor. Jack, who whined until Erik capitulated to let him into the bed. Jack, who preferred not only to be with his new person, but needed to sleep on him half the night. Perhaps, Erik thought, as he moved the pup off to the side for the umpteenth time, he should have paid the extra cost to get one day shipping on the dog crate. By seven, when the obnoxious buzz of the alarm went off, his hangover was far worse than a few glasses of wine might account for.

"Note to self: Find a different alarm tone for phone." Erik tapped the phone's screen, rolled out of bed and was reaching for his pants as Jack, tumbling out after him, headed for the door. They made it outside just in time.

Chapter 9

Comes the Dawn

The hot shower felt good. She wasn't sure what time the power had come back and it didn't really matter. She had hot water for both a bath and tea, she'd slept the best she had in days and the sun was cascading through the windows. Storm, still resentful of the intrusion the night before of a D. O. G. into her territory, had complained loudly at the back door as soon as the first rays hit the floor and was probably out looking for drowned mice or rats. Sara hadn't returned, as she'd hoped would be the case and her ghost had been absent as well. It was turning out to be a splendid day.

Her first class with Marc wasn't until eleven. She had plenty of time to throw a load of clothes in the wash and spend some time on the computer looking up a paper on *Isotope analyses of Merovingian and Viking age human remains* from the *American Journal of Physical Anthropology*.

Right now, however, she just wanted to feel the warmth spreading over her body and breathe deeply a calm she desperately needed. She didn't hear the door of the cottage nor the door to the bathroom open.

"So what was your little party all about last night?" Sara's voice was as cold as the air she was letting in.

Rhyjl squeaked and jumped. "Crap, Sara, you scared the hell out of me! Glad you're home, but couldn't you have waited until I was out of the shower?"

"I suppose. I don't have much time though, and I have to share it felt more than a little awkward to walk in to my place last night and find a party going on without my knowledge."

Rhyjl felt a wave of heat rising and it had nothing to do with hot water. Turning the shower off, she reached past the curtain for the towel hanging nearby. When she'd wrapped it around herself, she yanked the curtain back and glared.

"Don't you mean OUR place, Sara? And since when do I need your permission to have company over. You never ask mine before dragging in whatever guy you're sleeping with."

"Well! Too much partying last night has made someone very grumpy wumpy. We can discuss this when you are in a better mood."

Sara exited and went to the kitchen to rummage around.

Rhyjl followed leaving a wet trail of footprints.

"No left overs?" Sara slammed the fridge door. "Nice friends!"

"What's this really about, Sara?" Rhyjl went over to her tea cup and drank the dregs.

"Who were those people?" The cupboard thwacked shut setting the dishes rattling.

"What does it matter? What were you and Tony …"

"Troy!" Sara turned, stomping her foot.

"Okay, Troy! Were you planning on staying here? It didn't sound like it from what he said."

"No, but there is enough gossip going around this campus without everyone knowing that the Medical Examiner's car was parked outside here half the night.

God, Rhyjl, this is giving me the creeps!"

"I doubt it! But that's beside the point. It doesn't reflect on you. You weren't here and have nothing to do with any of it. I don't care what people think about me."

"Nothing!" Sara grabbed a knife, slicing it down on the table hard and leaving a deep V groove. "It has a lot to do with me. It was my lab, my class! This is my home! You are my roommate, and I thought good friend. Now you are taking it all over like I have nothing to say about it. Don't deny it! You, yourself, said it had nothing to do with me. What? You want to be Super Sleuth now! Think you have all the answers?"

Rhyjl dropped into the chair, her head shaking. "Do you know what you sound like, Sara?"

"No, why don't you tell me. You have all the answers." Pulling bread from the second cupboard, she ripped open the plastic sack pulling two slices out for the toaster and sending a third flying under the table.

"Look, Sara, I don't have the answers. People think I do, but I don't. We didn't have a party last night."

"Oh yeah, from the amount of food and wine bottles it sure appeared like it." She was now battering through the silverware drawer. "Don't we have any clean knives?"

"Power was out. I haven't had a chance to wash the dishes yet."

"So why were they here?"

"We were going over theories of who, what and why this happened. Theories, nothing more."

"And did you have any theories?"

"This is getting us nowhere, Sara." Rhyjl surrendered her pounding head into her hand. "Could we just drop this? I'd like to get dressed."

"What theories, Rhyjl? Don't you think I at least deserve to have some idea of what's going on?" The toast popped up and was ignored.

"I think we might have come up with some good ideas. I'm not thrilled with some of them, but I don't want to say anything until there is more proof. As you said, there are enough rumors going around." Rhyjl walked toward her room. "I'm getting dressed. But maybe you could answer one question for me?"

Sara, feet planted, arms akimbo, stood glaring at her.

"What do you think would be accomplished by someone hiding a dead person in the lab?"

"I don't know, Rhyjl. You tell me when you figure it out."

When Rhyjl returned dressed and groomed, Sara was gone. The toast remained neglected in the toaster. Rhyjl sighed, dropped the toast back into the appliance knowing it would come out blackened, but not caring. At least it would be warm. With enough butter and some honey, she could manage it.

*

"Hey Rhyjl," A young fellow with the physique of a bull was charging out the side door of the Anthropology building as if fleeing a fire. "I'd think twice about going in right now. Kendricks is back and she's one unhappy camper."

Catching the door before it closed, she stood at the landing leading up the stairs. Even from this distance it was hard not avoid the clash of angry voices. She couldn't hear the words, but it didn't take a psychic to know what it was about. She considered what Marc suggested and thought twice. Or three times, but who was counting. She couldn't avoid the office forever. The way Kendricks held grudges, it might not be until the next century before this was resolved to her satisfaction.

Well, she thought, dismissing the stairs for the straight shot down to the office, I'm thankful I had a good night's sleep. This day is going downhill fast. She navigated the hall leading to the office slowly and nodded to several other students exiting from the direction of the squall. With each step, she wondered how she would handle the barrage of anger coming for her. Flee like a coward or stand and fight? Or, would she just stand and take the tongue lashing while doing her best not to flinch? She wanted to believe she'd hold firm giving as good as she got. It was probably more realistic that she'd take the beating and go home to lick her wounds after.

At the top of the landing, the voices were clear. Rhyjl knew it was only because the two combatants were longtime friends and associates that Amanda Kendricks was able to get away with screeching at the Department head. The halls and office had the look of a ghost town. Her foot falls sounded hollow as she proceeded. Not a person was in sight except Magena who was standing at the copy machine and turned to place her finger to her mouth as Rhyjl entered.

"The fact remains, Marc, that bitch shouldn't have been anywhere near my lab and she had no business taking over my class."

"And for the eleventh time, Amanda, I'm telling you, she was doing you a favor!"

"Favor! Like hell! My class is shut down. My lab specimens have been confiscated and are at this moment in the hands of some inept Medical Examiner. All on the say so of that incompetent T A of yours. Tell me again what kind of favor that is?" The last was punctuated by a crash and a plethora of invectives describing Rhyjl.

"There was a crime, Amanda. If Rhyjl hadn't discovered it, someone else would have, such as you."

"What evidence do we have there was a crime except her word? I'm telling you, Marc, that bimbo made a mistake! I wouldn't have found a problem and neither would anyone else. BECAUSE there isn't one!"

"I have confidence in her abilities, Amanda. I still …"

"Confidence! The same kind of confidence you had in Jenny! The sickening, sweet Jenny, who just happened to screw us over at the National Archaeology Symposium!"

"Shut up, Amanda! Before you make even more of a fool of yourself!"

"I'm not the fool, Marc! I was never the fool!" A door slammed. Glass shattered. Mags flashed around the corner of the counter effectively barricading the hall and any view of the open office while simultaneously shooing Rhyjl back out into the hall and out of sight.

"Mags! Send out a notice that class will be held in room 223. I'll be taking over Marc's lab until mine is released."

SLAM! Crash!

Mags sucked her lips between her teeth. It was a look that was rare. It meant that more than one person in the room had reached her limit. Hands on her hips, Mags turned to look down the hall and survey the damage. Peaking around the door frame, Rhyjl waited until Mags abandoned her defensive stance and took up her command post, fingers dancing on the phone pad.

Creeping in on kitten's paws, Rhyjl approached the desk.

Mags held up her index finger. "Maintenance, we have broken glass from a shattered door. Could you send someone up immediately? Thanks." She returned the hand piece to its cradle.

The sound of Amanda Kendricks' voice was still razor sharp emanating from her office. Magena looked up and again cautioned for quiet. "I'll make bets," she whispered, "the Dean is getting an ear full."

"Is she really taking over Marc's lab?" Rhyjl whispered back. If she was, Rhyjl would be shut out from her research and from Marc's class. She couldn't imagine Kendricks allowing her access even when Marc was in residence. Without access to the class …

"I don't think it will go there. She thinks she's a queen, but Marc still calls the shots. Just stay out of her way today. I would if I could."

"Maybe you could put some kind of curse on her." Rhyjl wished her sentiment was only a jest.

"Rhyjl, honey, someone already did that the day she was born. Now scoot before the Dean cuts her off and she storms out looking for her next victim."

"But my class. Marc?"

"I'll explain. Not that it will be necessary. He can give you a call or drop an e-mail off later."

Rhyjl knew Mags was correct. Perhaps, if Kendricks wasn't so well known for her explosive tantrums, people might take her more seriously. As it was, it worked against her. No one really listened, and if they did, they often didn't take her side of the argument. This storm would blow over, just like the one last night had. She just needed to wait it out. But just as with last night's storm, when the debris was removed, irreparable damage would still remain.

When she exited the building, she paused, shutting her eyes and turning her face to the sun. The light bathed her and played upon her eyelids creating a warm red glow. She took several deep breaths. To say the episode upstairs hadn't turned her body into a bundle of knots would be a lie. She needed to quiet her mind from the litany of disastrous directions this could take. Magena's reassurances were nice, but not solid. Dr. Amanda Kendricks, in spite of her volcanic reputation, was still highly respected in many circles. Up till now, Rhyjl hadn't done much more than ruffle the woman's feathers. This incident went miles beyond that. Dwelling on it and playing each and every scenario over and over again, would accomplish nothing.

Perhaps it was finally time for that good novel. Something she could lose herself in. Something as distant from her circumstances as possible.

After the madness on Monday, the bookstore was strangely empty. Only three people were milling around and she was one of them. The other two appeared to be student workers mainly trying to reorganize what was left of the once towering stacks of texts. Wending her way through the maze of shelving, she made for a small back section known as light reading. Personally, since starting college, she never seemed to have much time for fictional reading. There was even less time once the academic year started. It was probably true for other serious students as well. The human mind and eyes can only endure so much and after reading volumes of tombs just to meet class requirements. Picking up something even considered light was punishing. At the moment, however, she appeared to have more time than she'd like.

The shelves were neatly arranged by alphabetical order of the author's name rather than topic. Several best sellers were featured prominently. John Grisham, Clive Cussler, Nora Roberts and of course the one author no bookstore in Maine would be without—Stephen King. She'd heard once that King had retired a few years back, but there were two books that were recent. She picked one up, not because she was interested in reading it. That was the last kind of novel she wanted at the moment, but to satisfy her curiosity. Yes, there was the publishing date just inside the book cover. It had come out earlier this year. Putting it back, she passed over the Grisham novel and picked up a Jayne Ann Krantz. Romantic murder mystery. Nope! She didn't need a murder mystery either. She liked the cover on the Nora Roberts. It looked like a fun read about ordinary women and men who were anything, but ordinary, and fighting the good fight against evil in the Irish countryside. Taking it from the shelf, she looked as if she was trying to gage its weight by the way she let her hand rise and fall while it was in her grasp. Was she really in the mood for a romance, when hers was anything, but rewarding?

She paused remembering Alice's comment about Erik. There could be something there if she let it. Why was she so adverse to him? He was attractive, gentle … observing him with the puppy, she'd seen that. He was bright. Came from a good family. Looked to have a good career. So why? She knew the answer. He wasn't what she wanted.

The combined radiance of the sun streaming in the windows and overhead lights that only moments earlier had been so bright was waning. Ugh, she wasn't ready for more rain. And why was her eyesight faltering? Squeezing them shut, she massaged her right thumb and two forefingers gently over them. Too much wine. Except it wasn't the wine. She'd done this before. Stepped from one time into another. A ghost!

Oh, god, not here. Not around other people. Please! She was no longer holding Nora's book, but another. It was a smaller paperback with an albino dragon against a blue background. Anne McCaffery's. *The White Dragon.*

Cracking open the book to find the publishing date, she felt strong arms encircle her and a familiar voice caress the back of her neck. "I wouldn't recommend it, Sweetheart."

Wanting to pull away, she felt herself melting into the sturdy, warm embrace. She felt incensed. Why was he doing this, putting them both in jeopardy? What if someone took notice? Why wasn't her body responding to her?

"I know your addiction to fantasy, Love, both in books and in bed. But with your research, and shared time with me, do you really think you have time?" His voice was deep, rich and lazy. He was teasing, pulling at her. The invitation to come to bed with him was unmistakable.

This was what she had wanted, wasn't it? How long had she desired this moment. Anne McCaffery's book was forgotten. Turning, she looked into his face. His desire was raw, primal. Four long, long years of working together. Her mentor, her lover. Soon it would be over. She'd have her PhD. No longer would she be his student. She'd be on equal footing, a colleague. Then this illicit love affair would no longer need to hide in shadows.

"Jenny, Jenny, Jenny. My sweet Jenny. Not here,

not now. Meet me in an hour. I'll be waiting!"

Her breath caught. Her heart swelling to capacity.

Sunlight burst through the cool evening gloom. Nora Robert's fell from her hand. Tears freely tracked down her cheeks. This was what betrayal felt like. She'd faced betrayal from her father. That had been expected. This, this was something different. She had trusted Marc with her whole being. Thought him decent, a man of integrity. The blow to her mid-section was excruciating.

She held herself in check, refusing to succumb to the desire to run as fast and far from the book store as she might. She'd not make a fool of herself! She'd already suffered from too much unwanted attention. She needed sanctuary. Needed time to think.

The path through the woods skirting the campus center, was dappled with sunlight and shadow. Here, she did let the tears fall fast and furious. God, what a fool she'd been. What was it with the men in her life? Betrayal, after betrayal after betrayal. Her father, Marc, and even her grandfather. Though she had never known the last, he had left her this legacy with no one to guide her.

For the second time in as many days, she was fleeing Main. In her headlong flight across campus, she barely noticed the glances many students shot her way or the broken boughs and leaf clutter scattered across the usually immaculate grounds. Through tears, she kept seeing Marc's face except it wasn't the face she was so familiar with, but younger, more striking, finely carved. The angles hadn't softened with age. There was no graying at the trim temples. Instead, he had black, seductive locks.

This time it was too much, too close! The overlap of her feelings with the other were overwhelmingly allied. She wasn't this Jenny! She was running full out now.

Heedless of where she was going. She only wanted solitude. She wanted to be washed clean of what she had felt while connected to Jenny. That insatiable hunger that allowed caution to be thrown to the wind. She'd never known that before and didn't want to experience it again. No one should ever let their mind succumb to that extent, to the mindless will of hormones.

Arriving at her cottage, she slid to a halt in the wet leaves. Her heart groaned. Her solitude was to be denied. Parked next to her rust bucket, was the shining dark blue Tesla. Erik and the puppy were playing a game of tug-o-war with a scrap of rope. At another time, she knew she would have been warmed by the scene. Not now. He was just another man. Another betrayal waiting to happen. She was sure of it. Silencing the clear, small voice that would deny her assessment, she firmed her jaw and went to meet them.

"Don't you have classes or a lab today?" Her voice was as chilly as the meager breeze coming off the Atlantic.

"Whoa, and good morning to you, too."

"I'm sorry!" Was she? "It's been a tough morning." She opened the door she felt like slamming in his face, but she didn't.

"Anything I can do?" He and the puppy trailed at her heel.

Leave! "Not really. The expected fight happened this morning when Sara returned. Kendricks is back and raising hell. I've been banned from Ma ... Dr. McClellan's lab until things blow over. God only knows how long that will be. No," she turned to him. "I don't think you can do a thing."

"I can listen," he offered watching her cross to the table and stand, her gaze focused out the window over the sink.

The puppy was sitting at her feet, looking expectantly from her face to the rope offering he'd placed at her feet and back to her face. His paw reached out brushing her pant leg.

"You are so smart, aren't you?" Her features softened for a moment. "Too bad you're a male."

"Okay, so one strike a piece against me and the dog."

"Sorry!" This time she was. "It's just been ..."

"A bad day." He finished for her. "Yes, I know."

"Actually, I have some research to do. I think I was wrong about the age of the woman."

"Really, what makes you think that?" He was about to seat himself and decided it wasn't a good idea by the expression that crossed her face.

She picked up the rope and tossed it carelessly across the room. The puppy scrambled eagerly in its wake. "Have you named him, yet?"

"Jack. What do you think?" He stood studying her face. She'd been crying. There were faded splotches on her neck and cheeks. On another day, they might have been attributed to the cold. Today wasn't that cold. Her lovely, and yes, angry eyes were also red rimmed. He felt an unexpected rage festering. He wanted to get his hands on whomever had hurt her. He wanted to hurt them back.

"Jack." The puppy lifted his from his prize to glance back. "It suits him and he seems to have accepted it. But listen, I really do need to have time to check my suspicions."

"I won't keep you except to ask a favor."

"A favor?" Just what she needed. "What?"

He smiled as Jack dropped between them in

apparent confusion as to whom he should give the toy. Rhyjl reached down to retrieve the soggy cordage, patted the pup's head and sent it flying toward her bedroom.

"Jack. I don't have a crate for him yet and nowhere to secure him. I was hoping you might not mind pet sitting?"

She acquiesced with an audible sigh. "Sure why not. He can keep me company while I work on the computer. Can't you fellow?"

This time, there was no hesitancy. Jack deposited the rope lovingly on her shoe. His big brown eyes imploring her to accept it, accept him. Erik could identify.

*

She pulled the book up from several sources. The earliest publishing date for McCaffery's book, *The White Dragon,* was in 1979 and while she liked the cover better than the others that came up, it wasn't what she'd seen in the store. Marc would have only been around seven years old. Hardly a man seducing a female student. The next issue date was in 1989. Again, wrong cover. Marc was surely an attractive teen, most likely well on his way to charming the ladies, but not a professor. The next date hit all search parameters dead on. 2002. Bingo! Now to search for a PhD candidate for that year named Jenny, more likely Jennifer.

After hours of searching with no results and several interruptions from her charge, she decided a long walk out to the point and a lunch break were in order.

They shared a tuna sandwich which Jack inhaled. This, plus the piece of bread his sensitive nose had ferreted out from under the table, hadn't blunted his appetite. When she could no longer withstand his begging, she made a second just for him. "Good thing your person is well off. You are going to cost a fortune to feed." She rubbed his head. He panted, tongue lolling off to one side in gratitude.

The sun was well on its course toward evening and was barely visible above the stunted coastal pines. She hated the loss of daylight this time of year. The colors were lovely. The air was crisp and no longer saturated with draining humidity. The ticks had gone into hibernation along with the mosquitos. Still, she was dreading the coming of the long nights.

She'd thought about finding something to make a makeshift slip lead for the pup. Obviously it wasn't needed, as he frolicked after one leaf then another, but never straying more than a few yards from her. He was such an amazing creature. How could anyone have had a reason to toss him out on a stormy night? Thank God, Erik had come along to the rescue. But then that seemed to be one of Erik's talents. For a fleeting moment, she gave in to the wonder of what it might be like to have him take her in. She just as quickly shut the fantasy out. She didn't need anyone. Not her father, if he were even still alive, not Marc, and not Erik. She had always been strong. She just needed to focus.

Jennifer hadn't come up on any of her searches. Yet, she'd been here. She'd had a relationship with Marc. She'd been working on her PhD the same as Rhyjl. What had happened?

Woman and dog came to the point. The ocean still had the remnants of the storm to its coloring. In the distance, The Fisherman, sat off the point, his ores at rest. What did he see? What brought him out to that place day after day? She lifted a hand to wave. Once again he surprised her and gave her a half salute. Jack neared the edge of the bank, barked, and backed away with a low guttural growl, then hid behind her legs and whined. Maybe he didn't like the waves crashing below. She knelt down even though the sparse grass and leaves remained wet, and hugged the puppy close. "I'll protect you." She soothed, rubbing his floppy ear.

When she looked up again, the man and his boat were gone. The turtle islands were bathed in the late afternoon sun and a chill was creeping into her limbs. It was time to return home. Maybe Erik had returned. Maybe it would be safe to seek out Mags and see if she had anything to tell about the mysterious Jenny.

*

Erik read the e-mail for the second time. So, according to his source, there were any number of scandals associated with the Anthropology Department over the years. Most, involving students' pranks. Then there were the reported improprieties by none other than Doctor Amanda Kendricks and usually dealing with her temper. Rhyjl was correct. Kendricks had made a lot of enemies. If the woman hadn't been seen that morning back on campus, Erik might have wondered if the mysterious bones could have belonged to her. Fitting that a professor, so hated, could have been laid to rest in her own lab. It wasn't her, though, so he wasn't really any closer than he'd been before.

He quickly typed a response back to his old friend and mentor; the one person who had been a key reason he'd applied for the job at DEU. His finger hesitated on the send button. He pulled out his phone instead.

"Hi! Yes, I got the note. Are you going to be around this Friday? No, no, everything is fine. Yes, this is about the bones found in the lab up here. How did you hear about it? It was my understanding the University was trying to keep it under wraps until there was something official. They're making a big deal about it on the TV networks? Since when? No, I didn't know. I don't have a television and haven't really been paying attention to the news. Hey, I thought I might drop down Portland way this Friday and get your thoughts on some things. Oh, that would be great. Around noon then?" He finished off by asking about the grandnephews and Trina.

TV. He didn't like the sound of that. Why hadn't he thought of it before? He supposed the cops and the University were trying to keep a lid on it. After all, as far as he understood from the conversation the night before, it hadn't officially been ruled a death. Someone had spilled the beans, however. He had a good guess. Unfair and as prejudice as that might be.

Therefore it shouldn't have shocked him when he pulled up after his trip to town for dog food, that several film crews from six, eight, thirteen and Fox 23 were congregated around Rhyjl's door.

His first response was to go to her aid. She shouldn't have to endure this bullshit. It was not Rhyjl who stood at the door with microphones surrounding her. Sara, looking gravely serious and at the same time radiant in the limelight, was answering the shouted questions.

"Miss Fields can you tell us why the police have taken the specimens from the bone lab?"

"There is a strong theory that bones of a murder victim may have been scattered among them."

"Channel six news, Miss Fields, why won't the

University issue a statement? Are they trying to cover something up?"

Sara gave a coy shrug of her slender shoulders and a smile to match. "I'm sure I don't know. You would have to ask them. It's possible that everyone was waiting for Dr. Kendricks to return. It is her lab. She would be the best person to confirm the bones were tampered with."

"Fox news. Rumor has it one of the students made the original discovery. Can you tell us who that might be?"

"Yes, it was my good friend and roommate."

At this point, it appeared as if an all-out storming of the cottage door might ensue.

"Is your roommate here!" A vigorous shout rose.

Erik was ready to move to the defense again, imagining Rhyjl trapped inside like a hunted bird. His forward momentum halted when Sara replied. "No, I'm sorry, she is out for the afternoon."

"Yes, I just bet you are." He muttered, returning to his car. He drove down the road to one of the student parking lots, not caring if he got ticketed, and parked. He had a good idea where Rhyjl and Jack might be. If he hurried, maybe he could head her off and whisk her away to the safety of his place.

Jack pulled out of Rhyjl's arms announcing Erik's appearance quite vocally. Rhyjl had been kneeling on the ground. She pulled herself up brushing the dampened leaf debris from her knees and smiled. Whether it was from the antics of the puppy leaping up and doing clumsy attempts at pirouettes or him, he didn't care. He was just glad she could smile.

"Hello, I'm sorry you had to come find us. I didn't know when you would …" Her explanation died when she saw the concern in his eyes. "Is everything okay?"

"Not really. I'm glad you were out here and I'm glad I found you. We need to head back to my place." Erik reached for her hand.

She pulled away. "I don't take orders, Erik. Why do I need to go to your place?"

"Because you don't really want to go to yours."

"You are being a little dramatic and cryptic at the same time. What's wrong with my place?" She folded her arms and hoped she looked solid. In reality, she felt like her bones were turning to water.

"Someone has notified the media. They have your place surrounded and are voracious. So c'mon. My place is just across campus. I'll get you and Jack settled then come back for my car."

"Oh, god, Sara is going to be livid!" Rhyjl fell into step with him, the puppy falling in between them.

"I wouldn't count on it. Right now she is the star of the show."

"Well, she said she didn't want to be left out. Guess she got her wish."

"I'd say. In spades, if you asked me."

"So other than heading to your place, do you have any ideas?" They had broken out into a jog. Well, at least she and Jack had. Erik's stride was carrying him easily.

"I'm making it up as I go. As I said, first we need to get you someplace they won't be looking. Second, I'll get my car and hope what's his name hasn't ticketed it."

"Billy."

"Huh?"

"The name of the security officer working today is Billy. And I doubt it. If the media is surrounding my place, I'm sure that's where he will be. Crowd control and all that." Remembering how the old guard had puffed himself up when the police had arrived the other morning at the bone lab, she could only imagine how important he'd feel backing down the news folks.

"Another seeker of his fifteen minutes of fame?"

"Yes, I suppose, or just a man over his prime who wants to feel valuable."

*

They approached from the path overlooking the ocean. The scene caught her breath as well as her imagination. What had she been expecting? It wasn't this, this beautiful Cape Cod perched on a rocky point looking over the wind tossed Atlantic. Wind sculpted pine and maples created a vibrant color contrast to the hues of weathered gray exterior. All the time she had spent at DEU, she had never known this home existed. How could she have missed it?

"I'm afraid I haven't done much with the place. I'm still in the process of moving in. As it is …" He rambled on reciting a list of things he had or didn't have. All she could see was the well-trimmed green expansion that ran from the white railings and steps of the covered porch spreading like a carpet to the expanse of mottled sea. Windows ran the full length of the front, or was it the back of the house? From there you could watch the morning creep from slumber to throw back the darkness, welcoming a new day. She saw herself walking the widow's walk, her hair free in the wind. Come evening, she would swing on the porch, the cares of the day riding the clouds on the horizon to oblivion.

"It's stunning, Erik." She breathed.

He felt something awaken inside. She was pleased

and the amount of pleasure that gave him was boundless. "As I was saying," he opened the door and stood back for her and Jack to precede him. "I only have one bed at the moment. You are welcome to use it and Jack and I will take the couch in the front room."

Jack padded proudly across the hard wood floor and disappeared through a doorway. The sound of water being lapped echoed through the empty space.

"Oh," she said, turning in a wide circle taking in the whole room and knowing exactly how she would furnish it. "That won't be necessary. I'm sure they will be gone in a short time."

"You don't know the media the way I do. They are nothing more than a pack of hounds on the scent of blood. The kitchen is over this way." He ushered her in the same direction Jack had taken.

The rest of the house might be lacking, but it was clearly obvious where Erik's priorities were. The kitchen was designed to be efficient yet casual. A nice table for four sat in a nook overlooking the view. There was a small wooden wine rack with two empty slots sitting on the counter along with a state of the art espresso machine. A white paper sack with the logo Perfection Confections was sitting next to it as well as a crumb splattered paper towel.

"Breakfast!" He hurriedly waded up the paper towel, tossing it in a container under the kitchen sink. "You'll find an assortment of teas and hot chocolate in this cupboard. There are still a few sweet rolls in the bag. They might be a bit dry, but I've found if you wrap them in a paper towel and stick them in the microwave there," he pointed to the appliance suspended above the stove. "Thirty seconds and they come out almost tasting fresh."

"Erik, I really can't." Even though she wanted to,

she needed to get back to her own space.

"Hey, they are only sweet rolls."

In spite of her tension, she laughed. "Silly, I'm not talking about sweet rolls. I'm referring to staying here."

"Look," his hands reached out to take her arms, turning her to face him. "I'm not one of your professors. You are not my student. There will be no recriminations from the school. Besides that, who needs to know?"

She tightened with the blow. He was speaking as if they had an affair going. Had he conjured this whole thing just to get her here? "Erik, I really do need to go back home. I'll stay until dark."

"Look, just think about it. I'm going to go back and get my car. It's got some frozen things that are probably melted by now and more importantly, Jack's food. He hasn't been fed today.

"He had tuna sandwiches with me," she confessed. "Okay, I'll stay until Jack is fed and the frozen food has been rescued. But," she emphasized as he smiled broadly, "only until dark. I've got things at home that need doing." I want to be alone. In my own space in case she comes.

Erik slipped out the front after admonishing her to only use the back entrance if she or

Jack needed to go out. He also cautioned her not to let anyone know where she was. "Trust me on this would you, please. Until we find out who the leak was, you can't let anyone know."

Left to her own devices, she thought a little exploring wouldn't hurt.

The house, while giving the appearance of an earlier time, was fairly modern. Nice! No residual energies left behind except the very benign ones of everyday living that every place had. She was gradually learning to recognize and come to terms with what she called static that most people only glimpsed in a very limited way. These were the senses that other people might describe a room as being cold, warm, restful, or cramped. If you asked them why, they would probably just shrug it off or tell you it was the color or the furnishings.

The large open concept on the main floor, was skirted on one side by a master bedroom and bath and the kitchen on the other. A large fireplace dominated the center of the room. Across from it was a leather sofa with matching end tables that appeared to be new. In one corner, wedged between the windows and a large cluttered desk with three oversized monitors, was a serious black leather CEO chair. An indication that Erik's preference was not the magnificent view which had so captured her. Then, not everyone needed to feel openness.

It wasn't that she was claustrophobic. She enjoyed her snug little cottage. No, it was the absence of being crowded by people. Less crowded, usually meant less chance of stumbling across lingering energies to trip her up or catch her unexpectedly. That was the crux. She didn't like surprises. She could work in the lab or out in the field. That was fine. She knew what to expect. She could put her guard up and only let in what she needed. Jenny had caught her off guard. Well if that *was* who the mystery skeleton belonged to. Until the episode in the book store, she'd been fairly sure it was Melinda. What she really needed was more time with the bones. Instead of blocking her instincts, she could open herself and let their story sink in. That wasn't going to happen, was it? Without the bones to make a solid connection, the energies were no more than trailers for a movie.

She liked the ambience of this house. She liked it a

lot. There was warmth and laughter. The people in this house had been happy. It warmed her. Made her smile. Erik was a lucky guy.

Jack barked twice before the door opened. She hadn't heard a car. Duh, it was electric.

"They are still there," he answered her unspoken question.

"It's getting dark. What can they hope to accomplish?" She took two grocery bags from him and led the way to the kitchen. He followed with a large sack of dog food.

"A story. The lead in on the nightly news. They need to sing for their supper and right now you and the bones are the song." He set the bag down and pulled a small knife from a case attached to his belt. Jack, heavy pawed, was doing his best imitation of a graceful happy dance.

"He's smart!"

"Well, thanks. I like to think so." He smiled, zipping the knife across the top of the bag.

"Jack, not you." She teased. "Where's his dish?"

"Still on a plane or UPS truck. There is a bowl up in the cupboard there on the left of the sink. It should do for now."

The only bowls she could find were some oversized cereal bowls. Taking one down, she handed it to him. "You'll have to fill that twice or perhaps three times you know. Haven't you got something bigger like a mixing or serving bowl?"

"Nope!" He said, taking the bowl and dipping it in to the bag. "I haven't had the need to mix anything and I'm not using my mother's china. I haven't had time to get everything yet as I told you. So I kind of wing it. When a need comes up, I order it. I'm a great fan of Amazon Prime."

Jack demolished two bowls' full with barely a pause. By Rhyjl's predicted third, he had gone from standing to lying down with his paws placed on either side. Now it was a slower, more thoughtful crunch, crunch, crunch.

The half-gallon of Moose Tracks ice cream had only begun to soften around the edges. Two bottles of Oak Leaves vineyards White Zinfandel, presumably to replace the two bottles he'd taken the night before, were chilled from their close proximity to the Moose Tracks and a package of organic frozen peas, also slightly thawed. In the other sack were two thick cut T-bone steaks, a foil sack with buttered garlic bread, an onion and a small package of Portobello mushrooms. "Were you expecting company?" She knew the answer, but wanted to hear his explanation.

"I confess when I was getting dog food, I had thought of offering Jack's sitter dinner as well."

"Was this before, or after, the discovery of the media encampment?"

"Before." He deftly pulled the cork from one of the wines to let it breathe. "Why are you looking at me like I've grown two heads?"

"Erik, are there really TV crews surrounding my place, or is this a ploy?"

He stopped mid stride to the stove, turned and studied her. His somber mien told her she had crossed some line, but she wasn't sure what. "Rhyjl, let me make this perfectly clear. I like you. I like you a lot. I want to get to know you and I know of only one way to do that—to spend time with you. This situation you have found yourself in is unfortunate. It cuts deeply that you would think I'm the kind of guy to take advantage of it. I have offered to help in any way I can and that includes offering my home. I also pay my debts. I'm new to this area. Just like my home, I haven't settled in yet. I appreciate your help with Jack."

He took up the cork and punched it back into the bottle with the heel of his hand. "Get your things. I'll take you back."

"Erik, I don't, I mean I didn't mean to hurt you. You've been great. It's just ..." She stretched out her hands toward him them let them drop to her side,

"Save it." He handed her jacket and scarf over. "If I remember correctly, the cottage windows aren't very secure. Is there a way you could get to your room or Sara's without being seen? They will be watching both doors."

Chapter 10

Never What They Seem

The tense silence inside the Tesla was stifling. It felt like it was sucking the life out of her. Out of them. She rolled down the window hoping the cool air would help. It didn't. Then she saw the blaze of lights where her cabin was located. Night had been turned to day. People stood around holding coffee cups to ward off the cold in their hands. Their breath steaming like the cups they held.

"Oh, no! I can't get in there." A sob caught in her throat. Tears welled up and spilled down her cheek.

Erik didn't respond. Somehow, her judgment of him had turned him to stone. He drove past the lane that lead into the cottages, only to pull off to the side of the road as soon as they were past where the halo of lights ended.

"How long will they stay?" She asked the silence.

"Until they get what they want or some other more enticing new story breaks." He offered, turning off the engine. "They camped in front of our house for almost a week and continued to pop up at odd times for months afterward. But then Boston Arnesons are always good copy." His voice was laced with venom. Old wounds scraped open by anger bled out around and between them.

This was not the time nor place to ask. "I'm sorry, Erik. So, so sorry and I don't mean just because of what must have happened to you, but especially for my mistrust. You've been nothing, but kind. I do appreciate all you have done, believe me. It's just …" What could she say? I'm screwed up! Sorry, but I think most men are selfish bastards! "I haven't had the best of luck when it comes to men. Today, I got hit with another let down. Someone I had allowed myself to get close to and trust."

"I take it," he turned the ignition and the car purred back onto the road, "you have given up on the idea of trying to get into your place?"

Had he accepted her apology? His voice didn't reflect it. The hard cold edge was still there. "I don't see how. Where are we going?"

He'd turned the car on to the highway leading to town. "There's a few places still open. I suggest we should pick up a few things for you."

"You don't have to do this. I could maybe get a room at the motel." She didn't have the money. If he'd let her borrow his cell phone, she might be able to reach her grandmother for help. Surely the clerk would take a card over the phone?

"You're correct, I don't. As for a motel, I'm sure they've already made sure management has been paid handsomely to report anyone like you checking in with or without your name."

"You're serious!" Shivers skittered down her back. This was unbelievable.

"Does anyone outside of Alice know who I am and that I've been with you?"

"No, I don't think so. I suppose there might have been some people who have seen us walking on campus. Why?"

"You're sure you haven't told Sara." Glittering pinpoints of light announced the close proximity of the town just over the rise.

"No, she was too upset about us all being there. I don't think I gave her any names."

Then unless you have more objections, I think we should go back to plan A. They pulled in front of a small boutique that was expensive and mostly for the tourists. The only reason it hadn't shut down was the leaf peepers who were still traveling through trying to catch those last vestiges of color. "Erik, I can't afford this place." She didn't know a lot of students that could, with the exception of Sara and that Bannerman jerk.

"I'll buy. No strings attached." He got out of the car and then leaned back in. "What size?"

"I can come in." Her hand already moving to the door handle.

"Look, trust me. The less you are seen, especially with me, the better." Reporters are better at ferreting out information than the CIA."

He had no idea what he was doing. He'd never bought clothes for a woman in his life. He passed the attractive and well-dressed middle-aged clerk a story about buying some things for his sister's birthday. With a sly smile and knowing nod, she took Rhyjl's size and asked what he had in mind.

"A night gown."

She led him over to the lingerie rack, pulled out three skimpy, gauzy things and held them up for his inspection.

"Ah, no. Something with a little more substance." Her brows knit, then raised realizing she'd misread him.

Her next choice was a soft teal cotton that was ankle length, trimmed with soft embroidery, and lace. He liked it and his smile let her know she had a sale.

By the time they were finished, the clerk had

packaged a soft grey cashmere sweater, a paisley tunic, a pair of jeans and classic black slacks. He dealt out four hundred dollars and pocketed the coin change.

Getting back in the car, he tossed the bag in her lap. "I'm sorry, you'll have to wash your, uh, under garments. I couldn't quite bring myself to buy those."

There wasn't enough light to see what the sack contained, but just from its weight, a lump formed in her throat and tears stung her eyes for the second time that evening. Jack apparently sensing her discomfort, pushed his soft muzzle past the head rest of her seat to rest it upon her shoulder.

"Drug store next. Any preference on toothpaste?"

*

Pulling up to the front of Erik's home, Rhyjl's heart sank. There, sitting low and lean, the sports car waited along with its passenger. Looking to Erik for direction, she was at a loss when he smiled broadly. "A woman of her word. *And*, she made it in good time. Punctuality and brains. A rare combination."

Exiting the Tesla, Rhyjl was pleasantly surprised to see Alice emerge out of the sleek Scion. She, too, had a large shopping bag. They were once again a threesome. The tension that had been coiling like a snake ready to strike, eased.

"Don't look so surprised." She sidled up to Rhyjl as they took the steps leading to the porch. "I don't always drive the body wagon."

"I just didn't expect anyone else to be here. Well, and to be honest, I was terrified they had found me." Jack came bounding up as they opened the door and pushed past on his way to the kitchen.

"Love the dog." Alice smiled indulgently as her focus trailed the pup. "Um, yes, I saw the committee of vultures when I passed your place. Erik's idea to bring you here was the right one. I can tell you that Tanner is frothing at the mouth. God help whoever leaked this when he finds them." Alice flowed over to the leather couch and dumped the bag she'd been toting. "I didn't know exactly what to get. Erik, sweet boy, had to be blushing when he called and asked if I could pick up a few personals."

Placing her packages next to Alice's, Rhyjl looked over the parcels. Had she just jumped ahead to Christmas? Except she'd never seen so many gifts in all her life. "Thanks, but you really didn't need to. I could have done as Erik first suggested and washed things out. I'll pay you ..."

"Nope, not a chance. Besides, one of my first rules: Never, ever, turn down a good looking man who offers you a steak dinner and good company. It's my pleasure. And to be honest," she slipped her arm over Rhyjl's shoulder, hugging her. "Erik told me you think you have more clues about who our victim might be. How could I resist?"

The steaks were grilled to perfection. The spinach salad and garlic bread accompanied by the freely flowing wine and conversation made for a perfectly normal and enjoyable evening. There was only one hitch: How many normal people sat around discussing murder?

"So you think this Jenny or Jennifer person might be the same person my source said there had been a scandal over ten years ago? Erik held the wine bottle up. Rhyjl refused the offer of a refill shaking her head.

"Yes, I think it might be. The age of the victim would be about right, guessing that she would have been around my age and then add ten years."

Alice nodded. "That would fit my assessment as well. Erik, did your old professor say more about what the scandal was?"

"No. Other than it had involved both Dr. Kendricks and McClellen, who wasn't the Department head at the time. He said it was quite serious and there had been a lot of heated debate on what actions should be taken. I guess in the end he wasn't happy. The student was expelled and Kendricks and McClellen were given a minor wrist slapping and obligatory warnings."

"And you're sure, Rhyjl, they didn't mention a last name?" Alice setting her glass down, folded her hands in the child's church pose and tapped the steeple against her lips. "How many women with the name of Jenny could there have been in the Archaeology program ten years ago? Not many, I'd imagine."

"I came up with four. Two undergrad in the Archaeology program, one undergrad under the Anthropology side and one grad student working on her PhD in Archaeology. I'm leaning most heavily in her direction." She wanted so much to share why she knew, beyond doubt, which of those women was lying, at this moment, in Alice's lab. "The latter was working pretty closely under Kendricks and the Belize project at the time."

"And what was her name?"

"Matheson." I was going to do a further search when I got back from my walk, but, well."

"No reason we can't do a search now." Erik stretched his legs before rising and crossing the room to his desk. "One Jennifer Matheson."

Both women sat in contemplation as the computer

whined and whirred to life. "Makes more noise than his car," Rhyjl mused.

Alice laughed. "Probably has more power under the metal, as well."

"I heard that!" Erik piped from behind a glowing screen. "Spoken like a true sports car owner."

"I'd challenge you to a race, Erik, but my momma always told me never to compete with men. Their egos are far too fragile."

"Ouch," Rhyjl's hand flew to her mouth to stifle the giggle.

"Mine always told me to let ladies go first. Being the weaker sex and all." Erik shot back. "Uh-oh, this could be a long night. So far I've found close to a hundred Jennifer Mathesons."

Alice got up and crossed to stand behind him. "Can you narrow the search criteria to just those with PhD degrees?"

He tapped the keys. Ten names came up. "Better, but if she was expelled, did she ever get hers? She might have just given up and become a happy wife and mother. You know—Screw academia if it's going to screw me. It does sound like she got the shaft."

"Well let's check them anyway. Um, two lawyers. Maybe being screwed, as you so politely put it, caused her to change her major. Alice quickly scanned the information. "One is too young, the second, she might be an option except it says she's been a professor at Harvard for the last eight years. Unless our Jenny was brilliant, wealthy and well connected, I don't think this is our gal. What else do we have?"

Erik scrolled the screen down. "This one has a PhD, but it looks like it is in the field of physics. That's a big leap." He shook his head. "Now perhaps this one." Erik pointed to the screen. "She has a doctorate in Psychology. Psychology, Anthropology, not so different."

"Ah, now we might be on to something." Alice thoughtfully tapped her lips as she read. "She's only been practicing about five years. That would have given her five years to recoup after a huge setback. Right age, mid-thirties.

"What do you think, Rhyjl? Rhyjl? Rhyjl! Christ!" Alice was running across the room as the last exclamation left her throat.

Rhyjl, lying half on the sofa and half on the floor remained unresponsive. Jack, having been content to be at her feet all evening, was whimpering softly and nuzzling her hand.

"Erik help me get her on the couch and then call 911." Alice pushed the reluctant puppy back.

Erik knelt in Jack's place, lifting Rhyjl easily to the sofa. When he paused, she pushed him aside the same way she had the dog. "Okay, Professor, now would be a good time to make that call!" She ordered, checking for a pulse and respiration. "God, pulse and respiration are off the chart. You'd think she was running a race."

He'd only taken a step or two back. He reached in his pocket and pulled his worry stone rather than the phone from its holster on his belt. He'd wondered about it from the moment he'd first read her papers. Rhyjl and his mother were so incredibly alike in the way they saw things. Of course, she might have mimicked his mother's work. There were lots of others who had. But that little niggling voice of his had said otherwise. Her other behavior should have clued him in as well. That she avoided being in crowded places. Her unease even when they had been having a friendly chat. Her reserve when he had wanted to be with her.

Alice was now looking at him as if he'd grown two heads. "Damn it, Erik, if you aren't going to call, give me your phone!" She held out her hand expectantly. It was the move of a surgeon expecting the instrument to appear immediately.

Erik shoved her hand away. "She's okay. Just let her be."

"Since when are you a doctor of medicine? I'll get my phone." She sprung from a kneeling position, and headed toward the door to grab the purse she'd left on the floor by the entry.

Erik blocking her, grabbed her arm. "Alice listen."

"Erik let go before I do something we will both regret." She jerked back.

His grasp held firm. "I've seen this before. Not with her," he pointed with his free hand in Rhyjl's direction, "but with someone else. Give her a few minutes. She's in a kind of trance state. And no, I'm not crazy!" He addressed the latter to the look of incredulity on her face. "The best thing we can do right now is to just sit close by, and keep her from hurting herself if she starts to flail about."

"What? You think this is some kind of epilepsy?" She jerked her arm again. "You're wrong, Erik."

On her third attempt to pull free, he released her, sending her pin wheeling backward until she caught her balance.

"I wasn't sure before, but I am now. She has the same condition my mother had. Please, Alice. Trust me."

Chapter 11

Past Reflections

It had been a long day. The meal sated her hunger in more ways than one. She was full, warm, and content. When was the last time she'd known that? Jack sat at her bare feet, a fuzzy, soft foot warmer. She liked the feel of her little buddy. Stroking him, talking to him, having him hang on every word, or so it seemed. She was enjoying listening to Alice and Erik poke and prod each other with good natured jabs. Erik had started a fire in the fireplace across from the sofa. The flames danced, leaping and twisting with abandon, along the logs. There was nothing quite like a real fire. No matter how people had tried to capture the same hypnotic affect with gas and lights, there was something about the real thing that just escaped defining or capturing.

Erik was at his desk scanning one of the screens. His face was bathed in a glowing white aura that made each angle and curve more visible. Alice, slightly leaning over his shoulder, was exquisitely beautiful. Rich mahogany hair cascading over the sapphire of her blouse was silk over silk. She was no longer the well-manicured professional. Tonight she was a woman who had dressed soft, seductive. Had she done so for Erik? They looked so well together. So perfect.

The insidious familiar pang of being on the outside always looking in, wrapped around her. Reaching down to pet Jack, hoping the touch would cast away the cold, she saw the shift as the room blurred from firelight to harsh sun.

The anger was pungent between the two of them. The greedy bitch wanted more. She always wanted more and would always be the kind that wanted more. She'd give her half her asking. She paid her well for the work. She'd give her this last amount to buy her silence. Taking her purse from the table, she dug through to find her wallet. "I only have two hundred on me. That will have to do." And it would, because if she thought she'd get a penny more ... Well, she could just go to hell.

The harpy was still yelling at the top of her lungs. Certainly someone from hotel management would be knocking at the door any minute. Drawing a deep breath for strength more than courage ...

The fire sliced past her left shoulder blade, then turned to brittle ice. Her analytical mind traced the pain and knew she would bleed out in minutes unless by some miraculous chance it had missed the aorta. Turning, she stumbled into the flash of the blade. Throwing up her right arm to stave off the next blow as well as postpone her fall, she knew it was better than useless. She was a dead woman. Dead and for what? A paper, a stupid paper and revenge. Had the accolades of her peers and the look on Amanda Kendricks face been worth it? Marc, the only man she had really loved. Her husband, good, kind, stable and trustworthy. Why hadn't she loved him the way he deserved? Her students, her own work. All gone. Flowing out of her for what?

The blade continued to strike. She was in shock now. The blood loss too substantial. There was only the slightest sensation of dull thuds each time it struck anew. Oh, Jackson, I'm so, so sorry.

*

Someone was holding her wrist. Alice? Her body was sore and cold. Oh so very cold. She was shaking. From the pain. Alice was yelling at someone. Was it her? Erik, his back to the glow of the fire was dark, handsome. He held that thing in his hand. The one he always pulled from his pocket. A stone. Some kind of agate. It was a gift from his mother. He was worried. Both of them were. Why? Why was Alice screaming for Erik to call 911?

Oh, God, it was more than a dream. She'd had an episode! She was lying on the couch. Jack was pressing hard. Alice kept pushing him back. How could she even begin to explain? Alice was leaving her. Jack moved in. Alice moved for the door. Erik wresting her to a stop, blocked her retreat. They were struggling. Jack's whine was more guttural.

They think I'm having a seizure. Good, good! Let them believe that. No, not Erik. What was he saying?

"I wasn't sure before, but I am now. She has the same condition my mother had. Please, Alice. Trust me."

"What do you mean condition?" Alice stood glaring at Erik.

"It's hard to explain. I think it would be better if we just … Oh look, she's come round."

"Rhyjl!" Alice moved with alacrity. "How are you feeling? Any nausea, headache?"

"I'm okay. Really I am," she pulled her arm protectively across her chest as Alice attempted to take her wrist again. "It was just a dream. All this talk about murder and the media camping at my door." She shook her head to dislodge the sticky webs of the vision. "Seriously!"

"Honey, that was more than a dream. Can someone elucidate a little here for me. You are obviously not telling me the truth and Erik seems to think you and his mother share a condition." Alice sat back on her heels. When Rhyjl kept her own counsel, Alice turned to Erik expectantly. "Okay, if someone doesn't come clean, I am calling 911. Got it?"

*

"When my mother turned sixteen, she started seeing ghosts. She thought she was crazy. She became more and more withdrawn. She threw herself into her studies at school and the rest of the time, she spent studying the occult."

"Erik this is not the time for creepy stories." Alice interjected.

"It's not a ghost story. It's a story about how my mother discovered her condition, her gift."

Alice rolled her eyes, sighed and plopped down to a cross legged pose. "This is going to be a long explanation, isn't it?"

"Could be." Erik pulled the stone from his pocket again. "As I was saying, she pretty much isolated herself. One day her mother was agitated with her daughter's behavior and accused her of being like her grandmother. My mother was confused. She didn't think she had anything in common with either one of her grandmothers. Well, one thing led to another and it came out that Mom's real father had died in Korea. Her parent's hadn't been married at the time, so her mother married a longtime friend who agreed to raise the child as his. My mother's real grandmother was some crazy old lady that lived in

New England and made her living telling people's fortunes. I guess the son was embarrassed by his mother's chosen profession and had joined the military to escape."

Erik walked to his desk and pulled the leather chair over to the sofa. "Anyone like a drink? With the doc's approval." He nodded to Alice and waited for their responses then disappeared into the kitchen to return minutes later with three wine glasses hanging by their stems in one hand and a bottle of white wine in the other.

Pouring the wine, he continued. "My mother earned a scholarship to Harvard and when not busy with her studies, set out to find her grandmother. She found the old woman living in poverty and dying of cancer in a shack in New Hampshire. They spent the summer break together. My great grandmother taught my mother all she knew."

"So you are telling us your mother was a clairvoyant?" Alice asked.

"No," Erik looked directly at Rhyjl, "My mother was Claire Blackwood."

Rhyjl didn't realize the glass left her hand until it was shattering on the wood floor sending a terrified Jack running and Alice yelping as the contents splashed over her clothing.

"Claire Blackwood is your mother? Dr. Claire Blackwood who is still considered the leading expert on Neanderthals!"

"I think *was* is the operative word, Rhyjl. So you are one of those Arnesons, the prince and heir to the family Dynasty?" Alice carefully brushed glass shards from her slacks. "I'm sorry, Erik. That last was uncalled for. Your mother's death was a real tragedy. No wonder you knew how to deal with the press."

"Oh my god, Erik, your mother and her whole crew

were taken hostage and killed by terrorists."

"In their country they are religious extremists." Erik said, dryly. "Don't anyone move, I'll get a towel, and please someone keep Jack back if he has the courage to come out from hiding before I get back. I don't need any vet bills at the moment."

"You had no idea who his parents were or are?" Alice was frowning down at the wet patch on her blouse.

"I'm sorry about that." Rhyjl winced. "I hope it isn't ruined."

"No, it shouldn't be. Thank goodness it was the Chablis not the Cabernet. Back to Erik. You didn't know?"

"No. Why should I? I know about Dr. Blackwood, but how … I don't even know who the Arnesons are. You seem to, though."

"Yes, well it's kind of hard to grow up within The Beltway and not know who the Arnesons are."

"Beltway?" Rhyjl asked

"She means the Boston Beltway, Rhyjl. It's an area outside of Boston proper that is bordered by I-495. Unfortunately that's not the only place we are well known. My father has a place in the Hamptons as well as Martha's Vineyard."

"So you really are rich!" She said it as though it was a dirty word.

"Guilty." He mopped up the glass and wine at her feet." Or at least my family is. "Everything I have was either left to me by my mother or I earned on my own. Dad holds the remainder like a carrot over my head hoping I'll acquiesce and help run the family businesses."

"Um," Alice gingerly wiped herself with the other towel Erik had brought, then stood. "If you'll excuse me, I think I'll find the bathroom. My, my," she mused, walking away. "Erik Arneson. And here I'd heard you were some kind of recluse."

"Why didn't you tell me?" Rhyjl leaned down near him.

"Well in a way, I did that first afternoon." When she flashed puzzlement, he added. "The bit about the forks, my grandmother's need to impress? I didn't elaborate, true. Probably because it is a sore spot with me and I wanted to cultivate an interest in me not my family's money. Because, Rhyjl, I want to be seen as something other than one of 'Those Arnesons' or Claire Blackwood's son."

He had. The way he'd tossed it out, she'd gotten the impression of money, true, but not wealth, especially the kind of wealth that they were now speaking of. So okay, if it made him uncomfortable, she'd switch topics. "Erik, you said your mother had the same condition as me. But I don't -"

"The bones talk to you, Rhyjl. You see the people. You *see* ghosts."

"I think you've had too much wine." She'd had too much wine. The room was getting uncomfortably warm all of a sudden.

"Rhyjl," he folded his hand around hers. "It's alright. You can trust me. What did you see? I know you've been seeing the woman's death. It's pretty strong energy she's left behind if it can affect you here." His hand swept in a wide arc indicating the whole of his home. "Who is she and who killed her?"

Her further denial would serve no purpose. She was still trying to take in that he was wealthy and the son of one of her idols. He was right. It had changed how she felt about him. Not that she liked him any more or less, but in a way she couldn't quite put her finger on. If that weren't enough, he was also revealing that his mother had the same ability and more importantly, he wasn't afraid of that. She studied his face for any sign of guile. He would either be very good at cards or he was being honest.

"I'm not sure, Erik. I did sense her death. I know how she was killed. I don't know who except that it was a woman. A very angry woman."

"Could you describe this woman?"

"Yes, can you?" Alice had entered the room on a breeze.

Rhyjl hung her head. This was all too much, too fast. She'd gone from only one person other than herself knowing her secret, to double that in a matter of minutes. She remembered looking at the clock on the fireplace mantel just before she'd slipped, thinking that it was still early at a quarter to eight. Now the hands were only a few minutes past that hour. Minutes, and her life was now changed forever. The question remained, how it would be changed?

"I know her."

"The murderer?" Alice deposited herself next to Rhyjl on the sofa and slipped Rhyjl's free hand between her two.

"I want to believe it was Kendricks. Whatever, Kendricks is up to her eyebrows, but the voice. The angry voice I heard screaming at me." Rhyjl shuddered. Could it be, or was she just combining an earlier vision with this one. She didn't like this business. "I don't know, I need to think about it."

Alice squeezed her hand. "You said Kendricks is part of it. How do you know?"

"Because Jennifer was thinking about her as she

died. She was also thinking of someone named Jackson. I think he might be her husband."

Erik was up like a shot.

"What was she thinking in connection with Kendricks? Did you get anything in particular? I can't believe I'm even saying this."

"Join my club." Rhyjl gave a weak smile.

"So let's think! Why would a woman's dying thoughts be of Kendricks? A husband, yes. Children, yes. The person murdering her. Probably. Are you sure it wasn't Kendricks?"

"I don't know!" Rhyjl pushed up from the sofa and walked to the fireplace. "I need the bones! This other is only echoes, impressions. If I have the bones, I can see clearly."

"And Tanner will have my job if I try to get you in or them out. He's not the believing sort, trust me."

"And you are?" Rhyjl turned and raised a skeptical eyebrow.

"I'm open. I've see a few things I couldn't explain. I believe, as I think I told you, that there is more on earth than meets the eye. Have I ever met someone who can see a person's life from touching bones? Nope! Can you teach it to me?"

Rhyjl's laugh was brittle. "I don't think so and believe me, it's not all roses."

"No, I suppose not."

"I've got it!" Erik shouted. "Dr. Jennifer Jackson. She married prior to getting her PhD. She works out of University of Texas, Austin. Mayan Archaeology. Says she also does her field work in Belize."

Silence blanketed the room. As Alice had mentioned earlier, the operative word in this case was past tense. Jennifer Jackson was scattered around a coroner's lab waiting to be pieced back together. Rhyjl let that settle in. The woman's dying thoughts had been sorrow for not loving a good husband, regret that she had come to her end because of revenge, and her knowledge she'd let her students down. It was always a bitter taste in her mouth when the people she studied died with so much remorse. The strange thing was, they were often people who should have had no regrets. Jennifer Jackson by the sound of it, had married well, received her degree, established a distinguished career. Yet, often it was the people who had less to lose, had actually had less in life, that left life with joy. Like Mattie.

Mattie had been a slave all her life. She had only known freedom from what some of the old folks had said. Their stories had sounded like children's stories, unreal with happy endings. But they were the stories Mattie dreamed about when her aching body rested upon the straw bed in her corner of the shack she shared with the man she loved. Then he had died by the master's hand and she was left with nothing more than a swollen belly and heartache. But Mattie had clung to the stories and had promised that one day her new child would know that freedom.

On the night he came wailing strong into the world, she held him only for a few minutes, then kissed him goodbye. The smuggler woman came for him. She and the midwife had promised he would be taken north to freedom. When the master came the next day, they told him the child had died in birth. He would not believe them and when they could not produce a tiny body, he beat them all. Mattie did not die in sorrow. Her last thoughts had been of the man she loved, the children she had born, and the child she believed would find freedom. No regrets.

Alice broke the hush. "I think it's time I'm off. I'll figure out a way to get this information to Tanner without bringing into play your special ability, Rhyjl. We can put it down to super sleuthing, using gossip and the internet. If we are wrong about this being the correct Jennifer …"

"We won't be," Rhyjl sighed.

"One more thing," Erik held his hand up. I just found a notice for this big convention of Archaeology people. It says Jennifer was one of the key speakers."

"So," Alice slipped her sweater over her shoulders, "what has that to do with this? Didn't she show up?"

"Oh, she showed up. It was about four weeks ago. But for a Mayan specialist, I think the topic she spoke on seems a bit strange. Her paper was on *Divergent Cultures Among Slave Populations in Haiti*. Isn't that where you told me the bones were from in the lab, Rhyjl?"

"Yes," she whispered. "It is also Amanda Kendricks' life work."

Chapter 12

Cabin Fever

It felt strange to log on to a computer that was Erik's. Not as strange as it had been waking up in a bed twice the size of her own with the smell of fresh brewed coffee permeating the air. Most people she knew, would have found that pleasurable. They probably hadn't had to brew so much of it to get their father sober after a binge. Disgusting by association.

Erik had been charming, but then when wasn't he for the most part? She'd never considered herself opposed to mornings, yet his boundless energetic cheerfulness had her groaning inwardly and wishing she could stuff her head back under a pillow.

Jack's enthusiastic greeting when she opened the bedroom door was also a little overwhelming. He circled her several times before pushing his head between her legs looking for all the world like a small carousel character. On the way to the kitchen, his tail thwacked and smacked everything within two feet of his prancing body.

Erik was happy to inform her the puppy had slept at the door all night and admitted it was the best night's sleep he'd had since the dog had arrived, even if it was on the couch. He certainly didn't look worse for the wear. He was showered and smelled something like the sea. He was still wearing the same shirt and pants as the night before. She supposed that was her fault. He would have been too polite to come in to his bedroom closet for a change.

His banter was light and cheery. He'd scrambled eggs and bacon, had a kettle on to boil for her tea and a cup sat waiting next to an assortment of teas. Two glasses of orange juice sat on the table and a plate with a stack of buttered toast occupied in the center.

Over breakfast, he talked about the weather. They'd had their first frost. The green expanse stretching to the sea, was glittering white in mute testimony. Alice had called. She had contacted Tanner. He was checking into Jennifer. She also didn't know if she'd be able to stop by as planned. It seemed some energetic reporter was tailing her. UPS should be arriving with several packages. Best not to answer the door. They could leave them on the porch. He reminded her for the third time since she'd arrived, that she and Jack were to stay close to the house and in the back.

She knew he was only trying to be careful, but by that time, she answered him, "Yes, Dad." in the petulant voice of a bored teenager. He'd responded in kind by patting her hand accompanied by an indulgent smile. Then he informed her he would be picking up a cell phone for her. She would have protested, but had learned by now it was a useless gesture.

She walked Jack. Played a little tug-o-war and worked on sit and stay. He was smart and it didn't take long for him to master his first lessons. That or his previous owner had taught him a few things. Somehow, considering what they'd done, she found that unlikely. In a way, they were both just castaways.

After wandering around the house exploring the main floor and the second, she returned to the kitchen, gave Jack a fresh dish of water and rummaged through the refrigerator. She found some left over pizza and some salad fixings which reminded her of the ingredients in her fridge. Would Sara have eaten them or would they still be there when she returned?

Thinking of Sara sent a little chill skittering along her skin. The voice she'd heard. It sounded so much like Sara's. For the second time, she wondered if that was because Sara had pulled her from her first vision, thinking it was only a bad dream? She tried to recall what had happened, but it all seemed so hazy. If only she could get to the bones. Even one could clear this mental fog. Surely, Alice could sneak something out. A mere fragment.

She warmed the pizza in the oven as she tossed the salad. It would have been quicker had she used the microwave, but often when she was around microwaves, she ended up with headaches. She didn't know why, but then that was par for the course. She didn't know why she responded to half the things around her the way she did.

That brought her thoughts back to Erik's mother. Here was a woman she would have given anything to study with and now to find out Claire Blackwood might have also been able to give her answers to this, this—What had Erik called it? Condition? Yes, condition. That was as good a word as any. Over the years, she'd seen it as a curse, a blessing and of late, more of a nasty disturbing irritant. Once again, however, she had been cheated. There would be no help from Claire Blackwood.

That thought made her a little sick. Here she was wallowing in self-pity, when Erik had lost his mother to a horrid and cruel death. Long ago she remembered reading how as a boy, he had been an unofficial part of his mother's team. It was along the same lines as Mary Leakey's children. It was all a part of Claire's biography. Meeting Erik, she'd never have made the connection. She didn't even remember that Erik's dad had a different name. It wasn't important since he never appeared to have an interest in his wife's work. Sobering thought. Did Claire have regrets when she died? Anguish at leaving behind a son? Remorse that her team had suffered at the hands of evil men? Perhaps misgivings for a life that was rarely spent with her husband? Another thought squirmed uneasily in her mind. Had Claire known there was a risk that summer so long ago and left Erik behind for that reason?

Morbid thoughts. If only there was something to read that didn't have anything to do with physics and engineering. Remembering Erik had told her he had left the password to his computer on the desk. She went to check it out. She'd never seen a system set up quite like he had. The mouse curser even rolled from one screen to another. It was a bit unnerving. He'd only made one request, that she not send anything out that would indicate her whereabouts. That included checking or using her email account. "A good snoop could locate you from an IP address."

Would someone really go to those extremes? It wasn't like she was wanted by the FBI or CIA. Tanner already knew where she was. Alice had made sure of that. Her fingers typed her address in then hovered over the enter key. Frustrated, she dropped her hands to her lap, then raising them, she scrubbed over her face and back along her hair, washing the temptation away. It was his house, his computer and his request. He was just trying to protect her and possibly himself. That thought hadn't occurred to her before. What had Alice said? One of *those* Arnesons!

"I'm sure he is just thrilled to be involved in

another macabre death of an archaeologist."

Jack's deep soulful eyes looked up from his place at her feet, or more realistically, halfway on her feet. His tail thump, thump, thumping a beat of his own. God, she was really beginning to love this dog. Love, wasn't something she could afford at this point in her life. Not for the dog, not for anything or person.

Reaching down to pet his head, she cooed. "Let's go for a walk," Before she had even grabbed her jacket, he was bounding for the door.

It wasn't much of a walk when you were restricted to a yard not much larger than the house. Granted, it was a big house at what she guessed was something over 2400 square feet just on the main floor. She played a game of running back and forth, Jack bouncing beside her and then it settled into a game of fetch with a stick Jack had found. It helped the restlessness some, but not really.

She missed going to the point and wondered if the fisherman would be out today? It was a nice enough day. Better than a lot of days she'd seen him out in his rowboat just off the point. Staring out from Erik's yard, the headland where Main perched was just enough to block her view. She looked longingly at the path that wound its way up and through the rocky bits of shoreline. Erik had felt secure enough to lead her away from the media using the path. Why wouldn't she be just as secure using it to go back? She might even be able to get close enough to her cottage to see if they were still around. If they weren't, she could at least sneak in long enough to grab her computer. Then she could be doing some of her research. Chewing on her lip, she heard Erik's warning about not using the net, yet, she could be proofing her written material or looking over data she had already downloaded.

So what could she do to get past the open area near Main? She didn't think anyone would recognize the way she was dressed. Jeans and a jacket were standard student attire. Too bad her jacket didn't have a hood she could pull up to hide her face. If she did, well who would notice someone walking along the path with a dog? Unless she ran directly into them.   Hood. A hoodie? She didn't have one herself, but Erik did. She'd seen it hanging in the hall closet when she'd gone to get her jacket. If she put on his oversized dark green hoodie, she could be anyone including a guy. Other than Erik, Alice and possibly Sara—had Sara even noticed the dog that night?—no one else would put two and two together. That's what she'd do. She'd swap out her coat for his hoodie and be off to the point and back in a blink of time.

With the roar of the waves as a backdrop, she didn't hear Erik calling her name until she opened the back French doors.

"Ah, there you are. I'm finished with classes for the day. And I did manage to get through to Magena Loring to let her know you wouldn't be coming in. Smart lady, she didn't ask me any questions other than if you were all right. She also relayed that between certain persons in the department and the media it was just as well."

The heavy weight she'd been carrying around gained a few pounds before settling in her midsection. "They are still looking for me then?"

"Well, you and any other info they can get. I tried to warn you."   Erik squatted down reaching out and enfolding Jack into his arms. "There's my good boy. You take good care of our girl, while I was gone?"

Jack's whole body wriggling with pleasure, just about knocked Erik over.

The delight of the whole scene almost diminished the significance of the "our girl" statement. Almost. She wasn't his girl. She wasn't anybody's girl.

"Erik we need to talk. I can't stay here!"

"Why?" He stood to gaze at her with eyes almost as soulful as Jack's. The hurt was written clearly there.

Rhyjl turned and paced across the floor to stand looking out at the cold sea, the blue sky. Anything, but Erik and Jack. "You want something from me I can't give."

"Have I asked anything except to help you?"

The combined sound of his foot treads on the plank floor in harmony with the soft padding and clicking of the puppy's paws, told her they were coming for her. In moments she might weaken. She might accept what he hadn't asked for, but was offering never-the-less.

"Not now, Erik!" She turned to face him down. "Not now and maybe not ever. Please understand we can be friends. I appreciate you helping me. But it can't be more."

"Rhyjl," he reached out to touch her and dropped his hands as she took a step back. "Rhyjl, I understand. Really I do!" he added when he saw she was ready to protest. "And I won't ask any more of you than I already have. But please you can't leave. I don't know why, but something inside of me keeps screaming it's dangerous for you."

"You getting a little psychic on me, are you?"

"No, I don't think that gene is dominant in me. It's a form of intuition, however. Threads of logic that intertwine sometimes to give me a clearer picture. We don't know who this murderer is. We do know that it must be someone with access to the Anthropology department. My guess is that whomever that might be, they are around here. You opened a can of worms when you discovered the bones. I don't know if they were ever supposed to be found or not. What I do know, is they weren't supposed to be found by you or at this time. I just know it. So I'm guessing whomever planted them is not too happy with you right about now. Would you say that is a fair assessment?"

It was. She walked over and plopped, very un-lady like, on the sofa. "I can't stay here forever! Erik, I'll go nuts. There is nothing for me to do here. I feel like I'm in prison."

"No one said anything about forever." He sat as far away as he could on the same sofa. "A few more days. Just a few."

"Ha! What makes you think it is only going to be a few more days?" She pulled her knees close and hugged them to her.

"Alice turned everything we came up with over to Tanner. She called back to say he'd done some checking on a few things. First, you were right about Bannerman's lady. She's not our victim, although she was a victim in another way. She is dead. They were finally able to reach her parent's in Europe. They were there trying to get over her untimely death. It seems she died of a heart attack linked with her anorexia."

Rhyjl's thoughts traveled to the young woman she'd seen in the lab. The one who was frail and lost. She didn't know her. Had never known her. Except for a split second. A vibration. But was that true? That girl had spoken to her. Had interacted with her. Had apologized for Bannerman's behavior, for god's sake. How was that even possible? Did he have another girl? Was he the sadistic type that preyed on women with eating disorders? Her head was spinning. None of this was happening. A tear trickled down the crease between her cheek and nose.

"Did you hear me?" Erik had inched closer. He wanted to reach out. To take her in his arms and stroke that singleton tear. He couldn't though, could he? There was a wall there that he didn't know how to breach and it wasn't just about her unusual ability. It was deeper. He'd like to clear that away, too, but he didn't know if it was in his power to do so. Some things in life were not easily changed.

She dashed the tear roughly away. "Yeah, Melinda is dead from a heart attack."

"No, I'm referring to the information about Dr. Kendricks. She's been taken in for questioning. I guess Tanner is pretty convinced our deceased is Dr. Jennifer Jackson."

"So why take in Kendricks?"

"Well, I don't have all the details, mind you, because Alice doesn't have them all. But, I guess no one has heard from Jennifer Jackson since that symposium that was held in Chicago a few weeks ago."

"But she is married. Didn't her husband report her missing?"

Erik's lips went pencil thin. "Rhyjl, not all married couples … well, not all are close. There can be a lot of reasons. Sometimes, it's just that they have different goals, different interests. Jackson, the husband, is the head of pediatric medicine at one of the hospitals in Austin. It's not like he can go gallivanting around with his wife to Belize. He knew after the conference she intended to fly back down there. He didn't know she was missing until the police informed him. The thing is, her tickets were used. Someone using her name did try to check in to the Chabil Mar in Placencia."

"Someone tried?"

"Well, see that's the thing. I guess this is a very luxurious hotel but not very large. Jackson was a regular and has been for years. When the woman using Jennifer's passport tried to check in using her reservations, the management knew it wasn't her. They asked her to wait while they checked the reservation. They called the police, but by the time the clerk returned to the desk the woman had left."

"So who was it? Didn't they have any kind of surveillance?"

"Yes, but other than a woman with blond hair, there isn't much they could get. She was wearing a sun hat that kept her face partially hidden from the camera."

"Okay, this is all really interesting, but what does it have to do with Kendricks?"

"Well it seems our Dr. Kendricks was also in Belize."

Chapter 13

Revelations

Erik looked one final time at the domestic scene framed on his front porch. An intriguing duo: a woman he couldn't take his mind off and a dog that had pawed a pathway to his heart. Two weeks ago he hadn't even know Rhyjl and Jack existed. Now, he couldn't imagine his life without them. He wished she'd come with him. Wished they were both making the trek to Portland for the day.

He knew she was restless. Even the movie he'd streamed on his computer last night hadn't taken the edge off. If she'd had any more episodes, she hadn't said anything. But then, would she? Had his mother ever struggled like this? He couldn't remember. He didn't think she had. She'd never spoken to his father about it. Was that because it was a private thing? Something so emotional that there were no words to explain it? Or in his mother's case, they had no reason to talk?

Rhyjl had seemed truly puzzled that married couples could be apart for weeks and not speak or even know what the other was about. It wasn't because her parents had an ideal relationship. He didn't need to be clairvoyant to glean that. She hadn't said much. Just a comment here or there. Mostly it was by what she didn't say. She talked about being with her grandmother in Montana. There was a passion for that place and the woman. Never a mention of her parents being there. He wondered which one she'd taken her gift from. Not the grandmother, no. If that had been the case, surely the older woman would have helped her understand. He'd gotten the strong impression that she been mostly on her own in that department.

Prior to the movie, they had spent the evening unpacking boxes from Amazon. They'd assembled the dog crate which Jack inspected dubiously, played tug-o-war and keep-away with the new dog toys. Not the pup. No, the two of them. Jack had loved the bubble wrap until his puppy teeth made it pop. Then feet scrambling, he slid behind Rhyjl for protection. They'd laughed. They'd had fun. Still, there was always that wall. An iron curtain blocking all light as well as movement. Was she aware of it? Did she create it on purpose? He suspected the latter.

*

The car hadn't even made it out of sight before she was regretting her choice. How would it have hurt for her to spend the day with him at friends? It wasn't a life time commitment. Yet, when he'd asked, that's how it had felt. She was surrounded by Erik Arneson. She had his dog, his house, was sleeping in his bed. He'd even set her up with a cell phone and showed her how to use it. But who could she call? Alice? Tanner? Erik? She'd thought about her grandmother, but how would she explain without causing worry?

Last night had been something out of a fantasy. She couldn't remember the last time she had allowed her defenses down enough to frolic and play like an unencumbered child. And talk! Oh my, how they had talked! He shared what his life had been like living in all the foreign places his mother's work had taken them. Reminisced about fantastical adventures with a girl they had taken in and who'd become like a big sister to him. She'd recognized the name accompanied by grinding envy as soon as he'd spoke it. Dr. Ayla Denkel had literally taken over Claire Blackwood's work. It wasn't general knowledge Ayla had gotten her start playing and watching over a boy who saw life as a full out adventure.

She shared her time with her grandmother. While considerably less adventurous than his, she loved her life on the ranch. The open spaces. The freedom to get on her horse and ride for hours. The sky seemed bigger there, the air cleaner, the trees taller. And most of all, less complicated.

She knew he deliberately tried to keep the evening on the light side, including the comedy they'd watched on his computer. They'd both had enough of the mystery by that point or, he at least had sensed that she had.

In spite of his efforts, when it was time for bed, her sleep, like her dreams, became fragmented. At some point, she woke to Sara's voice, a full moon bathing the bedroom in quicksilver and shadows. Had it been Sara's or the murderer's? She might well be done with the mystery, but it was far from done with her. The pain, anger, betrayal and then the deep, deep remorse echoed through all her dreams. The betrayal and remorse were mixed with memories of her own mother. The pain and anger, her own, and too often made manifest with scenes of her father. In one dream, she saw Jack run out into the road to be run over by a speeding car. She woke crying and drenched in sweat. Why had he been out there in harm's way? Why had he been alone! Only dreams, and yet they left their mark by leaving her even more restless than she had been during the day. She wanted to get up and make some tea, but was afraid she might wake Erik. It was then she began to feel her life was too intertwined with him in subtle ways she didn't fully understand.

*

By the time he made I-95 his thoughts had switched lanes as well. Still focused on Rhyjl, but via a different route, his mind kept tripping over something she'd said in passing. They'd been speaking about Maine and how different it was from other places. She'd mentioned a fisherman she'd seen every day out on the point and her concern and admiration for his audacity, even on stormy days. He hadn't given it much thought at the time. And true, he didn't know much about the ways of fishermen, but he kept coming back to the dedication of the man. That thought flitted around the periphery of his musings of other topics he intended to speak with Jim Braxton about.

It was still strange to pull up to the toy strewn yard of the house his old professor and mentor now lived in. Always so neat and orderly, it was odd to imagine he now lived with his niece and her family of three rambunctious boys. But times change. Jim had retired from Boston University about the same time his niece's husband had been killed in Afghanistan. Jim was their only family. It seemed like the right thing to do.

When their mother opened the door, Erik was struck again with her beauty. Trina never aged. She was still the girl he'd thought he might someday marry. Of course he had only been twelve and she four years his senior.

"Erik! As usual you're late!" She admonished while shaking her well-manicured finger in front of his nose. Her smile belied the scolding and was one of delight.

"I couldn't let you think I'd changed," he teased. "You don't know how many odd looks I got from your neighbors down the block when I parked there for the last half hour."

"Unca Ek!" a towheaded sprout wrapped his arms around Erik's legs. "You bing me sumpun?"

"Um," Erik pulled the large white sack out from behind his back feeling like an underdressed Santa. "I think there might be something in here with your name."

When packages had all been handed out, hugs and thank yous exchanged and boy's dispersed to play with their new toys, Trina led him to her uncle's den while she went to get the lunch started.

"My boy!" Jim Braxton hefted himself out of his chair and wrapped big bear arms around his favorite pupil. "So glad you could make it. I can guess from the commotion followed by silence you must have brought the boys more toys. Just what they need." He shook his head and returned to his chair. "Sit. Sit and tell me what's going on in your neck of the woods and what's your involvement?"

Erik's discourse kept mainly to the facts. A friend had taught a class and while doing so, had found discrepancies amid the specimens. She reported it and, well, he got caught up in it.

"And your relationship with this friend?"

"She's just a friend. She's in need of help."

The old man shook his head again and had the same twinkle in his eye as when he'd remarked on the excess of toys. "Always the Boy Scout, hey! I think I know better."

"Okay, yes, I'd like it to be more, but she's not ready."

"And you think that when you help get her through this she will be?"

"Possibly. I don't know. What I do know is that because of her, I'm caught up in it as well. It's been interesting puzzling it out and even helping out the Medical Examiner and cops."

"Well, you always were one for a good mystery or puzzle." Jim folded his hands over his belly and leaned back. "Your email was a bit cryptic, but you think this has something to do with some scandal around ten years back?"

Erik got up from the chair he'd been sitting in to walk over to the window. It looked out on nothing more than neighboring houses, but it wasn't the view he was focused on. "I think it has to do with—and keep in mind this isn't to leave this room—a woman named Jennifer Matheson.

"Ah yes, bad doing that was. A young and promising woman many said. She was working on her PhD and claimed her two mentors stole it and published it as their own."

"Let me guess, the mentors were Kendricks and McClellen?"

Jim nodded. "It came mostly down to their word over her's. Yes, they admitted that her thesis was very close to their work and not by coincidence. They claimed plagiarism. They had plenty of documentation to back them up.   Then the girl claimed she had an ongoing affair with McClellen. It wasn't taken seriously. By that time people saw her as just grasping at any ol' straw."

"And your thoughts?" Erik turned to gage Jim's

demeanor.

"I don't know. I didn't really know any of them well. The girl not at all. Oh, I'd heard plenty of rumors about Kendricks. As I told you in my note, she was always known for a bad attitude. But, she publishes regularly and her work seems solid. That's her reputation. McClellen? Well, he's an odd duck. Young, brash! He's been known as a chance taker, often going about things in an unorthodox way. For all of his idiosyncratic methods, his work is exceptional, as you might guess, or he wouldn't be where he is now."

*

Rhyjl pulled up the Archaeological Institute of America website and scanned the different symposia and conferences listed. She found the conference Erik had discovered earlier. It was unusual because it was done in conjunction with BAAS or the Belize Archaeology and Anthropology Symposium. The key speakers were all known for their work in the Caribbean and especially on the Mayan culture. The topic was Intercultural Traditions and was hosted in Chicago by the University of Illinois Urbana.

What were the chances?

Rhyjl went to the closet and pulled out the green hoodie she'd seen yesterday. Jack, immediately on the alert, jumped up from his cozy new dog bed thinking it was time for his walk.

"Okay a quick one, but then you're going to have to kennel. I've got some things to do and you can't come with me."

She ran the dog for a few minutes, but didn't play

with him as she usually did. Her mind kept going over comments Sara had made over the last few months. She had to get back to the cottage. The answers were there, she knew it.

Jack was not in the least happy about being locked up in his crate. She could hear his pitiful howling until she made the first dip beyond the back yard. Then it was drown out by the surf crashing on the rocks below.

It didn't take her long. She didn't run into anyone on the path and it didn't appear there was anyone interested in looking in her direction when she did notice others milling around outside of Main. Soon she was enclosed in the dwarfed wind-torqued pines. From there it was a quick shot to the fork that would take her to the cottages or continue along the cliff.

Either the news people had given up or had found someone else to harass for there was no sign of them. She slipped cautiously in the back door of the kitchen. No one was home. The place was a complete and total disaster looking for all the world like a tornado has passed through. What had Sara done!

Going to her room, she found all her drawers turned out, the sheets and blankets torn from the bed. Someone had turned everything inside out, but why? Sara wouldn't have done this. Were members of the media this crude? She didn't want to take time to figure it out. Who knows they might come back.

Sara's room didn't look any different than the usual mess which further confirmed that she had been the target and it hadn't been random. Sara's laptop sat on the dresser next her massive collection of makeup and jewelry. Rhyjl booted it up and waited. While the machine whined to life she kept an ear out for any sound. It was then she realized she hadn't seen any evidence of Stormy. Calling softly, she went back into the main room. His bowl sat empty. A growing uneasiness settled in the pit of her stomach.

It didn't take long to find the email confirming the air travel to Chicago. She had remembered correctly that Sara had gone to Chicago the same week of the Conference. Her finger was paused to tap on the pad closing out the mailbox when her eye caught an address for @austinutexas.edu. She opened it and read: *I've sent the last file as requested and I still haven't heard anything back from you. We had a deal and I expect you to keep up your end. I'll be traveling to Chicago for the show. Will love watching Kendricks' face when you take her down.*

"Oh my god, Sara, what have you done?"

*

Trina put on a great spread for lunch and endured the good natured teasing by Jim that Erik should come more often so PB and J sandwiches would get a break. He spent a little time with each boy and the gifts he'd given them. Jason and Jon took to their new tablets like fish to water. And it was slightly embarrassing when Jeremy, the four-year-old beat him unmercifully at go fish.

He and Jim talked about Erik's pet project until the same old argument broke out about Erik starting his own company. And then it was time to wind it up. "Before I go, I have two questions. Are there any of Mom's old friends around that still do underwater archaeology?

"Um, let me think. Chris … Chris? Oh hell, it's tough getting old. He used to work out of University of Mass, Amerhurst. Botsaris! Yes, Christou Botsaris. I don't know if he is still working. We, ah, kind of lost track after, well … What do you want to know that for?"

"I'm playing a hunch."

"With other people, that would mean gambling of some sort. You don't gamble. What's up your sleeve you aren't telling me?"

Erik explained about the fisherman's odd behavior and the theory that had been formulating on his drive down.

"Does this friend of yours, well, is she like your mother?"

It wasn't Erik's place to tell. That choice belonged to Rhyjl.

Jim stood and patted Erik's left shoulder with his right hand. "I'll take your silence as a yes, and don't worry. I'll keep it the same way I did your mother's. That's only one question. You said you had two."

Erik had wondered about it from time to time throughout the years. His relationship with Rhyjl had brought it to the forefront again. "After being around here for the day and remembering all the time and patience you had with Trina and me while we were growing up, it's obvious you love kids. Why didn't you ever marry?"

"Erik, you already know that answer. There was only one woman on this earth for me."

*

She heard the car drive up, the door slam and the crunch of the gravel on the path. There had been just enough time to close down Sara's computer and make for the back door. Fortunately, Sara, well she assumed it was Sara, had closed all the curtains.

"Rhyjl?" The bang against the door had to be an

object. It was too heavy to be someone's hand. "You can't hide forever. We need to talk." Another crack reverberated. "Do you hear me?"

Oh, I hear you, Kendricks, Rhyjl thought as she eased out the back door and headed down the path.

So Sara had sabotaged Kendricks by using Jennifer. But how had she found out about Jennifer in the first place? A more cunning and malevolent thought eventuated. Had Jennifer been biding her time all these many years waiting like a spider for just the right person, the precise circumstance? A dissatisfied student, someone she could corrupt somehow? But how would she know? There must be someone on campus who kept her informed. Someone who had their finger on the pulse of what was happening. Quickly dismissing the name that leapt to the forefront, she hurried down the path. It could be any number of people. As Erik had said, it was a small campus and it had been even smaller when Jennifer had been here. Engrossed in her thoughts, she didn't realize she had missed the fork back to Erik's and was almost to the promontory until she heard the restless roar of the waves.

What was she to do now? Should she head back to Erik's and wait for him to get home? He said he expected to get back around this time. She needed to reach Tanner. Dumb, dumb, dumb! Why hadn't she thought to bring the cell phone Erik had given her? Because she wasn't used to having one. Because she didn't think she needed it. In her mind, she could see it sitting on the counter back in Erik's kitchen, where she had pushed it aside like a moldy cracker.

She stared out at the islands. She saw the fisherman wave. She neither saw nor heard any answer to her dilemma. And then she did hear the faintest sound over the waves, over her troubled thoughts. A snap.

The explosion across her back sent her reeling out into open space. Her arms pin wheeling frantically found no hold. The water was black! So very, very black. Her scream dying in her throat as the waves slammed then swallowed her whole.

Light exploded out of darkness. She felt strong arms lift her from the deep. His voice rough. "Not your time, lass. He comes for you."

*

Erik called the cell phone for the seventh or eighth time. Still there was no answer! Where the hell could she be for all this time or was she just ignoring it? Driving past the cottages he realized the media had given up residency. But there was someone at Rhyjl's. He didn't recognize the vehicle. Possibly one lone sadistic bastard still hoping his prey would show up. Well, he could wait until hell froze over except it wasn't a he. The woman came around from the back of the house and she wasn't looking too happy. Erik punched speed dial again.

Soon as he pulled in to his drive and parked the car, he heard Jack's wolf-like baying. Taking the steps two at a time, he threw himself at the door. Jack's howl diminished to a whine. Why was he kenneled? "Rhyjl! Rhyjl!" His stomach knotting, he ran to his room hoping against hope she was sleeping, maybe even having one of her episodes. Anything was preferable to what his vivid imagination was conjuring. There was only one logical reason she'd have locked Jack up. She'd gone somewhere she didn't want him to accompany her. But where? Jack's incessant whine was gaining in volume. "Okay, okay, I'll let you out while I try to think."

As Erik unlatched the kennel door, the pup leapt past flying toward the French doors. His paws skidding, he careened crashing so hard into the doors, it was a wonder he didn't break the glass or his own bloody neck. "Whoa, give me a second, boy!" Erik scrambled after him, reached the double glass doors, opened one, and had a repeat performance minus the crash. Jack flew down the stairs straight for the path.

The headlong dash swept them precariously along the trail, past Main and into the woods. In spite of the adrenalin rush, Erik was flagging. When they reached the fork, the puppy paused just long enough for Erik to gulp air into his burning lungs. Then, they were off on another chase straight to the overlook. Of course! Her favorite place!

They rounded a corner breaking into the open. Hope failed along with his diminished stamina. Leaning over, hands on his knees, drawing ragged breaths that didn't seem to fill his need for oxygen, he watched the puppy pace back and forth near the cliff's edge, nose to the ground. She'd been here. The puppy had her scent, but they must have just missed her. She might be at her cottage. He thought of the blond woman he'd seen earlier. Had Rhyjl been waiting the intruder out in order to get in and get her things? Is that why she'd left Jack kenneled? It was hard to be stealthy with a fifty pound bundle of energy at your side.

"Jack, boy, she's not here. Come Jack, come!"

Jack was having none of it. Coming to a stop at the edge, he let loose with sharp, demented barking.

"Jack she's not here! Come on!

Straightening from his tripod pose, he watched in

horror as Jack vanished over the precipice!

Erik ran to the edge. Miraculously, the pup was working his way from boulder to boulder. "Crazy dog!" He breathed. His momentary relief, however, was short lived as he saw Jack's objective. Her face half hidden, the waves tossing her legs as they ebbed and flowed. She was dead! Oh, God! Noooooooooooo!

Chapter 14

Taking the Fall

Tanner was the first on the scene. He called to Erik as he worked his way down the uneven bank of stones.

"She's alive, but barely. I've haven't moved her. I don't know what's broken!" Erik shouted to his inquiry.

By the time Tanner reached the man, dog, and woman, he wasn't holding out much hope she would remain that way. It was written plainly on his face. Erik held a struggling Jack back as Tanner lifted the coat Erik had stripped from himself to cover her back. He winced, then let it gently fall back over the wound.

"She's not doing so well. But I'm no doctor." Tanner paused, and looked back up the climb he'd just descended. "The paramedics should be here shortly. How'd you find her?"

"Jack, our dog. He found her."

Tanner raised an eyebrow. "So you are the boyfriend?"

"We're friends, yes."

A loud commotion of voices and clattering overhead drew their attention. "Down here!" Tanner yelled.

From that point on, it was a nightmare played out in slow motion. The paramedic and the two EMTs helping, were solemn to say the least, as they called out thready vitals and negligible shakes of their heads. The Sheriff stood at the top raining questions down upon his deputy's head, who was scribbling notes and taking mental calculations.

Erik could have told him the length of the fall and rate of descent, if the man had bothered to ask. He'd calculated it again and again, trying to hold on to sanity while waiting for the help he'd thought would never come. Each breath she took was a fine thread of promise he clung desperately to.

"Mr. Arneson? Sir?"

Erik looked up expecting to see his father. Why was he here? Except Arvid Arneson wasn't there.   Tanner was addressing him. Was looking at him expectantly.

"Doctor. Dr. Arneson." Erik corrected.

"Sorry, Dr. Arneson. I was told Ms. Martin was staying with you. Is that correct?"

"Yes, Alice, I mean Dr. Merks and I thought it was best until all the hullabaloo died down."

"So you weren't concerned for her wellbeing other than the media circus?"

"No, I mean yes."

"Which is it," Tanner pressed.

Erik had taken off his belt to make a makeshift lead for Jack, yet he still knelt beside the animal on the cold stones, his hands wound in the thick fur. Releasing Jack, but not the lead, the pup made a lunge toward Rhyjl. Erik rose to his feet bringing the dog up short.   "Both. At first it was to keep her away for the press. Later, I became concerned that she might be in more danger."

"Can you tell me why?"

"Her discovery had upset a lot of people. It had opened up a Pandora's Box from the past. The more we dug up, well, the more I was afraid we might be treading on some people's feet."

"Which is one of the reasons, amateurs like yourself shouldn't be messing with an official investigation."

Erik's rebuttal was so vitriolic, the detective actually took a step back. "Don't lecture me, Detective! You wouldn't have half the clues if Rhyjl, Alice and I hadn't been spoon feeding them to you."

"You don't have much faith in the law do you?"

"None! If you'd been doing your job, she wouldn't be here right now!"

"If you and she had let us do our job, she wouldn't be here right now."

It was easily escalating into a testosterone show down. Tanner was tough. Erik was tiring. "We might not work as quickly as you all would like, but my methods are solid and when I close a case, it's air tight. Not full of innuendo and suppositions."

"Innuendo? Suppositions!" Erik could feel the cords in his neck bulging. Another trait he'd seen in his father more times than he cared to remember. "*She* discovered a murder victim. *She* told you it was a woman, before Alice even had time to check the remains out! *She* gave us names and leads to follow! Not *you*, Detective! *HER!*"

Jack was emitting a low rumble deep in his throat. His body was wound tight and blocked next to Erik. He might be afraid of a popping plastic bubble, but there was no fear now. It was as if the puppy was drawing bravery from Erik's energy.

Tanner didn't so much as twitch. "Yes, she did give us all those, but let me add, those things would have all eventually come to light if you and your girlfriend hadn't played detective. The one exception being the initial discovery."

"Sir?" One of the EMTs broke in. "We are ready to transport if you two wouldn't mind moving."

*

Lifeflight of Maine took off just as the sun was turning the tops of the trees to liquid gold. Cameras flashed and at one point, Erik thought he had shoved a reporter in the face. Tanner had been joined by Alice. Was it a good thing she was here or a bad? His mind was in frequency hopped spread spectrum mode. Tanner was leading him to a blue sedan. Was he under arrest? Alice had taken control of Jack and was only steps behind.

"No comment! No comment!" She and Tanner chorused.

When the doors shut, the motor started, and Jack's head drooped into his lap. Erik looked in the rearview mirror and caught Tanner's eye. "Where are they taking her?"

"Maine General in Augusta."

"I've got to get there!"

"Slow down champ." Tanner slowed and hit the siren. Two more news vans grudgingly gave way. "She's in good hands and my guess is she'll be tied up in surgery for quite a while."

"Take us to his house, Mike," Alice's hand reached in Tanner's direction. "He can get cleaned up, I'll help him figure out what to do with Jack here, and then I'll ride with him in to the hospital."

"I'm not sure that is the best idea, Alice. You've seen the feeding frenzy. Back at his place you are liable to get swarmed. I think I should take him straight to headquarters."

"Oh yeah, brilliant idea, Mike. I can see it now, Erik Arneson, heir to the Arneson fortune arrested for murder!"

"But he's not!" Tanner argued.

"Yes, well, tell that to the press. We all know how accurate their reporting ethics are when it comes to headlines."

"I want to go to the hospital." Erik interjected, in case anyone was interested.

"We will, Erik, but first we need to get you into a hot shower and dry clothing. You're soaked, chilled and covered in blood."

Erik looked down at his soiled attire. He'd torn a large hole in his pants climbing down to Rhyjl. His knees were soaked from kneeling on the tide swept rocks. His hands were still covered in blood, her blood, and so was his shirt where they had rubbed while taking off his jacket. The jacket he'd laid over her to try to keep the last of her body heat from escaping. Where was it now? It didn't matter. He'd get another.

"Besides there's Jack to consider. While you are getting cleaned up, I'll contact a veterinarian friend of mine and see if she can board him for a day or two."

"I don't want him boarded!" He knew he was sounding like a petulant child, but the idea of leaving Jack in some strange place after what had happened. Well, it just didn't seem right.

"She's right, you can't take the dog with you to the hospital and I get the impression you won't be spending much time with him for at least the next twenty four hours. So unless you've got some other idea, the vet sounds like a good bargain."

"It'll just be for the night, Erik. I can pick him up tomorrow, or you can, after we know she's out of the woods."

So his life was being planned for him just as it had been following his mother's death. Go here. Do this. It will all be for the best, you'll see. No matter how well intended, it hadn't set well with him at the age of sixteen and it sure as hell wasn't sitting well with him now. Just as it had been then, however, it was now. He couldn't see any viable alternative.

*

Tanner had been reluctant to leave. Erik surmised it had more to do with his concern for Alice than for him. They had a thing going and it wasn't limited to their professional relationship. The media was camped at his door, but at least Alice was right. He wouldn't be tarred as the villain. Victim, however? Yeah, Erik Arneson, victim. He didn't need Alice to interpret that headline. *Son of Slain Archaeologist Wrapped Up In Second Archaeological Mystery.*

He went through the movements. Showered, changed and fed, the last being somewhat dubious. Was beer part of the food group? Malted barley, hops and brewer's yeast. It should qualify. He grabbed a fist full of tortilla chips.

Alice was sitting on the sofa. She'd fed Jack and now he was content to sit at her feet. "Did you get something to eat or should I make something for you?"

"Yep," He held up the chips. "What about you?"

"I grabbed some of those as well." She confessed.

"Then we're good to go?"

"I called Dr. Swarsky. She's expecting us. She'll keep Jack at her kennels rather than at the office. He should fit in just fine. She raises Newfoundlands. Has he had his shots?

"I'm afraid I haven't gotten around to that yet. Been kind of busy." Erik braced himself before opening the door and looked at her with a question.

"Right. I guessed as much and told her to give him the once over."

Alice nodded. The door swung open. Blinded by lights, they and the dog fought their way to the Tesla.

They lost some of their entourage at Swarsky's. The rest dropped off one by one. Erik wasn't a fool. They knew where he was headed and had more than likely phoned ahead alerting their team waiting at Maine General.

For the second time that day, Erik was speeding along highway 3 on his way to Augusta, his mind racing over all the different outcomes this day could bring. Alice had interjected thoughts of her own from time to time: a comment about the heavy traffic, something else about a good restaurant they could all go to when this was over. It was meant to distract him. To take his mind from those furtive glances the EMTs had passed between each other and the paramedic. He appreciated her attempts. He just wished he could dispel the gut feeling that he was the only one who really believed she could pull through. She had to! He could see no alternative.

By the time they reached South China and joined with 202 and 9, the car's GPS digital readout showed another twenty five minutes travel time. Those remaining minutes seemed interminable. How long since the medical team had taken off with her in the helicopter? The drive by car was just short of two hours. Had the copter cut that by half? He and Alice had lost maybe forty minutes all totaled. By his calculations that meant she'd been in surgery for the last hour. He continued to crunch the numbers as the miles ticked by. A slow driver. A stop light. Seconds lost. Long, long seconds.

Tanner and the media were waiting for them as they pulled into the visitors parking. He and five uniformed officers escorted them past the doors into a private waiting room off the surgical floor. When they closed the outside world out, and left uniforms outside the door to keep it that way, Tanner turned to Erik. "I'm doing this as a courtesy, you understand?"

Alice, sensing the tension, thanked him and asked the question they all needed to hear.

"I'll tell you what I know. She's in pretty serious condition. Several broken bones, a concussion, numerous contusions. They've got the internal bleeding under control and fortunately even though it looked really nasty, the knife didn't cause any serious damage. She's one tough and lucky lady. They told me to expect several more hours in surgery. Then she'll be in ICU. There's always a chance of infection and evidently she took in a lot of water. They'll have to monitor closely for pneumonia."

Tanner set his hand on the door handle then paused. "Erik, you said you hadn't moved her, correct?"

"Yes, I left her the way I found her. I was afraid if I moved her, I might do more damage. Why?"

"That's what has been bothering me. See, it's all wrong. If she'd fallen where you found her, she wouldn't have survived the rocks. As broken up as she is, she didn't land on them. My guess, especially after they found so much water in her lungs, is that she hit the water."

"But that would mean that someone moved her back on shore." Alice who had been pouring two cups of coffee from a glass pot, joined them. Offering one cup to Erik and a second to Tanner, she said, "If that's true, then why leave without getting help? Unless, it was the killer."

"No benefit." Erik took the coffee, nodded his head in gratitude and pocketed his Turritella agate. It had been his talisman since his mother had given it to him their last time together. "If they had wanted her dead, and clearly they had, then why pull her out of the water and leave her breathing?"

Tanner refused the cup in kind with a gracious smile and shake of his head. "That's pretty much my thinking as well. We have a third party involved. A witness, who it seems, may be responsible for saving her life. A witness that for some reason doesn't want to be known."

*

Hours ticked by. They drank coffee until Erik was sure his eyeballs were swimming in it. Alice immersed herself in her Kindle, only surfacing to make bathroom breaks or start the coffee maker for the umpteenth time. He checked through his e-mail on his phone, returned a couple inquiries from students and wrote a thank you to Trina. He didn't even need to check the time to know the eleven o'clock news had aired, when a call came through from his father. He ignored it and the four that followed, but picked a fifth one up from Jim.

The headlines Jim related were pretty much what he had expected except the one from MSNBC. *Arneson heir held for questioning in brutal attack on college co-ed.*

He assured his old friend and mentor that, yes, there had been an attack on the young woman they had discussed earlier, but in no way was he being held or a suspect. "I came home from your place and found her. No, we don't know much else at this time. Yeah, I'm pretty shaken. I'll let you know more tomorrow."

*

"Alice?"

"Um?" She didn't bother to look up from the Kindle.

"I think I may have seen the murderer."

The Kindle dropped to her lap. "What? Did you just say you saw the murderer?"

"Yeah." Erik stretched his arms above his head and stood. His limbs were stiff and sore. "She was at Rhyjl's this afternoon."

"But why didn't you say something earlier? You need to tell Tanner."

"Tell me what?" Tanner walked in, located the coffee, picked up the pot and set it down with a grimace.

"Erik thinks he saw the murderer at Rhyjl's!"

"That so, Doctor?" The detective scrubbed a hand over tired eyes. "When were you going to tell me this?"

"With everything going on, it slipped my mind. Besides, I don't have proof, and I thought you weren't interested in speculation, Detective."

"I'm not. What I am interested in is what possible witnesses might have seen."

"When you finish your hair splitting guys, would Erik elaborate, please?" Alice put the Kindle on the table. She then picked up the pot, emptied the dregs to make some fresh.

"On my way home today, I passed by Rhyjl's to see what vultures might be hanging around. I saw a white GMC Terrain parked out front."

For a split second Tanner's passive expression clouded. "Go on. Anything in particular stand out about the vehicle? You wouldn't have happened to get a license number by any chance?"

"Nope." Erik shook his head. "I assumed it was just a stubborn reporter until I saw the older blond woman coming from the back of the cottage."

Tanner was fully engaged, a hound who had finally gotten the scent. "Can you describe her?"

Erik shut his eyes and bowed his head. "Medium height. Five-five, five-six. Weight—a little harder to tell—but I'd guess maybe a hundred forty or fifty. Blond shoulder length hair."

"How old?" Tanner and Merks said in unison.

"Now that's really hard for me."

"Narrow it down.   Twenty, thirty, sixty?" Tanner pulled his phone from his pocket and was tapping away.

"I'd say somewhere between forty and fifty. Could be sixty. Women are good at covering up their ages."

"Don't look at me when you say that." Alice glared at him.

"Anything else you can tell me about her? What she was wearing?"

"Pants, coat. I think the coat was beige or light brown. The pants were red, no, more of a wine color."

"You said this afternoon. What time specifically?"

"Maybe about twenty or thirty minutes before I found Rhyjl and called 911.

I don't remember much more, other than she was

really angry."

"How do you know that?" Tanner pressed. "You didn't talk to her, did you?"

"The look on her face. The way she walked. She was fit to kill." It took Erik a moment after Alice's quick intake of air, to realize what he'd said. But it was true. Whoever the woman was, she was out for blood.

"Oh, Erik!" Alice moved to embrace him in a hug. "I think you just solved the mystery."

They stood in silence as Tanner placed the call. "Tanner. I want a BOLO out on Doctor Amanda Kendricks."

Chapter 15

Fortune's Hand

"The doctors say you can come home at the beginning of next week." Alice moved one of the numerous bouquets that had arrived over the last couple of days. "Well, what I mean is, back to Erik's. He's arranged for you to have in home care."

"I can't, Alice! He's already done *too* much for me, flying Grandmum out, paying the hospital bills."

"And you will continue to let him because this isn't about you."

"What do you mean, not about me? Cripes it's me we are talking about, here. My bills, my life, my grandmother."

"No, dear, it's about him. He's doing this because he needs to, just as he needs to breathe. You are a very lucky girl to find someone like him. I hope you know that."

"But I don't want him. I was never looking for him." Well, at least the last statement was true. The jury was still out on the first. When she thought she was dying, her last thoughts were of Erik. She thought it was his strong arms lifting her from the water. She knew it was him who would find her. He was her first thought upon waking in the ICU. She'd been hurt and yes, angry that he wasn't there until a nurse explained that only family were allowed.

"Whatever you say." Alice moved a few cards and poured fresh water into the Rhyjl's cup. "Here." She offered the cup to Rhyjl.

Sipping on the straw and wincing because her throat was still raw from the tubes they'd only taken out the day before, she knew Alice didn't believe her. What did it matter? She didn't like this conversation or the direction she felt everyone was pushing her in, including Grandmum. "So tell me again about Kendricks. Did they really arrest her?"

"She had the means, the motive and was in all the right places at the right time. I'd say it's pretty much a closed case even though she is screaming she is innocent to high heaven. She even had the murder weapon in her lab. Forensics found both Jennifer's blood and yours on the blade.

Rhyjl forced herself to breathe remembering the cold heat slamming between her shoulders.

"Sorry," Alice grimaced, her demeanor crumbling when she realized her faux pas. "I shouldn't have said that."

Rhyjl would have laughed had it not hurt to do so. "It's okay. Occupational hazard for people in our lines of work. Remind me to tell you someday about the Thanksgiving I ruined my junior year when I went into great detail on the evidence of abuse and illnesses apparent in the poor bird's bones."

"Oh, god, you didn't!" Alice laughed.

"I did."

"You've got it bad, haven't you?"

"'Fraid so. Never was invited back to that friend's house again."

"Oh? Why?"

Rhyjl joined Alice in the laughter despite the pain. It was good to be alive. To talk of ordinary, or maybe not so ordinary things.

Erik, standing at the door watching, was awash with pleasure. Two days ago this moment wouldn't have been possible. The majority of the blunt force trauma of hitting the water had caused extensive damage to her right side. With both her arm and leg in casts and elevated, tubes coming out of her throat and just about every other part of her torso, Rhyjl had been limited to tapping on the tablet Alice had brought in. The miracle of her voice and laughter was worth more than all his money could ever have bought him.

"Private joke or can anyone join in?"

"Erik!" Alice reached out to him and pecked his cheek when he came to her. "I didn't expect to see you until later today."

"My new TA took the lab today. He's coming along quite nicely. Smart, imaginative. He'll go far. How's our girl?"

"Great!" Alice leaned in closely to his ear as if giving him another kiss and whispered, "Feisty!" When she pulled away, she continued, "Doctor Zorski said he thinks she will be ready to go home next week."

"Really? That's great news! Maggie will be thrilled to hear."

"Um, excuse me! I am here!"

"Yes, indeed you are!" Erik left Alice's side and moved to take Rhyjl's hand. "I see you have more well-wishers. There's at least three new flower arrangements."

"Yes, we're going to have to get a bigger room for her if this keeps up. There's even one from your family, Erik. It's the big oriental arrangement ... Is there something wrong?"

"Nothing." Erik would have thrown the damn thing

out the window. What the hell was his father up to now? Hadn't he told Arvid to go to hell when he'd gotten tired of his cell playing the theme from Dracula? "I'm just surprised."

"The card was signed by someone named Ingrid." Rhyjl offered. "Didn't you tell me that's your grandmother's name?" The tension remained even though he forced a smile. The lips were thinner, less generous. His eyes lacked their earlier mirth.

"You've a good memory. Yes, Ingrid. Named after her favorite actress or so she thought."

"One of my favorites as a kid." Alice interjected. "What? Why do I feel like I've grown two noses? We are talking about Ingrid Bergman, right? I've seen her and Humphrey Bogart in every movie they ever produced."

When Erik cocked an eyebrow and Rhyjl raven winged two, Alice added, "Yes, well, I guess I'll be moving on and leave you to talk. I'll be back this evening. Maybe I'll even sneak in some good Ben & Jerry's instead of the stuff they have here. Later!" Grabbing her coat, she was out the door.

"You don't like old movies," Erik took off his new Merino Shearling jacket that arrived from Orvis the day before.

"I don't think I've watched many. We didn't own a TV while I was growing up. You?"

"Had one in just about every room of the house. But I was usually too busy building models or …"

"Or Korebe in the villages of Turkey?" Rhyjl smiled.

"You were listening!" That pleased him. "Yes, Korebe until I was about ten, then Aslik when I got older."

"Do you ever think of going back?"

"I do go back quite often, as a matter of fact. Ayla and I are still quite close."

"And do you still play Aslik?"

"No, I'm not into gambling or fortune telling these days. However, I did play a hunch the other day and it paid off. It's what I wanted to share with you today. I think you'll be very pleased."

"Erik, I, I don't want to throw cold water on your enthusiasm, but I can't continue to take funds from you I have no hope of repaying. Alice already informed me of your plans to pay for my continuing care. I'm sure I can get help from the state of Maine."

Erik's yawn was cavernous. "You finished?"

"Am I boring you?" she snapped.

"Look, Rhyjl, you don't owe me a thing."

"That's what Alice said."

"But," he held up his hand. "If you did, as of next week, you'll have more than enough to pay me back if you insist."

"Psychiatric ward, I believe is two floors up. Erik. You should check in."

He looked like a kid at the circus. "Remember the fisherman?"

She wrinkled her forehead then a slight nod.

"Well, I had a friend of my mother's do a little underwater snooping. He's a Maritime Archaeologist named is Christou Botsaris. He found something very interesting and since it was your idea, you own the largest share of the treasure. Christou's rough guess is that it will probably add up to several million, give or take. Of course the government will probably take their unfair share."

"Treasure? Several million? Now, I know you've lost it. Are you trying to tell me that the fisherman was looking for Crossbones Jack's treasure and you had some friend of your mother's get the jump on him?"

"Well, in a way. My theory is that old Crossbones and Captain Archambeau were one in the same."

"There's a lot of people who think that, Erik. It's nothing new."

"No, probably not, but I think your fisherman and Captain Archambeau are also one in the same. I think he was out there every day with his treasure. Think on it for a minute or two. The good captain would have needed a secure place to stash his booty. On that, every treasure hunter agrees. But where would be safe while remaining accessible? Our captain is no fool. Hide it on land or on his property, someone is bound to find it, especially if he has to disturb the ground each and every time he wants access. Put it in the ocean, now. Secure it with a chain to a rock. A chain he can use to pull it to him. When he is finished fishing out some gold or a jewel or two, he rows out a few hundred feet and drops the chest back over the side. That chain would eventually, years after his death, rust away leaving very little if any remnants, or clues."

"I still don't understand. Sure underwater archaeology isn't my specialty, but wood rots. Sea creatures destroy and corrupt. Iron, as you pointed out turns to rust. How was there anything to find?"

"I don't have all the answers. Let's just leave it that Dr. Christou Botsaris is one of the best in his field. He knew what to look for and he found it! Why are you making this so difficult? You are a wealthy young woman."

Why was she making it difficult? Could she really be wealthy or was this some elaborate trick of Erik's to alleviate her guilt for taking his money? Perhaps this was all a dream? "I'm sorry, Erik. This is just too fantastical to be real!"

"Say's the lady who talks with bones."

"Then prove it to me. Bring me evidence I can see or feel."

"There will be time for that later. Dr. Botsaris will continue to work the area until it gets just too cold. He's become quite intrigued and wants to see if he can come up with anything else that he can use in a paper. It seems he has always been interested in numerous claims that pirates sought refuge in the northern colonies when things got too treacherous down the south. According to Christou, pirates at one time were more than welcomed in places such as Boston and Newport. The colonies were poor. Pirates brought and spent cold hard cash. There are even legends that William Kidd and Blackbeard were frequent players amid New England's jagged coastline ..."

Rhyjl lay there trying to grasp how her whole life might change if what he'd said was true. The rest of the time, she spent half listening to his discourse. Erik was either a fabulous actor or he really believed the story he was weaving. He finally wound down when the nurse came in to offer her more pain meds.

"She'll sleep now." was the nurses' polite way of telling him to get lost. He knew it was true, though he hated to leave. Now was a good time, however, to find her grandmother, he'd left shopping at the mall. At least Maggie was more than happy to use the cell he'd purchased for Rhyjl. They'd grab a bite to eat and then come back to visit after Rhyjl woke again.

*

Her dreams were confused. One minute she was on a pirate's ship, the fisherman calling out orders to a motley crew, except when he turned to face her, the fisherman was Erik. Then it was Erik at the helm of a Viking ship that was loaded with pilfered loot. "All yours, just for you!" He kept pointing to the gold and jewel encrusted cups and crosses. Then Sara was there in the ship telling her to wake up. Except the ship was a room, a hospital room and she couldn't move.

"Rhyjl, wake up!"

"Sara?" Her roommate's face slid into focus and out again. "Why?"

"Why am I here? I would think that was obvious. You know too much, Rhyjl. But then you always were the smart one. I knew it would only be a matter of time before you started putting the pieces together."

What was Sara talking about? What pieces? She didn't have any treasure.

"Oh hell, you're drugged. I wanted so much for you to understand. I didn't start out to kill anyone. She was no better than Kendricks in the end. I met her in her hotel room after I'd watched Kendricks almost have a stroke at the presentation. Oh, you should have been there. It was glorious! But then you see, Dr. Jackson couldn't have pulled it off without me. She owed me and she was trying to cheat me. I carry a knife in my pocket when I'm traveling. Never know when you might need to use it. Jackson laughed, Rhyjl. Said she didn't owe me a thing. The knife was in my hand before I even realized it and all I really wanted to do was to stop her from laughing, and then of course, I had to stop her from screaming. I wouldn't have had to stab you at the point and shove you over if you hadn't been snooping. I saw you through the window. Using my computer. That's when I was sure you'd begun to figure it out. Well that and the fact you hadn't come home. You never stay away from home, Rhyjl. Or did you stay away because little Cinder Rhyjl has finally found her prince? So Sad. Too late. Because now I'll just have to kill you again. The second time is easier. No, this will be my third time."

Had the whole world gone mad? First Erik and now Sara? Or was this all some hallucination more insane than pirate ships and Viking loot? Those were dreams. She'd known that even while they were happening. This was a nightmare and her eyes were open.

"You know the sad thing? You'll never get to appreciate my cleverness, Rhyjl" Sara's laugh was brittle like icicles.

"Don't worry. You probably won't feel much. I started researching methods as soon as you survived your fall into the sea. Lucky Rhyjl. Luck and brains. Everything I always wanted. Everything my parents wanted. But no. My brother has luck and brains like you. You've heard me talk about how he gets everything he wants. Never Sara! Until now. Clever, clever Sara. I did it all on my own. I made Kendricks pay. She'll go to prison for this you know. They even think she tried to kill you. Not part of my plan, but it still works."

She tried to speak. Her lips were dry, her tongue unruly. Something like chalk, no, old cloth.

"Did you like the way I made the bones look aged, Rhyjl. Tannic acid. I must have used over two hundred tea bags. I couldn't believe how fast you picked up on that. *I* was supposed to find them and cleverly make it look like Kendricks hid them in the lab. She played into my hand so beautifully. I didn't expect her to fly to Belize. We were on the same flight, you know. I'd used makeup to make myself an older Jennifer. Thank, god, for all those theater classes I took as a freshman and sophomore. I died my hair blond, used her tickets and passport. Kendricks even looked twice at me as we were boarding, but didn't make any connections. Those stupid people at the airports weren't the least suspicious."

Her whole body was vibrating. Sara's words sinking deeper into her conscious were stinging nettles. Adrenalin was very helpful for clearing the fog. Focus, focus, call out! Her fingers were already creeping along the woven cotton blanket to where she thought the call button was.

"Looking for this, dear Rhyjl?" Sara held the call mechanism in her hand. "I'm sorry I can't allow you to have it."

There was a clatter-clack as Sara released it and it swung from its cord repeatedly hitting the side of the bed railing.

"You were in surgery for a long time I hear. Air embolisms are often common in cases like yours. Of course finding information about the right amount of air to get the job done without raising suspicions, took a lot longer than I was hoping. You know you can find almost anything on the internet if you search hard enough."

Sara pulled a syringe out of her pocket and held it up for Rhyjl to see. "Just a couple of CCs in your IV and it will all be over quickly." Taking the clear cap off the needle, Sara slowly pulled the plunger back until the black rubber tipped end reached a mark halfway up. "Do you think this will be enough, Rhyjl?

How many times the last few days had she watched a nurse slip a needle into the small, faded yellow cap on her IV tube, being oh so careful to get the air out to avoid something like this? And Sara? Sara was going to end her life with a massive bubble. Her blood was pounding in her ears. Her tongue pushing and shoving at the cloth obstructing her scream. Her eyes locked with her tormentor, desperately pleading in hopes of finding the Sara she knew. The Sara who wouldn't do this.

Neither saw nor heard his entrance.   His passage, nothing more than a fleeting shadow until his hand stayed Sara's.

"I don't think so, Miss Abrams."

Detective Tanner's voice had never sounded so sweet to her ear. His hand restraining Sara's, as she struggled to carry through with her plan, was divine deliverance.

Chapter 16

Beneath the Surface

"I think I owe you a huge apology." Erik held out his hand to the detective. "What made you suspect her, Tanner?"

"Apology accepted, Arneson." Tanner grasped Erik's hand in a crushing vice and held firm until Erik shook free.

"Yes, Mike, how did you know?" Alice was sitting on one side of the hospital bed, Rhyjl's grandmother on the other. "I mean you had Kendricks. She seemed to fit all the criteria."

"As much as it hurts me to admit, I didn't know. I figured it wouldn't hurt to keep a plain clothes cop on to watch Rhyjl's room for a while. Tanner stroked his chin. "I did have Kendricks. She was a good fit. One exception, she kept saying she didn't do it."

"But isn't that what they all say?" Maggie McKenna entangled her fingers with her granddaughter's.

"Most the time." Tanner laughed. "Especially in the crime dramas. In real life? Not so much. We don't arrest people on speculation, as I said." He was looking directly at Erik. "So when we do, it's pretty much a grand slam with nothing left to do than get yourself a good lawyer and hope for a miracle. Kendricks wasn't about to go down that path. She admitted to calling the department and dropping that accusation against you, Rhyjl.

"What accusation?"

"An anonymous tip saying you had planted the bones. Her argument was pretty convincing. Enough that it shifted you to a person of interest for a time. Actually, she was pretty convinced you were behind everything, except she hadn't worked out the murder because she didn't really believe there had been one. She firmly believed you had set her up as some form of petty retribution."

"When in reality, it was Sara who was out for revenge." Erik shook his head. "What cleared Rhyjl?"

"Well, Rhyjl had motive along with a long list of others. It could be argued, unlike most those others, she had the knowledge to pull an elaborate hoax off. Once we had established the victim's identity, it didn't fly."

"So I was cleared before ..." Rhyjl shifted uncomfortably. The pain in her extremities was screaming for relief. She'd vowed never take pain medicine again. Better to be in agony than helpless in an induced brain miasma.

"The fall? Yes. After we arrested Kendricks, there were other things. The DA wouldn't be pleased if I say too much."

"Okay, but what clued you in to Sara? I don't think any of us had an inkling of that?" Alice flipped her hands over, fingers spread as if evidence had just flowed through them.

"I did." Rhyjl thought about Sara's voice being present in both visions of the attack. She couldn't explain that, so she offered up the evidence of Sara's journey to Chicago and the e-mail she'd found. "Unfortunately, I never got to share that."

"So you did suspect her!" Eyes round with shock, Erik growled and shot daggers her direction. "Why didn't you tell us?"

"Don't everyone look at me like that. She was my friend. Sure she hated Kendricks, but as Tanner says, there's a long list of us. My suspicions were that she had leaked the research to Jennifer, especially when I remembered her making a comment after summer break about disliking Chicago. I figured she had a part in it. I was sick thinking her selfish action might have contributed to Jennifer's death. But I swear, I never considered she was the murderer."

Tanner nodded. "So to sum up, there were too many loose ends. I don't like loose ends. They can unravel, and in this case, a few of them were already beginning. Sara had been part of that list. She'd actually made a pretty good suspect along with Rhyjl, means, motive. One of the Sheriff's deputies commented on the Red Head's temper. She also shared something else in common with Rhyjl."

"What's that?" Erik asked.

"Once we learned about the alleged pilfered research, there were really only two people, three if you included Dr. McClellen, who could have passed that information along. We checked passenger lists for all the major airlines going to Chicago and found Ms. Abrams. What we didn't find was a return. Our next step was to follow Kendricks. That became interesting when we discovered that Jackson and she had taken the same flight to Belize. There was no evidence of Jackson returning.

"So this Sara," Maggie said, "She goes down to Belize acting like Dr. Jackson to throw people off? But how did she get Jackson's bones back here? You can't just ship bodies can you?"

"No, Mrs. McKenna, you can't ship bodies or bones without special permits."

"Then how?"

"Yes, Mike, how?"

"We are still looking into that, but my best guess now, is Sara took a boat from Belize to one of the islands and then possibly flew or took another boat back to the states. Prior to that, she rented a storage unit near Chicago, bought a small chest freezer, and kept Dr. Jackson's body on ice until she could drive back with her car and deal with it."

"Cold!" Maggie hissed. "And to think, Rhyjl, you've lived the past two years with that woman. Makes me sick to think about."

"Then don't, Grandmum. The Sara I knew wasn't that way. Spoiled, yes! Selfish, yes! She had a temper, but so do I. I can't imagine what sent her over the edge."

"I think we know which straw might have broken the proverbial camel's back, but from what we've found so far, well, let's just say Sara Abrams was having a bad year."

"What will happen to her now?" Rhyjl asked.

"Hard to say. Her parents have hired some hotshot attorney. Innocent, by reason of insanity."

"Could that set her free?" Maggie McKenna's grip tightened protectively over Rhyjl's hand.

"It could make the difference between life in prison or an asylum. Hard to tell."

*

The press were waiting for them at the hospital entrance and then again when they arrived at Erik's home. Tanner, two sheriff's deputies, and even Billy, the campus guard, ran interference for them as she was taken from the ambulance into the house. Even so, she thought she might go blind from all the camera flashes. Alice, her grandmum, and a very exuberant Jack were waiting when they closed the door on the outside world.

The first thing she noticed was how the decor had changed from masculine functionality to something out of House Beautiful. Her grandmum's doing, no doubt, with just a hint of Alice. In a way, she almost regretted the loss. Beautiful as it was, it no longer represented its owner.

The ambulance attendants wheeled her into Erik's room where his bed had been replaced with what looked like a hybrid of hospital and ritzy hotel model. Seeing Rhyjl's dismay, and misunderstanding, her grandmother said, "It's only temporary until you get those casts off."

"Where are Erik's things?" she asked, noting that in their place were many of her personal items from the cottage.

"I've moved upstairs to the room right above you." Erik answered, coming through the door with two huge bouquets and trying to maneuver through dog and company. The gray shadows which had haunted his features were gone for the first time since her fall. His smile was again easy.

Jack had taken up his post at her bedside and was refusing to be budged. Sadly in the last five weeks, he had begun to lose much of his funny, endearing puppy look and was instead becoming a noble representative of his breed. And she'd missed it. She'd missed all of it! A single tear warmed her cheek.

"Are you in pain, honey?" Maggie asked.

"No, I'm just glad to be home." And the truth of it, she realized, was that she truly was.

About the Author

    JM Meigs has always believed that human and animal remains each have their own stories to tell. Combining her love of archaeology with her second passion of storytelling has led her to develop the Rhyjl Martin mysteries.

    She lives in the Pacific Northwest with her family and a menagerie of pets.